Doctor Wooreddy's Prescription for Enduring the Ending of the World

'The most substantial Aboriginal novelist to date', according to the Brisbane *Courier-Mail*, Colin Johnson is a Bibulman from the Swan River in Western Australia. He moved to Melbourne and after the publication of his first novel, *Wildcat Falling*, travelled widely in South-east Asia, the west coast of USA and UK. He was a Buddhist monk for seven years and is a member of the Maha Bodhi Society of India. He lives in Perth with his wife and son and writes full time.

Doctor Wooreddy, a Bruny Island Aborigine, witnesses the strange and threatening arrival of the Europeans when still a boy. He leaves his island in search of a life uncontaminated by the white man but after seven years his yearning for his land forces him to return. He finds the place desolate, with the surviving Aborigines ill, inert, bewildered. He is persuaded to join that splendidly comic character, the self-appointed missionary and spiritual redeemer, George Augustus Robinson, on Robinson's crusade to gather the remaining Tasmanian Aborigines for the Lord. With Trugernanna (Truganinni), his wife, his white 'Fader' and a small band of Aborigines he embarks on a tragi-comedy Pilgrim's Progress which can only end in the final segregation and destruction of the last black nation.

Colin Johnson does not attempt academic even-handedness. He looks calmly at the historical record and is able to imagine the world as it existed before European intrusion, as well as evoking the pain of seeing that world lost.

Doctor Wooreddy's Prescription for Enduring the Ending of the World

COLIN JOHNSON

HYLAND HOUSE MELBOURNE

First published in 1983 by
Hyland House Publishing Pty Limited
10 Hyland Street
South Yarra
Victoria 3141

First paperback edition 1987

The poster on page 170 is from the collection of the Queen Victoria
Museum and Art Gallery, Launceston.

National Library of Australia
Cataloguing in publication data

Johnson, Colin, 1938–
    Doctor Wooreddy's prescription for enduring the ending
    of the world.

    ISBN 0 947062 02 5.

    I. Title.

A823'.3

Jacket painting by Shane Pickett
Jacket design by Leonie Stott
Typeset by ProComp Productions Pty Ltd, South Australia
Printed by Brown Prior, Anderson, Melbourne

Contents

DEDICATED TO THE MEMORY
OF BOB MARLEY
JAH RASTAFARI!

1

The Omen

Wooreddy as a child and a young man belonged to Bruny Island: two craggy fists of land connected by a thin brown wrist. It was separated from the mainland by a narrow twisting of murky water. His island home abounded with wallaby and each tree held a possum. All along the rocky female coastline, clinging in mute desperation to the last vestiges of the land, shell- and crayfish hung waiting to be gathered. Wooreddy belonged to a rich island, but the surrounding sea was dangerous and filled with dangerous scale fish. Not even women were allowed to gather these creatures. It was evil luck to see one. They were taboo, for unlike the denizens of the real world, they swam in a different medium and never needed to feel or touch the earth. To them the land was death, just as to the Bruny Islanders the sea was death. This belief lay in Wooreddy's mind as he wandered by himself in the direction of a beach.

Around him lay the summer, peaceful and sunwarm on his skin. A breeze touched his nostrils with the different smells from the open and closed bush. With it came the slight smell of humankind. His tiny feet drifted him along towards a narrow bay arcing between two long fingers of points. Living on an island, he was never very far from the sea and a favourite spot was the beach toward which he was moving. Suddenly the breeze switched direction to blow in strongly from the ocean. The salt-smell caused him to think of that thing, neither male nor female, which heaved a chaos threatening the steadiness of the earth. It heaved like some huge wombat, and unlike the flowing darkness beyond the

1

campfires, could never be penetrated. It stood away from humankind. Wooreddy was only a ten-year-old boy, but he thought such thoughts. Born between the day and night, he had a fascination for things that lurked and threatened. He walked onto the beach thinking of charms and omens, mysteries and things hidden in the dark cave of the mind.

Though only a small boy, Wooreddy already had wriggled many times to the side of the few irascible old men as they sat theorising on life and its mysteries. On these occasions he had to pretend to make himself as tiny as an ant so as not to be noticed and chased away. Somehow he almost always managed to stay, intently listening with a child's mind which missed concepts but caught mysteries. They fell into his ears like raindrops and filled his head with things beyond his years. One such drop was *Ria Warrawah* which, or who, seemed to infest and affect all existing things. It, or he, or she lurked ready to strike down the unwary and on rare occasions hand power to the wary. This thing or creature was held at bay by the Great Ancestor who lived in the sky as a star. When *Ria Warrawah* became too strong and threatening, he subdued it with long flaming spears.

Sometimes the old men sat talking far into the night and Wooreddy stayed with them either sleeping or listening. Most times he missed much of the conversation as it meandered towards the dawn. It drifted in the darkest part of the night and became murky with *Ria Warrawah*. They discussed the taboo placed on its manifestation as a fish. To touch one meant death; to see one meant the itching sickness. Only powerful spells and charms could stop any harm. They detailed the forms and powers of this 'thing'. He, or she, or it was the sea and lived in the sea from which it sent manifestations as well as tidal waves to harm the land and those who lived on the land. But try as it might, it was held at bay by Great Ancestor. He had sent himself (or part of himself) crashing into the sea just off the eastern coast of Bruny. There he stood protecting the island. He also had sent them fire so that they could see in the darkness.

Wooreddy listened or slept while the information built into the foundations on which the adult character of the future Doctor Wooreddy would be erected. The child had

2

already learnt that the ocean must be confronted side-on and not directly. One had to be always alert for attack. But this day the boy felt so overwhelmed by the delightful charm of the weather that he began leaping and bounding along the beach like a kangaroo. He gave an extra-long bound and landed on something slimy, something eerily cold and not of the earth. Desperately he sprang away as his eyes clenched shut to keep out the horrible sight. He marched seven steps chanting a spell, then gave a yelp of despair. The last step had brought his big toe against something slimy, something eerily cold and not of this earth—and worse, it was spiky and wriggled. It was alive! He began to tremble violently. *Ria Warrawah* wrapped him in a transparent mist. He was lost! His hands shut out the world as his mind desperately searched through remembered snatches of half-understood conversations in an effort to find a potent protection spell. He tried a string of words. As the last one left his lips, there came a strange moaning from the sea, then gruff voices speaking in strange tongues which were followed by a sharp crack that made the water heave and lap at his feet. By magic his eyes clicked open to focus in a fixed stare on what had come from the sea. It was an omen, an omen, he knew—but what came from the ocean was evil, and so it was an evil omen. His eyes remained fixed on it. Shapes of thick fog had congealed over dark rocks, or a small island which floated a travesty of the firm earth.

Another boy would have turned tail or collapsed in a quivering heap of shock, but Wooreddy had been born for such sights. He watched the fog patches shift as they tugged the tiny dark island along. Such visions were rare and set a person apart. He had been selected and set apart. The future doctor felt the strangeness fill him. It became a part of him. Now remembered voices of the old men began murmuring in an effort to explain the unexplainable:

'Once in the time of our grandfathers and before the birth of our fathers, a small piece of darkness, fashioned by the very thought of *Ria Warrawah*, came floating along on the sea. *Ria Warrawah* manifested himself as a cloud and pulled the island along. He pulled to Adventure Bay and left it there. Our grandfathers watched from the shore. They saw

3

the black sticks by which *Ria Warrawah* had held it as he pulled it along. Then a piece of the island broke away and came crawling across the sea towards them. Our hidden grandfathers watched on. The creature touched the land. It carried pale souls which *Ria Warrawah* had captured. They could not bear being away from the sea and had to protect their bodies with strange skins. They spoke and the sounds were unlike any that had been heard. Our grandfathers remained hidden and after a time the creatures mounted their strange sea thing and went back to the dark island.'

This account explained the ships sailing past to form the first European settlement on the Derwent River, but it did not explain Wooreddy's enlightenment which he now endured. Nothing from this time on could ever be the same — and why? Because the world was ending! This truth entered his brain and the boy, the youth and finally the man would hold onto it, modifying it into harshness or softness as the occasion demanded. His truth was to be his shield and protection, his shelter from the storm. The absolute reality of his enlightenment took care of everything. One day, sooner rather than later, the land would begin to fragment into smaller and smaller pieces. Clouds of fog would rise from the sea to hide what was taking place from Great Ancestor. Then the pieces holding the last survivors of the human race would be towed out to sea where they would either drown or starve.

The boy stood in a trance and learnt that he would live on to witness the end. He had been chosen and would endure through the power of his Truth. It was a charm of awful power. He received it in this initiation and then it retreated to live on in a corner of his mind. He awakened with his back to the sea. The sun dissipated the fog, the breeze turned to flow from the land, bringing the scent of humankind. The smoke of the campfires awakened his hunger. His lithe, brown body charged off to the nurturing warmth of his mother. She sat mending a basket. He begged her for food and she gave him the tail of a large crayfish. He loved her for it.

Wooreddy waddled his way towards adulthood in an awful world that became less and less familiar. Before, uneventful time had stretched back towards the known beginning. Now, it seemed that something had torn the present away from that past. Many people died mysteriously; others disappeared without trace, and once-friendly families became bitter enemies. Night after night the piercing whistles of *Ria Warrawah* shrieked from the hidden recesses of the forest. No one could understand what was happening. Still the people endured and tried to live as they always had lived.

Wooreddy grew and reached puberty. Jokes were made about his sprouting pubic hair and the sudden uncontrolled erections which showed his manhood. Then, in the dead of night, the older men grabbed him and hustled him through just a few short metres of darkness to where a campfire gleamed. Once it would have been further away and hidden, but times had changed. His uncles held him down while a stranger thrust a firebrand into his face. Another man chanted the origin of fire and why it was sacred for him. Fire was life; fire was the continuation of life — fire endured to the end. He came from fire and would return to fire. One day it would take his spirit to the Islands of the Dead where he could live happily stuffed with plenty of wallaby, kangaroo, possum and seafood brought by his loving mate. But this was not all, for on those islands grew the cider trees exuding litres of sweet intoxicating sap which could fly his soul to where Great Ancestor's campfire flamed the sky with light. There he could live on with Great Ancestor in bliss. Fire was a gift from Great Ancestor and Wooreddy had been selected as one descended from that gift. Now while he lived he had to ensure that fire lived. They whispered his secret name, *Poimatapunna* (Phoenix), then detailed the coming of fire:

'Fire was sent to us by Great Ancestor. He gave it to two birdmen to bring to us. Long ago, the grandfathers of our grandfathers saw them standing on top of a high hill. They stared up at the strangers. They saw them raise their hands. Burning brands fell from them and among our people. The very earth began to burn and our ancestors fled across a river to escape. Much later they returned to their land and walked over the burnt and blackened earth. Many burnt animals lay here and there. They tasted some and found that they were good to eat. Then they knew that fire was good and from that day we have used it. And when we move over our land we burn it off in remembrance of that time. Never forget that your own campfire is descended from that first fire. It is a living sign of our connection to Great Ancestor and his many fires flickering in the sky . . .'

The recitation hesitated and the youth felt the burning brand pressed to his breast. It hurt, it hurt like—what else?—the touch of fire. He wanted to shout out his pain. Instead he gritted his teeth against it and endured the fire eating into his flesh. At long last the brand was withdrawn. His throbbing flesh throbbed in time to the continuing chant. Would the searing pain ever go away!

'Those two birdmen, those two messengers from Great Ancestor, did not fly off into the sky. They stayed on in our country and you will see the marks of their camping places. Near the *Lungannaga* river two women dived into the water for mussels. They did not know that below the surface lurked *Ria Warrawah* in the shape of a giant stingray. From his hiding place in a dark hole among the rocks, he watched those women. They swam down. They were very near. He dashed out. He lashed out with his spear. He stabbed and stabbed; he cut and cut; he thrust and thrust; he pierced those women through and through . . .'

Wooreddy, thoroughly miserable from the aching of the burn, now had to endure a series of parallel slashes across his chest. It was little consolation that the cuts from the sharp shell piece did provide a contrast to the dull throbbing. He wished to be anywhere but where he was. In an effort to see the blood trickling down his ribs, he rolled his eyes as the myth continued to unfold.

'The two birdmen came to the shore. They saw the great stingray basking in the shallows, gloating over his deed. He did not enjoy his triumph for long. They crept to him; they fought with him; they wounded him; they killed that evil thing!'

The miserable youth had to undergo further torments as the stingray was disposed of. To add to the burnt patch in the centre of his chest and the seven cuts on the right side, three more were engraved on the left. Later on in life he could earn four more, but now this was all that he had to endure—or at least he hoped so, for perhaps his knowledge of the ceremony was faulty, or a variant had been used. He eased out a sigh of relief as the myth flowed on.

'From the water, they took those two dead women. They were messengers from the Great Ancestor and had no fear of it. They lay the two women upon the ground and built a fire between them. Then they opened their chests and put into the chest-cavity some blue ants.'

Wooreddy shuddered as someone gently touched his wounds. He relaxed knowing that an ointment of fat and ash was being smeared over them.

'The ants stung those two women into life. They moved, and moved again as the ants stung them again, as the birdmen sung life into them. Then the two strangers filled the holes in the women's chests with mud and pressed the flesh together. The holes were no more. They fixed the women's wounds in the same way, and they were whole.'

The youth gave a slight smile as soothing river mud was put over his own wounds. The ceremony was almost at an end.

'*Ria Warrawah* raged at being deprived of two victims. He rose, he rose as a vast fog, to race in from the sea and towards the two birdmen. It might have been fast, but those two were faster. *Ria Warrawah* extended almost to them. Up they flew with those two women. Up they flew, and you can see them in the sky to this day.'

The ceremony ended at dawn and Wooreddy retreated into the bush to stay by himself while his wounds healed. He accepted the solitude as he had accepted the burning and slashing. In these days of tribulation and when the world was ending, tradition and custom were comforts.

When Wooreddy returned to the camp, he came as a man permitted to express the feelings of a man. Sex awareness often hit him like a blow from a club and he had, at times, to command himself not to proposition other men's mates.

7

Honour kept him from breaking the law and intriguing for relief. But his eyes often followed the swaying hips of a woman. Perhaps he could seek a mate from some stranger-community. This was permissible and some of the other men had foreign wives. He observed these matches and was deterred. The men, unlike those who married women from the customary groupings, seemed like shellfish collected in a basket. Foreign women expected their men always to return laden with game from the hunt. They expected their menfolk to be always attentive and when they quarrelled, the wife instantly threatened to return to her own country or to find a better man. Seeing this, and seeing it too often, Wooreddy put the idea of a foreign wife from his mind and began to look for a local girl for a mate. Or rather his father did the looking, while he suffered the pangs of lust and waited for the event to happen.

Women and marriage were not the only things he saw with that detachment which had become a mannerism from that day, seven years ago, when the omen had forced itself upon him. He watched a man burn his mate. He squatted just beyond the light cast by the fire to observe the cremation. The woman had been murdered by ghosts and this made her funeral of special interest. Everything had to be done just right, if the spirit, tormented by the loss of a young and healthy body, were to be sent away towards the Islands of the Dead. The family gathered the material for the pyre. The father belonged to a different clan from Wooreddy. One in which he could marry, he thought, as he watched the three daughters working. Moorina and Lowernunhe were past puberty and taken, but the third one was only twelve and possibly still unattached. She was a female with a strong will. Everyone had become aware of this when, as a child of five, she had dived after her sisters into the surf and almost drowned. He knew that a great future as a provider had been predicted for her—and much sorrow for her mate!

Wooreddy dressed his hair as he waited. He rubbed a plain grease over it, then searched his chin for any lengths of hair growing on his cheek. He found one or two and pulled them out. Dawn turned into morning, and the family members probed further into the bush for timber. Finally, Mangana, the father, determined that enough had been collected. He stood beside a shallow square dug into the earth and muttered a few incantations before beginning to stack the logs up in the form of a hollow cube. When he reached a metre and a half, he stopped and began filling it with twigs, leaves and bark. Wooreddy noticed that the structure had begun to sag at one corner, and sighed. The old ways were losing their shape and becoming as the cube. Mangana, he had heard, on hearing of his wife's murder, had only shrugged his shoulders and muttered: 'It is the times.' His words summed up the general mood of the community. No one had any trust in the future and they accepted a prophecy that passed among them: fewer babies would be born to take the place of the adults dying ever younger; fewer babies to be born, to be weaned, to die—and this meant fewer mature adults to keep and pass on the traditions of the islanders. Thus it was, and it was the times. Everyone knew this and accepted it. Wooreddy alone knew more. He knew that it was because the world was ending.

From a bark shelter hidden beneath the down-hanging branches of an ancient tree, the husband carried out the corpse of his wife. The three daughters began snivelling. Wooreddy was impressed by the solemnity of the occasion, by the sight of the man carrying to the fire the dead body of his mate. Mangana gently placed the corpse on top of the pyre. Softly Wooreddy moved closer to see if custom was being observed. The limbs were folded against the trunk and tied there with woven-grass cords knotted in the proper manner. He nodded: it was as it should be. He turned to where Mangana squatted at the fire, poking a long stick into the flame and muttering a short incantation until the end caught. Then he rushed the stick to the pyre and thrust it through the special tunnel which led into the heart of the cube. Tendrils of smoke pushed up past the corpse. A few licking tongues of fire erupted to dance into a hungry red mouth under the spell of the onrushing morning wind. The roaring flames carried the female spirit up and away from the land of the living leaving behind loss and sorrow. Mangana groaned out his pain. His daughters wailed out their pain. One by one the man took up his spears and broke

9

them. It was an abject sign of surrender. One disarmed oneself before an enemy of overwhelming strength and cast oneself on his mercy.

Mangana's wife had been raped and then murdered by *num* (ghosts) that came from the settlement across the strait. What had happened had had nothing to do with her, her husband or her children. It had been an act of *Ria Warrawah*— unprovoked, but fatal as a spear cast without reason or warning. No one could have protected her, and thus Mangana broke his spears and cast the pieces on the blazing pyre. This showed that he, and all who were associated with him, were at the mercy of forces which he could only try and propitiate through magic. He snatched up a sharp pebble and slashed at his chest. Blood dripped upon the earth. He flung drops into the flames. He groaned and raised his lacerated breast to the first rays of the sun. Black blood turned as red as the fire consuming his mate.

This was not the last tragedy Mangana was to suffer, or Wooreddy to witness. More and more people died and the frightened survivors huddled together. Family groupings had been created by Great Ancestor. From the first he had bound individuals together in biological groupings. No one was alone. But that was how it had been. Now some families were reduced to only a single member, and with all their relatives gone they were alone in a country of strangers. Wooreddy found himself in this predicament, but instead of giving way to despair he applied himself to rectify the situation. A thinker with a family was a thinker in custom; a thinker with only his thoughts to keep him company was an outcast. He could not live alone and needed allies. He was drawn to the remnant family of Mangana.

He spent much time sitting with the father. Now that so many custodians of lore had been swept away, Mangana could be classified as an elder. He might have knowledge and Wooreddy, a youth with too big a brain, wanted to get some of it. This, apart from his need of allies, was a strong enough reason to stay close to the older man. But Mangana did not pass on any wisdom. That which he might have once possessed had been destroyed by *the times* which had personally struck him such a vicious blow that he had been

10

knocked into premature senility. For most of the day he sat and watched the flickering flames of his fire which Wooreddy kept up. He sat subdued while ghosts roamed his land and marked it out as their own. Within and without there was no hope, and sometimes Wooreddy heard him softly moan as he probed the wounds of his sorrow. Too often silence settled on man and youth, and that silence was the brooding of *Ria Warrawah*. It hung between them that day when the thudding of tiny feet imprinted themselves on it. Wooreddy recognised the feet as those of Trugernanna. As always he was correct. Hunter as well as thinker, he could identify individuals by their footprints. Trugernanna flung her body into the clearing and stood panting before the two men.

Her father slowly lifted his face and asked in a monotone: 'Why haven't you collected some food? I'm hungry!'

The child answered in a similar dead voice: 'Three ghosts came rowing into the bay. They took first and second sister away.'

Mangana looked from his daughter to the youth. He began to speak perhaps with a slight intention of justifying his listlessness and his numb reaction to the loss of his two eldest daughters.

'*Num* come; they see what they want; they take it. It is their way. They do not know Great Ancestor and his laws. I remember when I first saw their big catamarans. I did not know what they were, or perhaps I did because they scared me. They scared all of us and they still scare us. We have lived in fear since they came and can do nothing to put an end to that fear. When we first saw them, we talked about them and decided that they were spirits of the dead returning. Soon we found that they were not our dead, but perhaps those of our enemies. They were under the dominion of the Evil One, *Ria Warrawah*. They killed needlessly. They were quick to anger, and quick to kill with thunder flashing out from a stick they carried. They kill many, and many die by the sickness they bring. Now all I have left is my little daughter. Once nine shared my campfire. Now it is hard to find nine members of my clan. A sickness demon takes those that the ghosts leave alone.'

Wooreddy seized on the last sentence and added it to his

11

own foreboding. The island was haunted and unsafe to humans. He must escape before he became a victim of the demon or the ghosts. He would not delay, and leave today. He would cross over to the mainland and flee far away from the *num*.

Trugernanna shuffled her feet and coughed for attention. Good or bad news focused attention on the bearer and she wanted the limelight. Without waiting for her father's permission she began to relate her story. Wooreddy could have ordered her to shut up, but he too wanted to hear the details.

Trugernanna was sitting on the beach watching her two big sisters diving for sea food. Relaxed and happy, they clambered to the top of a rock and stood looking down into the surf breaking at the base. They laughed for they had little fear from the sea. Then around the point came crawling a dinghy. It came to the rock on which the women stood and stopped bobbing up and down a few metres from the base. A lazy oar stroke kept it in position. Trugernanna, watching from the beach, became alarmed, but the women remained on the rock looking down at the three *num* staring up. Trugernanna reacted to her fright and dashed into the scrub. Safely hidden, she watched on. One of the ghosts held up a piece of soft skin. It was so soft that it fluttered in the breeze. It was of the brightest red she had ever seen. He flapped it, and his gutteral voice grated across the water to her. She listened, all ears, but couldn't even separate the individual words.

'Hey, my lovelies, come to our boat. We won't hurt you. We have this and more like it for you.'

The bright cloth held Trugernanna's eyes. She turned her gaze on her sisters and saw them look at one another. She guessed that they too wanted the bright skin. Both suddenly sprang from the rock and disappeared under the water. They came up next to the boat, held on to the side and stretched out their free hands. Trugernanna saw the *num* grab them by the reaching hands and haul them aboard. They screamed, but she did not see them put up much of a struggle. The boat began moving and disappeared from whence it had come. The girl ran off to tell her father.

Both men heard her out. Their bleak eyes stared into the fire as if a solution to their problem rested there.

12

2

Seek Allies

I

Many things had happened to the good Doctor Wooreddy since he had left his island home to flee to the South West Nation. Travelling along the coast road towards Poynduc he saw everywhere signs of the *num*. The Derwent River valley had been taken and from this they surged out to claim all that they wanted. Poynduc, a wide, shallow lagoon of a drowned river valley, was free except for a few timber-cutters, and the surrounding land of deep valleys filled with tangled undergrowth did not attract them.

The population of the South West Nation lived in villages scattered from Poynduc to the northern frontier at Parra-laongatek, a large, shallow harbour like Poynduc, where a *num* enclave existed. The villages were linked by a network of narrow coastal roads and the young man passed along these until he came to a village which knew his family. The future good doctor found the people too welcoming. He was accepted at once into the community as a full adult and even allowed to sit at the feet of the elder men who, even if they did not know everything, certainly projected that feeling. Their religion was much the same as that of the Bruny Islanders, though the presence of the *num* had modified it somewhat. The world extended far across the forbidden sea to the Islands of Ghosts, and around them, in the gloomy forests, lurked the many shadows of *Ria Warrawah* waiting to rush towards the humans if the fires began to go out. *Ria Warrawah*—they emphasised the collective rather than the he, or it, or she—had brought the *num* from their far islands to plague the humans. This was how things stood!

Wooreddy listened and made notes in his mind. It all seemed plausible and a variant of traditional theology. He was pleased with the knowledge of the older men and they were pleased with his interest in the old teachings. When he wasn't taking theology lessons, he went hunting. The Elders did not part with their knowledge freely; it had to be paid for with gifts of soft-meated wallaby (if possible) or possum. Wooreddy, an excellent hunter, earned enough to pay his fees as well as to support himself. This proved his undoing, or rather because he appeared to be settling down, it was natural that a woman be linked with him. This would keep him from pestering other women and also supplement his diet with seafood which only women were allowed to collect. One day, Wooreddy became conscious of a girl. How and why he did and why he continued to, he did not know. The girl, on her part, appeared not to be aware of him. His more and more frequent glances found her eyes elsewhere, never on him, and if he moved towards her she ran gracefully away to her home. But somehow she was often in his sight, and he could not help noticing that when she returned from the coast her bag was overflowing. Wooreddy's education had had nothing to do with women and their ways. He knew that a man and a woman came together to form a basic social unit and he had often felt the physical need of a woman—these were the only two things he knew. Now he found himself noticing a girl, so much so that she was beginning to dominate his mind. He felt that she was wholly or partly responsible for this, though he had no evidence to support this supposition. One thing that he was aware of was that she was a foreign woman and therefore dangerous!

Knowing that the older men knew everything, Wooreddy, finding one of them in a good mood, added to it with the gift of a few plump possum, then casually raised the subject of women. He waited for the answer expecting some sort of involved discourse on the sixteen attitudes of the mind as applied to women or perhaps just a grunt. He received the grunt, but this was followed by the older man shouting in the direction of his house, 'Lunna!'. His daughter reluctantly appeared and slowly came towards them. Her father smiled and whispered in her ear. This caused her to fling a

14

particularly nasty look at Wooreddy before fleeing to a distant group of women. The father laughed and invited Wooreddy to sit with him. They sat in silence. Wooreddy had been disconcerted to see that the man's daughter was the one which had been the object of his attention, or the one towards which his attention had been directed.

He did not know, but it had all been arranged. Wooreddy was a good catch. A successful hunter and a thoughtful man who would think twice before putting himself in the forefront of the battles which were becoming more fearful and bloody as the ghosts took more and more land. The South West Nation resisted and were losing too many men. Eligible mates were becoming scarce; the man's daughter was at the age to be married, and Wooreddy, though a foreigner, available and a proper choice.

The older man kept Wooreddy with him all that afternoon and that evening invited him to spend the night. He accepted the invitation and, when the fire died down to a heap of glowing coals, the girl came quietly to his side. But she only sat beside him for a few minutes before going to sleep with the other women. Wooreddy stayed on and after a few nights the girl remained by his side. He found himself with a mate and an extended family. Time passed gently in the village. Changes for him and the South West Nation (except for the constant loss of men on the frontiers) were rumours rather than actualities.

Wooreddy entered into full manhood as the regular rows of scars on his chest and the two irregular healed spear wounds on his side showed. Then, after seven years away from his island home, he decided to return. He longed to see the earth of his birth. The troubles there had become half-forgotten memories. He grimly smiled as he remembered leaving Bruny Island with scarcely a smear of red ointment on his head. Now his hair, plaited into many small rat-tails which swung about his face as he walked, was red with ochre. He had passed through combat and was entitled to hold the short, thick club in his right hand and clutch the long, clumsy spear in his left. Before the *num* spears were seldom carried, but now, since the crazed blood-thirstiness had affected them all, only a fool went unarmed through the frontier districts.

15

The South-West men had always been plotting and arranging, postponing, cancelling or marching off to fight the intruders who threatened the borders of their land. Over the twenty or so years since ghosts had settled the Derwent River Valley, participation in an action against them had assumed the status of an initiation rite. A man was not fully a man until he had sunk his spear in or thudded his club on the body or head of some hapless *num*.

It was expected of Wooreddy that he too would go on such an expedition. After giving the subject some thought he settled on one which he believed would be cancelled or postponed for an unknown length of time. This did not happen, and next day he found himself part of a column moving through the rainforest. The dozen men left the jungle, climbed up through the mountains and descended into the foothills on the other side. They grouped on a ridge and surveyed the village below. A harsh bare clearing had been eroded out of the trees and in the centre stood the alien square of a ghost hut. Wooreddy had never seen such a dwelling place. He examined it, noting the rough slabs of tree-trunks which made up the walls and the roof of flattened bark pieces held down by a framework of poles. A strange animal trotted out and barked once or twice. He had heard about such an animal. It was a *panoine*, and the people living along the frontier had them. A ghost came to the door, looked out, then went back inside. The men waited for an hour before drifting down the slope to surround the hut. Each man held a bundle of spears in his left hand and one poised in his right. The leader of the squad yelled. His spear thudded into one of the rough, wooden wall-slabs. They waited. They could hear the frantic barking of the animal inside the hut. They flung more spears at the walls. Some embedded themselves and quivered, others bounced off. Wooreddy began to find the attack a little tedious. It could last all day and night. He leapt to his feet, ran a few metres and flung himself down just in time to escape a musket ball. A comrade followed his example and no shot sounded. Did this mean that there was only one gun inside? Another man raced towards the hut and dived to the earth in time to escape the shot. Yes, only one was inside! All the men raced in to fling blazing firesticks onto the roof. The dry bark burst into flame with a whoosh. The *num* and his animal came charging out. He rushed directly at Wooreddy with his gun clubbed. The *panoine* snapped at Wooreddy's heels and tripped him up. This saved him from having his brains splattered across the clearing. The ghost did not get a second chance. Wooreddy lifted his club and brought it down. A sodden thud and it was all over. The *panoine* left off worrying his heels, sniffed at the fallen *num* and wailed. The men rushed into the hut, looted what they could find, then watched it burn before moving off. The animal attached itself to the party and followed after them.

On the return trip the men walked along carelessly. They bragged of past fights, heroes and cowards. Wooreddy did not join in the conversation. Then the talk shifted to tactics and weapons. Was it advisable or even permissible to use *num* weapons? This was a never-ending dispute and Wooreddy's carefully considered opinion met other carefully considered objections. The debate had dragged on for years and would drag on until no one was left to take sides.

Wooreddy smiled as he remembered how happy his wife's father had been to receive the strange animal as a gift. Now their village too had a *panoine*! He thought all this as he strode along the road leading south. Behind him followed his wife and children. She carried one in her arms, the other trotted at her side. It was a slow, leisurely journey and the woman had not once complained. Wooreddy, basing his opinion on what he had observed and heard about, found this strange. But he had no intention of being kept in a foreign woman's basket like part of her harvest. No, this would not happen, as it had happened to others he had seen so long ago.

II

Wooreddy stood on the shore staring across the narrow stretch of water. He saw the familiar dips and swells of his island and recognised the few thin lines of smoke as those belonging to his people — but at one point thick foggy masses of *num* smoke hung in the air like a bad omen. As he watched, fog streaked in from the sea to unite with the thick masses of smoke from the fires used to render down whale-blubber into oil. Things had indeed changed since the good doctor had been away. The island vanished from his view, and muttering a spell of protection, Wooreddy set about building a catamaran large enough to transport himself and his children.

Using the sharp *num* hatchet which had been his share of the loot from the hut, he hacked away at the bottom of reeds. He cut and collected a large pile. After laying them out and separating them into three bundles, he bound them together with the thin grass-cord his wife was twisting together. He went to the trees above the beach and using his hatchet cut out long squares of bark which he trimmed to the length of the reed rolls. These he bound around the bundles. If the voyage had been longer, grease would have been smeared over the outer surface of the bark to make them watertight. Wooreddy placed the long three-metre roll in the middle of the two shorter ones, then tightened them together with the net his wife had roughly woven. Now the catamaran had a canoe-shape with the bow and stern higher than the middle. Wooreddy hesitated to push it into the water. He trusted his work, but he did not trust the sea with all its lurking demons or demon, depending on the viewpoint held. He evaded any urge to ponder on the mystery and set about the ritual to keep it or them at bay. After patting mud into a square-shaped fireplace on the high stern of the catamaran, he lit a small fire there while singing the appropriate spell. The earth and the square shape of the fireplace and of the netting held the magic and not the fire. Wooreddy carefully finished the ritual and spell. Everything had been just right. A mistake, even a tiny one, might cause disaster. Gingerly, he pushed the craft into the surf until it floated. After putting the two boys aboard, he scrambled on. The catamaran settled a little, but still rode high fore and aft. His wife, Lunna, protected by her femaleness from the sea, pushed the craft into deeper water, then clinging onto the stern propelled it forward with kicks from her powerful legs.

Wooreddy's eyes clung to the shape of his approaching island. This kept his mind from the encircling water; it gave him solace, and then the earth, which had formed his body and given the hardness to his bones, did have the power to draw him back. This, in a sense, was what was happening now. He had not determined to return home, but forces had determined that he return home. One such force was that of the earth of his home. He dreaded what he would find there. Then he noticed that the catamaran, for apparently no reason, was making a wide detour around an open patch of water. His nervous eyes had glanced down for a second. Now they stayed on the water. Alarm thudded his heart. If he had been able he would have returned to the mainland at once. But then, what if he had returned to the mainland? Only the west coast remained free, and for how long? In the long run, to survive meant accepting that the ghosts were here to stay and learning to live amongst them, or at least next to them until—until the ending of the world! This was the only reason why Wooreddy wanted to live on—and in a friendless world! It was one of the reasons why he had left the relative peace and security of his wife's village.

He let the sight in the water enter into his mind. A bloody patch slowly spreading in circles of pinkish foam as a drizzle of rain fell from the grey sky. He shivered, feeling the presence of *Ria Warrawah*. The patch of blood turned a dull red, the colour of the ochre smeared in his hair. Just below the surface of the water, the dark body of a man drifted hazily like some evil sea creature. It quivered and turned dead eyes on him as Lunna's powerful kick sent the catamaran past and scooting towards what might be the safety of the shore.

At last they grounded. Wooreddy leapt out and raced to the shelter of the undergrowth. Behind him pelted his wife and children. Safely hidden, they stared back toward the beach. The waves marched in assault lines against the land. Wooreddy saw the smoke rising from the stern of the catamaran and remembered his vow always to protect fire. But he hesitated and caused its death. The waves had driven the catamaran broadside to the surf. Now they capsized it.

Ria Warrawah killed the fire. Then he found that he had left his spear behind. It floated in the surf. He left it there. He still had his club, and a spear, these days, was too much like a broken arm. Calling to his wife and children, he walked along the remembered track leading off this side of the bay. They followed it up over a rise, through thick undergrowth, then around the edge of a small cove. There another sight struck them a blow. The island, Wooreddy's own earth, had been taken over by ghosts. His wife and children huddled in terror at his side, but the good Doctor Wooreddy donned his cloak of numbness and observed the scene with all the detachment of a scientist.

On the soft, wet beach-sand a naked brown-skinned woman was being assaulted by four ghosts. One held both of her arms over her head causing her breasts to jut into the low-lying clouds; two more each clung to a powerful leg, and the fourth thudded away in the vee. Wooreddy could see only the cropped head of the woman and not her face. The ghost stopped his thudding between her legs and fell limply on her body for a minute, then jerked away, knelt and got to his feet. The doctor noted with interest the whiteness of the ghost's penis. He had accepted the fact of their having a penis—after all they were known to attack women—but he had never thought it would be white. He filed this probably useless piece of information in his mind and watched on. The ghost hid his unnatural organ in his pants, then reached for the arms of the woman. The one holding them, possibly eager for his turn, released his grip and she had her arms free. She did nothing. Experimentally, the other two loosened their hold on her legs. She remained still. The three stood up and watched as the fourth jerked out his pale, bloodless penis, knelt, and lunged forward.

'Hey, Paddy, leave a bit for us,' one yelled. The sounds drifted up to Wooreddy. He wondered about the grammatical structure and idiosyncrasies of their language as the rape continued.

'Arrh, Jack, got her all loosened up. Now she's just lying there enjoying every minute of it', Paddy finally grunted up, spacing the words to the rhythm of his body.

Wooreddy wondered if the ghosts had honorifics and

20

specific forms of address. Perhaps it was not even a real language?—but then each and every species of animal had a language, and so it must be! The kangaroos, possums and even snakes—and though it was not universally accepted, the trees and plants—all had a language. Even the clouds and wind conversed together. Some gifted men and women could listen and understand what they were talking about. It was even debated that such men and women could make them carry them to see a distant friend and after return them to their starting point. It could be true, for he knew that the whole earth murmured with the conversations of the myriad species of things and to understand what they were saying would be to understand all creation.

Paddy finished with a grunt and got off and up. Another took his place while Wooreddy wondered about the necessity of covering the body with skins rather than grease. It was the way of these *num* and could be compared with the strange custom of the North West Nation where women did not crop their hair. He thought about how different peoples held and shaped spears. Variations based on the series of actions of holding and sharpening which were individual to each person, and as they were individual to each person so were they to each nation and even community. Another *num* came and went—to be replaced by another.

The circle circled while the day flowed towards the evening. Wooreddy knew that he and his family had to leave soon if they were to make the camping place by nightfall. He was beginning to find the rape a little tedious. What was the use of knowing that the *num* were overgreedy for women just as they were overgreedy for everything? He could have deduced this from the record of their previous actions and they did appear fixed and immutable in their ways. At long last the rape ground to an end. The *num* without a final glance at the sprawling woman walked off to a boat Wooreddy had not noticed drawn up on the beach. They got in and began rowing across the bay like a spider walking on water.

A few minutes after they had left, the woman got to her feet. The doctor parted the mists of seven years to recognise the youngest daughter of Mangana grown into a woman of seventeen years. She looked a good strong female with the

21

firm, squat body of a provider. Unsteadily she managed a few steps, then stood swaying on her feet. Slowly her face lifted and her dull eyes brightened as she saw Wooreddy standing in the undergrowth. She glared into his eyes, spat in his direction, then turned and dragged her hips down to the waves subsiding in the long rays of the sun setting in a swirl of clearing cloud. He watched as she squatted in the water and began cleaning herself. Then he turned to his wife, told her to follow him, and waddled away with Trugernanna's glare, that dull then bright gaze filled with spite and contempt, in his mind. It upset him and dispelled his numbness which, fortunately for Wooreddy (though he often didn't realise it) was not the impervious shield of his theorising, and could be easily penetrated. Why had she looked at him in such a way? After all it had been the *num* who had raped her. He would never do such a thing! He thought on as he waddled along in that peculiar gait which had earned him the name, Wooreddy—*'duck'*—and finally concluded that it was a waste of time to try to divine anything about females. What was important about Trugernanna, he recalled, was that she was a survivor. This was what made her important to him—though she did have the body of a good provider!

The track ended in a clearing at the side of a long sweeping bay. Here he found Mangana much the same as seven years ago. He sat alone, smiling into his fire. Wooreddy waited until the older man glanced up and beckoned to him to sit. He sat and waited. Mangana looked across and smiled, not a smile of greeting, but one of resignation. To the old man's despondency over the loss of his first wife had been added that caused by the loss of a second. Now he filled Wooreddy in with the details, using the rich language of an elder. It was part gesture, part expression, part pure feeling allied to a richness of words moulded together in a grammatic structure complex with the experience of the life lived. It was a new and full experience for Wooreddy. The white cloud sails bulged, fluttered like the wings of birds and collapsed in a torrent of rain; a baby boat crawled from the strangeness of its mother ship-island; tottered across the waves on unsteady legs; dragged its tiny body up onto the shore—and reached out insect arms to Mangana's mate. Charmed, she enticed herself to it; charmed, she wanted the insect arms around her and her own arms around the soft body; charmed, she let herself be enticed by the infant-boat to the terrible mothership. Many legs walked the child to it and Mangana's wife was taken along to where the sails fluttered like seagulls, and flew out to sea. The loss of the mate was conveyed by a terrible feeling of emptiness, of the lack felt by the absence of a good provider not filled by the presence of a single young daughter, fickle and strange with the times and often not to be found and not to be managed. Mangana took up the subject of his daughter. With a finger he painted in the soft ashes at the edge of the fire her symbol and her actions.

She spent too much time watching the *num* and being with the *num*. From them she received ghost food, two whites and a black: flour, sugar and tea. He himself had acquired a taste for these strange foods since he rarely hunted and relied on his daughter for provisions. He projected the death of a son at Wooreddy. They lived through it right to the final ashes. Mangana left mental pain to wander in physical pain. He relived the time he had been washed out to sea. His waterlogged catamaran sagged beneath his weight and every wave washed over him. All around him the surge of the sea, the breathing of *Ria Warrawah*. A *num* boat came sailing along. Ghosts pulled him from the clutches of *Ria Warrawah*. This affected him even more than the other events as it involved a contradiction: why had the *num*, who allegedly came from *it*, saved him from *its* domain? Unable to formulate a theory to explain this, he now felt that he belonged, or at the least owed his very life, to the ghosts and thus existed only on their whim. They had claimed his soul and sooner rather than later would take it if he could not create a nexus to prevent them from doing so.

Mangana declared with more determination than he had so far shown: 'The *num* think they have me—but an initiated man is never had. He knows how to walk the coloured path to the sparkling path which leads to where the fires flicker in Great Ancestor's camp. There they are forbidden to come, and even now I am building up my fire there.

Wooreddy nodded. He knew that the older a man grew the more he received and found. Sometimes the old ones had so much knowledge that they could make the very earth tremble. It was even rumoured that they could fly to the sky-land while still alive. Respectfully he kept his eyes lowered. Here was one of the last elders of the Bruny Island people famed for their spiritual knowledge.

'My daughter, she is yours when I go,' the old man said suddenly to him, smiling with a humour which showed that he knew a little too much about Trugernanna—and about Wooreddy!

Wooreddy lifted his head in surprise and lowered it in confusion. He tried to mask his thoughts from the old man. Thankfully Lunna returned with her basket filled with abalone and four crayfish which occupied all of Mangana's attention. His daughter might have the body of a good provider, but she failed to live up to it. Mangana slavered for the succulent crayfish. His eyes flickered from them to Wooreddy's motions in heaping up the coals of the fire. His eyes lingered on the dark-greenish body of a giant cray as Wooreddy gently and lovingly (at least so it seemed to Mangana) placed it on the coals. He watched as the dark shell began to turn a lightish ochre-red. He openly sighed as Wooreddy with two forked sticks lifted it off the fire, placed it on a piece of bark and put it in front of him. It was delicious, and the first bite freed his attention. He smiled as Wooreddy gave the next one to his wife, and the third to be divided between his children. The younger man felt the eyes on him and would have blushed if he could. On Bruny Island the custom was that first (or, in this case, secondly) the husband took what he wanted and left the remainder for his wife and children. He, without thinking, had done what he had done from the time he had been married and then a father. Ayah! Indeed he had been caught like the crayfish he was eating and put in the basket of this foreign woman without even realising it. He consoled himself with the thought that it must be the times.

III

Bruny Island had become a cemetery. When Wooreddy had left he had known that his community was dying. Now he

24

found it all but gone. Only Mangana, he and a few females remained alive. The ownership of the island would pass to him, but this was meaningless. Bruny Island belonged to the ghosts. The land rang with their axes, marking it anew just as Great Ancestor had done in the distant past. He heard the crash of falling trees as he watched *num* boats towing to the shore one of the huge animals cursed by *Ria Warrawah*. Like all good animals, they had never got over their capture and often tried to return to the land. *Ria Warrawah* to prevent their escape had slashed off their legs, but this did not stop them from flinging themselves onto the beach. Huge and legless, they would lie helpless on the land, baking under the sun or wheezing under the clouds. They suffered, but never did they try to return to the hated ocean. These large animals, because they belonged to the land, could be eaten along with crayfish, penguins, seals and shellfish. The blubber provided the best oil for smearing the body and catamarans. After one came ashore and was eaten, the giant cradle of bones was flung back into the sea, not as an offering, but in contempt and defiance—to show *Ria Warrawah* that land animals would never belong to him.

Although Wooreddy went to the whaling station to get some of the flesh which the ghosts flung away, he took care that his woman did not go with him. Trugernanna and the other island women went there for both food and excitement. They often spent days at the station and when they finally came back to the camp, they carried with them ghost food. Mangana liked this food and had even begun to smoke the strange herb, tobacco, which his daughter had shown him how to use. He wore over his body a large soft skin which had been given to Trugernanna. He wore this as a sign of surrender and urged Wooreddy to do the same. The *num* were provoked by a naked body so much so that they often killed it. *Num* skins protected a person and if one continued to go naked one courted death. With such a choice before him, Wooreddy took to wearing a blanket.

The ghosts had twisted and upturned everything, Wooreddy thought one day as he went a step further and accepted a *num* skin from a ghost he found with his wife. This did not upset him much as the woman had so increased her demands on him that he had found himself a typical Bruny Islander saddled with a foreign wife. He still consoled himself with the thought that it was the times, and the *num* skin did hide his manhood scars. Not so very long ago, Wooreddy had prided himself on showing the serried rows of arc-shaped scars which showed the degrees of initiation he had passed. Now they had lost all meaning, just as all else had lost meaning. Such alienation brought lassitude and the sudden panic fear that his soul was under attack. To counter this, he pushed his way into the depths of a thicket and made a circular clearing while muttering powerful protection spells. Then he built a small fire in a pit in the centre of the circle, heated a piece of shell in the smoke and opened a number of his scars with it. Blood drops fell towards the flames. Anxiously he watched each drop hiss into steam before touching any of the burning brands. This was good: his spells potent and protection assured. Lighting a firestick in order to preserve the strong life of this fire, he took it back and thrust it into the main campfire. His wife was still absent at the whaling station.

Lunna finally returned from the embraces of the *num*. She carried a bag in which twists of cloth held flour, tea and sugar. Already she had learnt to boil the dark leaves in a shell-like container which did not catch fire and to make 'damper' by mixing the white powder with water and spreading it on hot coals. Wooreddy found that he liked the tea especially when some of the white sand-like grains were added, but the damper stuck in his throat. He preferred seafood, when he could get it, for sometimes when he ordered his wife to go and get some she appeared not to hear. Her large dark eyes would cling to whatever she was doing and she would ignore him. Once when he asked her she continued eating a piece of damper and he took up his spear and felt the tip. It was blunt. He went to the shelter for a sharp piece of stone, then remembered the hatchet and got that instead.

After sharpening his spear, he waddled off to the hunt without a word to his wife. She watched his bottom wobbling off into the bush and smiled. It was one of the things that had attracted her to him. It added a touch of humour which

26

helped to soften his stiff formality of manner. They had had a good relationship, but not as deep as it could have been. Perhaps it was because he belonged to a nation noted for their stiffness. She sighed and began thinking of the *num*.

Wooreddy, not thinking of his wife or his problems, began prowling towards a clearing which had been maintained for a long time and was still not overgrown. With his senses straining for the slightest movement or sound, he achieved a state of blissful concentration which smothered all disagreeable thought. In the clearing three large grey kangaroos hunched, nibbling at the tufts of grass. He crouched behind the trunk of a tree, thanking Great Ancestor that the wind blew in his face, though as a good hunter he had allowed for this. Wooreddy inched forward. One of the animals lifted a delicate face to peer his way. He stopped and after a few moments the animal bent its back to eat the grass. The stalking continued until Wooreddy judged himself close enough to risk a spear throw. Slowly he lifted his leg to take the shaft from between his big toe. Ever so slowly his arm rose as his leg descended at an angle to support his throw. With a lightning-fast stroke, which contrasted with his previous slowness, his spear flashed toward the prey. The force of the blow sent it sprawling onto its side. It leapt up and tried to bound away. It managed only a stagger. The long spear aborted its bound. The kangaroo recovered enough to hop away. Wooreddy trotted after the animal.

In the sudden joy at his success, he had forgotten his club, but no matter. He ran on in his curious duck-like gait which appeared clumsy but was effective. He quickly came upon the animal. It turned to face its pursuer with its back protected by the trunk of a thick tree. Wooreddy picked up a piece of wood as he circled the animal. At bay, it was dangerous. One sudden upward rip of a hind leg could disembowel him. If only he had a companion such as Mangana! Alone, he devised a tactic and ran straight at the kangaroo. At the very last moment he bounded to the left. Animals were like human beings and usually favoured the right side—but not always. He breathed a sigh of relief as the animal brought up its right leg. A fatal move: before the animal could recover he had bashed the thick stick down upon its nose, then belted it on one side of the neck. Wooreddy flung the carcass across his shoulder and took it back to camp. He would feed his sons real food, and not that white junk their mother too often served up.

IV

The island and the people continued to suffer. The darkness of the night-hidden land allied itself with the hidden, green, deep fears of the ocean. Wooreddy could feel it lapping about his middle and touching him with chilly fingers, cold as the white wetness he had once felt in the inland mountains. What had that been called? *turrana*. Now always he could taste salt on his lips and deep down his throat. The sea had invaded his body! This knowledge hit him one day as he was about to step on a snake which had no right to be on the snake-free island. His foot hit the ground a metre from the coiled black body in a rush of fear imagining a hissing death. *Ria Warrawah* had extended the boundary of his domain to include Bruny Island. He knew this for certain as he watched the coughing demon attack the few remaining people. *Ria Warrawah* sucked up souls and amid the vast sighing danger what could he do but chant the old protection spells, gash into his body extra-potent strength marks, carry about relics of the long dead, and hope—hope and watch the sun rise on another cloudy day of hopelessness? Day fell into day, and his numbness became a kangaroo-skin bag to hold his ever-growing panic. He told himself over and over again that he was destined to be a survivor—but, as he cast a glazed eye over the half-dozen people still alive and suffering, even his survival came into question. To survive, yes—but into what future? It lay ahead of him as dead as a fish tossed from the ocean. Automatically, he stared at the sea as he tried to imagine that his life—though not the old traditions giving it shape and meaning—would continue on aimlessly. He sighed and stared bleakly at the *num* crawling like insects on the very body of the devil. Behind him he heard the coughing

28

demon acknowledge the sigh of the ocean. The demon hacked at his wife's chest and he could do nothing. She might eject the demon, but the odds were against it. For some reason he thought of the female, Trugernanna and this caused his mood to lift a little. She would never come to a quick end. The boat pointed in their direction. Its wooden legs swayed the body from side to side. She was every bit a survivor as he himself was. The *num* were coming to them. She would go on and on, just as he would go on, until the end.

In the bow of the boat a *num* stood and, although his body swayed unsteadily, he still managed to impart to it an attitude of eagerness and readiness for action. Wooreddy watched uncaringly. Most *num* sat in their boats, this one did not — so what! Still, as the boat entered the surf, he felt an urge to flee into the safety of the bush. He stayed where he was examining the crew. He saw no killing sticks. This relieved him enough to wait to see what the boat would bring.

The bottom of the boat touched the ground. This was instantly followed by a shouted order from the now-sprawling *num* at the grey-clad crew who grinned as they shipped their oars. At last, obeying the order, they slipped into the surf and manhandled the craft to dry sand. The head ghost scrambled up, assumed his dignity and shouted again: 'Harder, you ruffians, pull harder there.' The watching Wooreddy repeated the sounds *sotto voce* and wondered what they meant. If he had the energy, he might learn the language. The main *num* jumped dryshod onto the beach, saw the Aborigine and stamped toward him with hand outstretched.

The Aborigine waited for the strange intruder to reach him. The *num* was short with a soft body plump from many days of good eating without hunting. Short, stubby legs marched that pot-bellied trunk over the sand with dainty, precise steps lacking the finesse of the hunter. Still there was something of the stamp of a sacred dance in the steps and this gave Wooreddy an interest in the visitor. His eyes brightened as his numbness lessened. The ghost's face, round like the moon, though unscarred, shone pink like the shoulder skin of the early morning sun. Sharp, sea-coloured eyes sought to bridge the gap between them. The ghostly eyes showed such an avid interest in him that he evaded those eyes by staring at the strange skin on the ghost's head. From under it, his hair showed rust-coloured like a vein of red ochre in grey rock.

The *num* grabbed, and succeeded in capturing Wooreddy's hand. It lay limply in the grasp, while the pink-petalled lips began fluttering out sounds which were gibberish to the man. 'Such a poor, poor creature! Such a wretched being bereft of everything we civilised people hold dear. How right I was not to listen to my wife and friends who sought to dissuade me from this charitable and necessary task. No matter what hazard, it is truly the Lord's work and I will persevere.'

Behind his back, the convict crew twisted their faces in mockery. Some of them had endured a visit from him in prison and were familiar with the style of his deliverance. They described it, in their colourful way, as a 'load of shit'. Perhaps it was their felt contempt which had driven George Augustus Robinson to the greener pastures of Aboriginal welfare.

Wooreddy's mouth hesitated on the way to a smile, then he saw the faces the convicts were pulling and grinned for the first time in months. The ghost still clung to his hand. Now he fluted: 'Me, me Mr Robinson.'

Wooreddy's agile mind discarded the pronouns and he repeated: 'Meeter Ro-bin-un.'

While behind him the convicts mouthed the words and even went into a little dance, Robinson pushed his left index finger against Wooreddy's greasy chest and, pronouncing each word slowly and distinctly, asked: 'You, you, your, name, what?' Loud snickers from the boat crew caused him to whirl around and shout: 'Don't stand around. Get that boat up on the beach'—then he turned back to the Aborigine and repeated the words in the same fluting tone, though now edged with anger.

Wooreddy politely answered: '*Narrah warrah* (yes)'

'Pleased to make your acquaintance, I'm sure, Narrah Warrah,' the *num* burbled enthusiastically, not caring if he was understood by the poor matted-haired apparition which stood before him with its nakedness partially covered by a dirty blanket. He had come to save such creatures and they would understand this intuitively. Already, this *Narrah Warrah* knew that he was their friend.

'I am your friend,' he said slowly, his voice dropping to a silky softness which oozed. 'Have no fear, Narrah Warrah'—a snigger from the convicts whipped a snarl into his tone. 'I have come to protect you from such scum as these ruffians behind me—' and he jerked a thumb over his shoulder. Wooreddy intuitively grasped what the gesture meant. He suddenly realised that here was an ally. The self-assured, pompous little ghost before him could be used to help him survive until the end of the world.

He accepted Meeter Ro-bin-un as his very own *num* with the same readiness with which Robinson had accepted the fact that he was destined to save these poor, benighted people. Such a *modus vivendi*, lacking all the essentials of a properly understood relationship, held infinite possibilities from rich comedy to equally rich tragedy. At first, Wooreddy was overjoyed. He had found a protector and also a subject of study. He tested out the relationship by making a gesture and then walking off into the bush. He was happy to find the ghost following, but his happiness disappeared when the ghost marched past him and took the lead. Robinson was defining their relationship from the beginning.

In the camp Wooreddy's wife, Lunna, sat naked and uncaring on a piece of blanket. The coughing demon hacked at her lungs. She didn't even lift her head when the *num* bent over her, his face filled with solicitude. A short distance away, one of her sons sat chewing on a tough piece of kangaroo meat while the other sat waiting his turn. They glanced up; their eyes filled with the image of the ghost, and with a united single shriek they were away into the scrub as fast as their little legs could carry them. The father called out, ordering them to return, but the sound of their feet diminished into the distance. Now and not for the first time, he wondered how he had fathered such boys. He remembered when he was their age and the sudden deep thoughts that had slowed his feet so that he more often found himself facing danger rather than fleeing from it. They had none of the qualities he cherished. It was the fault of their foreign mother. Wooreddy refused to acknowledge that his own stuffiness and indifference might have had something to do with their behaviour patterns. He hardly ever spoke to them and often ignored his wife as well.

'*Meridee bidai lidinee loomerai*,' he said explaining the sickness of his wife, but not his lack of concern—a concern which was expressed on the face of the ghost. But even that concern vanished when Trugernanna walked into the clearing clutching in each small fist an arm of the boys. Wooreddy had not been the only one observing the *num*. Trugernanna, hidden in the scrub, had studied him and decided that he was unlike the ones at the whaling station on the other side of the island. There, all that they wanted to do was take her off somewhere. At first she had found it flattering, but now it was just one of those things.

Away from the *num* the girl often went naked, but now she wore a kangaroo skin wrapped about her full hips. This was a new style which the women had adapted. The old fashion of draping the skin over the shoulders was gone for ever. Now demure in her rough skirt she shot a glance at the ghost and caught his look of approval. They liked females to be covered below the waist for most of the time.

George Augustus Robinson, destined by God to make the Aborigines the most interesting and profitable part of his life, leered at the forbidden fruits of the bare-breasted maiden who conjured up romantic visions of beautiful South Sea islands where missionaries laboured for the salvation of delightful souls. On this island and on the larger one of Van Diemen's Land, he too would be such a missionary. He went into his 'Me, Mr Robinson' routine and this time received a better response. The girl had been around the whalers and sawyers long enough to pick up quite a few words of the ghost language. She replied that her name was Trugernanna and set Robinson right in regard to the name of Wooreddy. In return Robinson smiled an expression which held more than that of the good shepherd at long last finding an intelligent sheep.

She spoke to Wooreddy and enlightened him about the *num*. Finally he had the proof that the ghost was indeed an ally. As Robinson quaintly informed Trugernanna: 'Me look after you, give you food, clothing—bad white man no longer hurt you.' And as the girl just as quaintly echoed: 'Bad *num* no longer hurt us' as she took the protector's hand and gazed up into his face with all the adoration of a child—though the fullness of her breasts belied the pose. Wooreddy found himself ignored. It annoyed him that the woman had captured all the ghost's attention. After all Meeter Ro-bin-un was his ally too!

V

Wooreddy and Trugernanna helped Lunna and the two children to shift along the coast to where Meeter Ro-bin-un had had erected a ghost shelter. It was right on the channel and at night they could see, gleaming across the water, the lights of the main *num* settlement. Robinson wished to acquire a working knowledge of the Bruny language and took every opportunity to learn from the people. He did not offer to teach them his language in return. This would come later. But the Aborigines had realised that they needed to know the ghost language and they too took every opportunity to learn new words and sentences. They found that the main difficulty was in the pronunciation, unlike Robinson who floundered in the complicated grammar structuring Bruny. He never did advance beyond a form of creole, though by this time so few people were left who spoke the language that it did not matter.

The Aborigines soon discovered that their ally considered himself superior to them. They were to be 'children' to his 'father'. The girl fell easily into the role expected and the word 'fader' constantly fell from her lips when Robinson was within hearing. But Wooreddy felt insulted. After all he was a full citizen, not only of his own nation, but of the South West too, and had he not collected, debated and even on one occasion refined a point of law regarding a custom of his people! He was a prominent citizen and a biological father to boot. What was this Ro-bin-un? . . . Then he saw and felt the sickness all around him and surrendered. It seemed a small price to pay for survival.

'Fader' gave him some white powder for his wife's sickness. He mixed it in water and gave it to her to drink. It did no good. She was so weak that she could not sit up. Her body flamed with fever, and to ease her suffering Wooreddy took a sharp piece of glass (shell was a thing of the past) and slashed the most painful parts of her body. The bad blood ran out. For a few days Lunna seemed better, then she had a relapse and died. Wooreddy performed the last rites and sent her soul on the first stage of the journey to Great Ancestor. Then his eldest son caught the coughing sickness and followed his mother into the fire. Wooreddy looked at his youngest son, acknowledged his responsibility, and decided to help him to survive.

Meeter Ro-bin-un did not like anyone going around naked like a human. He wanted everyone to cover their bodies as the ghosts did. 'Novillee, novillee' (not good, not good), he repeated over and over again to them in his atrocious accent. Wooreddy could see nothing wrong in showing the maturity of his manhood. What was wrong for the male to do was to neglect the hair. He took great care in keeping his locks smeared with the heavy ointment made from whale oil and red ochre. But now as he was going to see 'Fader', he pulled on a long shirt and then stuck a feather in his hair.

'Fader' met him with the outstretched hand which Wooreddy politely touched. He explained that he wished 'Fader' to take care of his remaining child and almost recoiled at the avid joy with which the child was received. To Robinson this was an important breakthrough. He wanted to separate the few remaining children from their heathen parents so that they could be educated free from bad examples. Now he complained of those bad examples to Wooreddy. They were not to wander where they wished, but were to stay with him, their only protector. Wooreddy replied as best he could in a mixture of Bruny and Ghost. He was stripping his language down to the bare essentials in order to be understood. All the honorifics, family designations and different grammatical constructions he would have used in conversing with a person belonging to the highly stratified Bruny society were unnecessary. The result sounded barbaric in his ears, but it did serve the purpose he had designed it for. And so he replied in this broken Bruny: '*Trugernanna, Dray, Pagerly maggera raege logana mobbali nunne*' (The three women have gone off to the other *num* for the last three nights). In the same style, though using a number of Ghost-words, he described the death of his wife and eldest son. He complained of the coughing demon and of how the island had become a place of evil. Meeter Ro-bin-un said: 'Nonsense!' Then he hinted (that is, if Wooreddy understood correctly) that they might be leaving shortly on a long trip. Wooreddy questioned him and verified it. They were indeed going on a long trip. How he longed to be away from this evil place! The tie between earth and man had been broken and he never wanted to return.

Meeter Ro-bin-un decided to go and save the three women from the ruffians at the whaling station. He dragged Wooreddy off with him. After he had slowed from the mad dash with which he started things, he pointed out shrubs and expected Wooreddy to give him their names in Bruny. After this he began to talk on things close to Wooreddy's heart, though he would never realise this. He talked down to Wooreddy on religion and much to his surprise found that these children of nature had some faint inkling of a creator god. Wooreddy equated the Christian god with Great Ancestor and gave the name: *Parllerde*. Robinson tried to elicit further information on their primitive religious beliefs, but the primitive form of communication he was using collapsed under the weight of abstractions. He did manage to learn that they also had the concept of the devil, called *Ria Warrawah*. This gladdened his heart, for now he had the two necessary terms for him to begin preaching the gospel to them.

The whaling station was a clutch of ill-shaped wooden sheds about a few large iron pots used for boiling down the blubber. Robinson marched right into the centre of the station, recoiled from the smell of rotting whale flesh, then recovered himself as the manager bustled toward him. Wooreddy, forgotten, hung in the background, his eyes moving in search of the women.

'Mr Robinson, I assume,' the manager said in the direction

of the on-coming Robinson who, steaming with all the righteous wrath of the Lord of Hosts, immediately began the offensive.

'Sir, it is disgusting, too disgusting for words,' he spluttered, fighting to control his pronunciation. 'Sir, 'ow can you allow your men to take advantage of these poor creatures? Sir, it won't be permitted, I 'ave t'ear ob t'gov'nor—' He paused to recover himself. 'Never fear, it shall be in my report. It won't be permitted sir, it won't be!'

The manager, recovering from his surprise, replied coldly in a middle-class accent to which Robinson was practising to attain. 'What won't be, Mr Robinson, and what exactly are you talking about?'

'Native women have been enticed into your station.'

'Enticed, enticed, that's a new word to describe it. Sir, we cannot rid ourselves of them.'

'Sir, if you read the gazette you will know that His Excellency, Governor George Arthur, has placed me in charge of these creatures. I have them in charge, sir! It is my duty to look after their welfare and to protect them from such types as your men. It is my duty to protect them, and protect them I shall!'

While the ghosts shouted at each other, Wooreddy wandered off. He looked inside the hut where the women stayed, or were put, when they visited the whaling station. They were not there. He looked down onto the ground to find the newest set of tracks, but the dust was too smudged for him to read the time. He returned to the two ghosts and waited for a silent moment to break into their wrangle. At last he made himself understood that the women were not there. Meeter Ro-bin-un stamped off, streaming words to the effect that he would send letters officially to each European ordering them not to interfere with the native women, or men for that matter. Wooreddy caught the words 'this letter' and remembered that they referred to the strange lines of abstract shapes which the *num* drew on thin sheets of bark called 'paper'. When 'Fader' had cooled down enough he tactlessly asked about 'this letter' and set him off again. He shouted out to the trees: 'I'll haddress ha circular letter to heach and hevery un o' t'ese reprobates. I will not hallow

36

t'em to co'abit wit t'a native females. I'll put a stop to i, t'at I twill.' Then he pulled himself together and in a clearer voice patiently explained to the good doctor that 'this letter' was magic and so was the bark called 'paper'. 'Put pen to paper,' he declared, 'and the waggon begins to roll and the house to be built.' This mystified Wooreddy still further. Finally gesture and repeated *num* words got the meaning across. How childlike they were, Robinson thought while the good doctor politely acknowledged the magic of the symbols scratched onto a thin sheet of bark with a stick dipped in charcoal. They might well be magic, he thought, declaring: '*Neire* this paper, *neire* this letter; good this paper, good this letter.'

'Extremely good, Wooreddy,' 'Fader' agreed holding the man's hand in his own pale paw. 'We will put a stop to this immorality,' he said squeezing the hand.

Wooreddy smiled in the warmth, nodded vigorously and urged: 'send this letter, send this paper.'

Robinson returned to the hut and wrote and wrote. Nothing happened; the women did not return. Finally Mangana got up one morning and ambled off in the direction of the whaling station. His daughter had been gone too long and he missed seafood and *num*-food. Wooreddy wandered off after him. Both returned after a week, but the women refused to come with them. Wooreddy began to doubt the efficacy of 'this letter' and 'this paper'. He began to pester 'Fader' with a continuing wail of 'Send this letter; send this paper, Fader and they will come'.

The ghost had spent long hours in acquiring his style of writing; and though it had been some time since the Governor had acknowledged his report or sent instructions, he still believed in the power of the written word just as he believed that faith would move mountains. Still he decided that he would personally deliver his next report and stir things up. Already he felt bored at being stuck on the island for over three months. He was a man of action and longed to be up and about. 'Things are about to happen,' he assured Wooreddy, as he bent his head to continue scrawling the long words of a long and tedious report.

In their own good time the women finally limped back to

37

the camp. After a day or so they planned to go fishing. Wooreddy had found to his dismay that the attractions of not having a woman were countered by the attractions of having a woman. In short, he needed a new wife. Women could brave the ocean and endure its cold pressure while they prised off abalone or grabbed the crayfish crawling along the very sea bottom. Trugernanna, young and agile, squat and strong, was a powerful swimmer who enjoyed her mastery of the watery element. She could fill this hole in his life. After thinking overlong in his usual fashion, at last he approached her father to see if his offer still stood.

Mangana seemed to have become all grey—his hair, his beard and even his skin was grey. He sat at his fire watching a few roots called 'potatoes', which Meeter Ro-bin-un gave out, darkening in the ashes of the fire. Wooreddy once had liked sitting with the old man, but since the ghost had arrived he had spent much less time with him. Mangana seemed senile and it was difficult to speak to him. In reply to sentences he usually grunted or muttered a single word or strung words together in meaningless sentences. Still he had to ask the old man's permission—he did so and waited and waited. At last the old man shifted his eyes from the fat possum Wooreddy had placed next to him and began to speak without the ceremonial opening which tradition had once demanded.

'Ahaha, *Ria Warrawah*, the darkness fleeing. My wives, my children—all but one gone! How dark the day is—and Trugernanna friends with those from *Ria Warrawah*. The Islands of the Dead! Does she wish to jump up over there where even the water is white and cold? Great Ancestor sits at his campfire in a sunny land and waits. Things are as they were, ever changing. They sicken and die on this island once our homeland. The dead roam whining in the night and it is best to leave them with the ghosts. That is right!'

Mangana fell into an ocean of sorrows and the younger man shared his pain. Then he began to speak again.

'Trugernanna, an ocean girl, a sea girl, a lover of ghosts. A ghost girl, a pale girl, she will live on longer than all of us. Go and eat her food, go and love her loveless body, go and share whatever she will offer. You and she are both foolish

38

enough to want life. It is for both of you and some of it will be enjoyable. Tomorrow is but a day away from Great Ancestor, he lives in me . . .'

The old man rambled on for an hour allowing the younger man to share the past of his life laid out in words and silences, gestures and feelings and things beyond Wooreddy's ken. When he left he felt himself floating in the old man's memories, but he had promised to bring him a fat doe kangaroo as payment for permission to court Trugernanna.

VI

'Motto nyrae parlerdi motti novilli raegewrappa. Parlerdi maggera warrangelli, raegewrappa maggera toogenna uenee. Nyrae parlewar logerna taggera teeni lawwai warrangelli. Parlerdi nyrae, nyrae raege logerna taggera teenni lawwai warrangelli; novilli parlerwar logerna taggera teeni toogunna raegewroppa uenee maggera uenee...'

'Fader' stopped his somewhat premature attempt at a sermon in Bruny and rose in eloquence and competence as he continued on in Ghost. His flow of moral rhetoric was directed at his convict servants carefully segregated from those he called his 'sable friends'.

One of his 'sable friends' had been stealing glances at another 'sable friend' throughout the attempt at Bruny. With the abrupt change in language, Wooreddy switched his mind off Trugernanna and onto the words he had heard. Within them must reside some sort of meaning. They seemed to mean that if you were good, that is, kept the laws of the Bruny Islanders, on death or after death you travelled along the sky-trail to where Great Ancestor had his camp; but if you were bad, that is, did not follow the customs, you stayed below in the sea or dark hollows with *Ria Warrawah*. All in all, if he had interpreted the mishmash of words correctly Meeter Ro-bin-un had just given a very simple account of the Bruny Island religion. 'Fader' also had seemed to imply that ghosts too could travel along the skyway, but this was wrong. Ghosts came from the Islands of the Dead (a halfway stop on the way to Great Ancestor) and when they left Bruny Island they would return there. But the good doctor, not content with the apparent meaning, sought a deeper and more esoteric meaning.

'Fader' could be relating a part of his own past as a human being. Then he had been 'bad' and thus after death failed in his attempt to reach Great Ancestor. Now his present life was a warning to all humans not to go astray. Using his excellent memory he recalled Robinson's words to check if they fitted with his interpretation.

'One good Great Ancestor; one bad demon. Great Ancestor, good! Great Ancestor stop sky; demon stop below fire (*this must mean that he stayed in the dark places of the earth and ocean*). Good men dead go road up sky. Good RAEGE (*perhaps num or ghosts*) dead go road up sky (perhaps this was a rhetorical question?). Bad men dead go road below (*across the sea to the Island of the dead, this meant*). Demon, fire, stop fire.' These last words puzzled the good doctor; tentatively they meant that the demon (*Ria Warrawah*) hated fire and always tried to extinguish it.

'Fader's' voice ceased its rolling and only the sound of the surf continued. Wooreddy left his musings and noticed that the *num*'s eyes glittered (he still could not think of the ocean without a qualm) like the sun shining off the sea.

Meeter Ro-bin-un was enraptured by the eloquence of his own sermon. He raised his arms and spread them as Wooreddy neared, and exclaimed into the blank faces of the convicts: 'Come, my child, God has not forgotten you. Poor pitiful child from a pitiful race friendless and alone in a dark and hostile world. Now you too have a father just as I have a father in heaven.'

'Yeh, fader,' the childman replied, as the ghost's rapturous eyes clung to him for some sign of recognition. 'Yeh, fader,' he repeated, taking the opportunity to try out his pronunciation.

If the man's repeated two words were not enough for the ghost, Trugernanna's seeming rapture equalled his own. She stood beside him, her face uplifted, her brown eyes fixed on his nose while her small body trembled under the sack-like

40

dress she wore. Such obvious adoration elicited from Robinson a deep red flush which had little to do with religious ecstasy.

He found himself feeling the same temptation he belaboured in others—but, unlike the others (he told himself) he would never take advantage of the trusting natures of these child-like creatures. He moved closer to Wooreddy and was relieved that the woman did not follow him. Then in the need to put space between desire and the object of desire, he indicated to the man that he wished to go to the narrow neck uniting the northern and southern parts of the island.

Wooreddy picked up his spear as Robinson raced off at a fast trot into the undergrowth. The man would have liked to question the ghost about the sermon, but the fast waddle he was forced to keep up made his breath rush in and out of his lungs like, like—again a sea simile came to trouble him—seawater in a narrow inlet. At last, and none too soon for the gasping Wooreddy, 'Fader' halted his headlong plunge, which had rendered him as desireless as his companion breathless. Wooreddy flopped down beside a bush and to excuse himself told the ghost that kangaroos liked to eat it. Robinson too took the opportunity to catch his breath. Wooreddy, after giving the *num* the names of a few other plants, took the opportunity to get onto his problem. '*Lubra logerner piggerder nene*,' he began in the pidgin dialect he had labelled 'Ro-bin-un' after its inventor. 'Fader's' ruddy face assumed an expression of concern as he heard the man mention his dead mate, and Wooreddy, observing that he had aroused the correct feeling, continued on to explain how a human male without a female was lost; he felt like that and had fixed on Trugernanna for a mate.

'Fader' smiled, and his mood and expression switched to jocular. 'You would like to have that one, eh? Can't say that I blame you. Might be good for her too! Keep her away from those ruffians at the whaling station. She'll make you a good wife,' rambled Robinson, and unfortunately brought Trugernanna to mind. His evil inclinations returned, and instantly his short stubby legs churned, rushing him away from his goal. Wooreddy waddled after him. Luckily he had tied a

41

charmed cord around his leg for energy—but not for speed, he found, as he lagged more and more behind Robinson as he charged towards the sea. The *num* came up against the steep slope of a hill and perforce had to slow his pace. He was clambering up as Wooreddy reached the foot. Higher and higher they climbed and slower and slower went Robinson until his companion caught up with him. They climbed up and over the summit, then down and along a wide crack below the lip of a cliff. Wooreddy shuddered and avoided glancing down at the lashing ocean which filled his ears, whooshing like his breath. His nostrils filled with sea-smell and his bare feet and ghost-skin leg coverings dripped from the hurtling spray. Then they were rushing off inland along a stream which rapidly became a swamp. Wooreddy became bogged in the clinging mud and left his trousers behind. Free of them he almost skimmed over the sticky mud. Now they scrambled up another hill, but this time the man had found his second breath and took the lead from the ghost. He even helped him over the steepest places and slyly when they reached the summit began a wide circle which would take them back to the camp. The sun was hidden by thick clouds and Robinson did not notice until the brush thinned, then he headed them towards the sea.

They came out onto the beach where a sharpened pile of rocks stood just offshore. The wind had died and Wooreddy felt that he could look at the stretch of water. It seemed less menacing. Tiny wavelets felt the sand grains and fell back. He saw three women standing on a low rock just above sea level. Each had a woven bag slung over the left shoulder. They climbed up the rock pile to stand sharply etched against the sky. Wooreddy recognised the lithe figure of Trugernanna—and so did Robinson! The woman held herself as straight as a child's toy spear, and the man decided that her small, pointed breasts were large enough to feed a manchild just as her hips were wide enough to give one birth. Robinson pushed down any carnal thoughts and sought to see the scene before him as an idyllic painting.

The women, in formation, flung themselves headfirst at the sea. Wooreddy gave a gasp. Such daring, he thought. Though the scene was very familiar, it always filled him with dread. Few men, if any, would have the nerve, or the courage, or potent enough charms, to dive headfirst into the domain of *Ria Warrawah*. The very idea gave him goosebumps. The women did not appear and he grew alarmed. No one was safe in the sea! Then their three cropped heads bobbed in the water, and towing full bags, they slowly made their way towards the beach.

Robinson's mouth went dry and his ruddy face paled as the women rose like succubi from hell to tempt him with all the dripping nakedness of firm brown flesh.

'God, let this chalice pass from me, let me not succumb to temptation and the snares of the evil one,' he whispered hoarsely as the dainty Trugernanna came to him, smiling around the wooden chisel clenched between her strong white teeth. The man with the ghost was more interested in the weight and content of the woman's bag. It bulged with oysters, and poking up from the bottom a large crayfish quivered spasmodically.

'Good, good, Fader,' Wooreddy exclaimed to the ghost.

'Very good,' the *num* replied, meaning not the harvest of the woman, but her body.

The object of attention was very conscious of Wooreddy's smile and the direction of his eyes. With his mate gone to the fire, he would be after a replacement. She scowled into his eyes, then turned to the silent Robinson and mock-snarled: 'No kangaroo, no possum, no man!' The good doctor smiled after her retreating buttocks. These words marked the beginning of their courtship. After all, she knew his skill as a hunter!

Trugernanna went to where her father sat cross-legged before his fire. She watched him watch a glowing coal fade and die. She only saw the coal fading, but he saw his people dying. One by one, two by two, three by three and more, they went, some quickly, some slowly to Great Ancestor or to *Ria Warrawah*. So Mangana thought, but his daughter had little concern for the contents of the old man's mind and his morose lines of thought. Very much the physical person, she enjoyed things she could touch and affect, and ignored anything like the wispy mind-traces of the aging. Now she stoked up the fire, waited until the sticks had become glowing

43

coals, then put on them the large crayfish and around it a number of oysters. When the shell of the crustacean had turned the red of the best imported ochre and the shells of the oysters gaped open like so many little mouths, she carefully removed them and put them on a piece of bark which she placed in front of her father. He stared at the food for an overlong minute, then broke off the tail and legs. He pushed the rest toward the girl. She ate, then went off to gather wood to last the fire throughout the night. Since that man, Wooreddy, the one with the funny walk, had given her father a *num* axe, she could even chop up the larger logs. Still they had been so long in this place that good, dry timber was becoming scarce. Carrying the last armful back, she found the man sitting with her father. This was not unusual, nor were the two possums roasting on the fire. She was surprised when she found that one of the possums was for her. Breaking the fragile body apart, she found inside a tiny baby. She popped the morsel into her mouth, enjoying the sweetest of all flavours.

Unlike other nights, Mangana retired early to his shelter. The two were alone at the fire. Trugernanna scowled into the flames, completely ignoring the man. They sat in silence for an hour, then the woman shot a hostile glance at Wooreddy and got up to make a fire in front of her sleeping quarters. She returned, put a large log on the main campfire, checked the supply of wood in front of her shelter, then went to bed.

The good doctor sat on at the fire. At last he moved. Not getting to his feet he hopped like a kangaroo towards where Trugernanna lay. The last few metres he covered in such exaggerated stealth that he managed to crack a twig. The sharp snap alerted the woman who was pretending to be asleep. She lay still until the man reached out a finger to scratch her on one firm breast, then she sprang up with a whispered string of curses: 'Get away, you ghost, you demon, you evil spirit. My father will take his knife and make a woman out of you, you mistake of a man that cannot even find the carcass of a rotting kangaroo for the bride price. Go and find a man to fit your womanhood. Go, or I'll scream for my father!'

Wooreddy's teeth gleamed in the firelight. The good doctor

knew the stages of courtship. On the first night should be only a slight touch, or if possible a scratch; on the second, the suitor might move his hand over part of the woman's body; and on the third, he could try to lie beside her—though this (unless they were already lovers) should be met with lamentation, the woman should threaten to do away with herself rather than stay with him. On the fourth night, the woman flees to sleep beside her mother and father, and repeats this on the succeeding night. On the sixth night the couple finally lie together, but without touching, and after an hour or so the man should leave in mock dismay and anger. They stay apart on the seventh night, but at dawn the woman glides into the bush and after a time the man follows her. They spend a few days away from the camp with the male showing his prowess as a hunter by keeping the bride supplied with food. If all goes well, they return married. Such was the tradition and both had the theory down pat. Trugernanna found herself enjoying the rituals which were heightening her emotions to the final point of relief in surrender.

Mangana was too listless to play the role of both father and mother, or even just the father. His daughter, as custom demanded, needing someone who would listen to her bewailing her fate, chose Meeter Ro-bin-un. If Wooreddy appeared in her sight, she immediately sought out her protector, her cheeks wet with tears. She accused the man of being a demon and even of killing his first wife. 'Fader' became overheated with the excited girl hanging from his neck while she tearfully sobbed out some wild accusation. Constantly, he had, figuratively, to take himself by the scruff of that same neck and force himself to play the role of father. The good doctor had filled 'Fader' in on his part and *Wooreddy* himself also had a role to play. One moment he smiled meaningfully at the woman, the next he crept up on her unawares, gestured angrily and acted as if he would carry her off by force. At other times he would scowl and turn away if he so much as glimpsed her. The nights moved along until by the fifth everything and everyone had become entangled in the mock drama of the courtship. Wooreddy often found himself trying to hide a partial or full erection.

The *num* trousers helped, but also hindered—the woman should notice in mock horror and show contempt for his erect penis.

The sixth and seventh nights were a time of trial for the good doctor. Fully aroused, he tried to grab his future mate, but she easily evaded his clutches. On the final dawn she ran off into the bush. Wooreddy filled in the waiting time by sharpening his spear or attempting to sharpen it. At last he raced off into the bush at the spot where he had last seen the woman. He found her tracks, lost them, found them again and eventually caught a glimpse of his prey through the trees. She had discarded her ghost wrappings and was her bare, lithe self. Now she disappeared and he could find no trace of her. Suddenly she materialised at his feet and sprang off. He followed closely.

Trugernanna came to the edge of a low cliff and scrambled down a narrow path which led to a shallow cave. This was to be the bridal suite. *Num* blankets had been spread over the rock floor for them. She sat down and ignored Wooreddy when he entered.

Finally, still looking at the floor, she muttered: 'A strong man would have carried food; a clever man would have found food.'

'A man in pursuit of game does not carry provisions with him,' Wooreddy answered, giving the standard response. He left to hunt.

It was not until late afternoon that he returned with six young possums. In his absence she had made a fire, but he had to cook the food. He did so, passed her half, waited until she had sampled it, then ate also. After eating, she went to the nearby stream for water and came back with a filled container from which he drank—then, unable to keep his hands off her, he grabbed. She struggled as he pressed his body against hers.

'Leave me alone, you'll hurt me,' the woman protested to no avail. She fell on her back as he entered her, then waited for him to begin as he waited for her. Wooreddy did not know that Trugernanna had only endured the rough embraces of ghosts, and so many older women had died that she had remained ignorant of the different sexual positions. The

46

man, almost twice her age and having already had one woman go to the fire, wondered at her lack of knowledge and movement. He decided to use the 'open legs' variations. They were simple enough for a novice to master and later they could progress to such variations as 'riding the canoe', 'climbing aboard', 'from the back', 'across', and so on.

The good doctor moved onto his right side and kept the girl on her back. Now he twisted her hips towards him and re-entered her. He pulled her top leg towards his shoulder and began a slow rhythm. This was the first step and a modification of the classical beginning. The woman remained on her back, but now he squatted right against her buttocks with both her legs over his shoulders. Holding her around the shoulders he began a faster rhythm, slowed, and moved into another position. Now both lay on their sides facing each other. Leaving out further variations he returned to the first position and contented himself with varying the rhythm.

Trugernanna was bewildered by so much movement. She had not experienced anything like it before. It reminded her a little of dancing. Then the man, now her mate, gave a long sigh which pushed his body into a series of jerks. She felt his nails digging into her back and marking out a line of half moons. Wooreddy had chosen a straight line rather than a curved one, as this was the good luck sign for a future filled with food. A curve meant a wish for children; an oval, faithfulness — both these things meant little in these times.

The woman accepted her fate with a numbness worthy of Wooreddy. In the past she had found sex to be a weapon useful for survival and felt little pleasure in it. She gave her body in exchange for things and that was where the importance lay. Her husband's love-making meant less than the rape that had been inflicted on her. She hated the men for doing that, and was indifferent to what Wooreddy could or would do.

Tradition ordained that the husband take his new wife over his land, explaining the landscape and earning her respect by showing his prowess as a hunter. Trugernanna watched her husband, armed only with a club, stalk a kangaroo, bring it to bay against a tree, then race in to deal the death blow. She appreciated the deftness that belied his seemingly clumsy gait. Each day Wooreddy made love to his wife, but her lack of response began to bore him. After all, he was a doctor with a knowledge of love-making and he had already been married. Now it all seemed for nought. Finally he accepted the fact that they were together, not for love, but for survival. One needed allies during the ending of the world, and he had coupled himself with Trugernanna and Meeter Ro-bin-un. This had to be enough, he thought, as he led his new wife back to the camp.

3

Flight from the Ill-omened Land

I

The good doctor, evaluating all that had happened, was
happening, and was about to happen, concluded that he had
to leave his homeland forever. The unity between man and
land had been severed by the agents of *Ria Warrawah* and
when he walked he felt he was stepping on the ashes of the
dead. His feet itched and shrank from the earth where once
the veins had drawn sustenance. His earth was polluted and
whether he sat, or lay or stood, his flesh crawled. He began
constantly scratching himself. He told his wife and she
heartily agreed with him that they had to leave.

Trugernanna had charmed her way into the heart of
Meeter Ro-bin-un. So much so that he decided to take her
across to Hobarton as an example of his prowess in civilising
the savages. Marching pompously along Macquarie Street
and feeling at least some of the eyes of the populace on
them, he swept his hand around at the town, then rested his
eyes on the small dark woman hobbling along behind him in
a long demure shift. She looked as sweet as a schoolgirl and
just as vulnerable—though even more available, he thought,
with a shudder at this forbidden conclusion. 'Look, look, my
child,' he began somewhat unsteadily—his voice steadied as
he spied an army officer coming towards them. 'Look, my
child, this is your future and the future of all your race now
living in miserable nakedness in the hidden fastnesses of the
island.' The officer coldly nodded as he passed. Robinson
continued to talk while he was in earshot. 'Under my supervision, you will become civilised and Christianised. You will
learn how to live in one of these houses and work for your

49

daily bread as it is written . . .'

'Yes Fader,' Trugernanna obediently lisped, as she tried to get the hang of walking in the constricting skirt. Her eyes fluttered from strange sight to stranger sight. Heavy, inert shelters and rough white faces everywhere in frightening profusion and confusion. Her eyes clung to a ghost female wrapped in many more layers of constricting cloth than she herself was. Her face was covered with white dust and ochre. Then two yellow-clad convicts heaved a heavy dray across her field of vision and the future loomed worse than the present. A drunken man lurched out of a low doorway, stopped with a falling forward motion, thrust a twisted face the colour of red ochre at her, then staggered toward her cringing form. Robinson stopped him with a gesture which showed that the girl was under his protection; but his too-visible repugnance for the state of drunkenness and those in it caused the *num* to guffaw loudly as he stumbled back from whence he had come. Robinson's opinions on low-life vices as well as the Aboriginal problem had trickled down to the bottom of what passed for society in Hobarton. He wanted to be known, and he was! Many thought him mad; others a religious crank, and the rest a pompous bore. But the Governor of the Colony, George Arthur, held similar views to those of Robinson and the power lay with him. Robinson was on the way to an interview at which he would parade for inspection one of his better-looking charges.

The Robinson-Trugernanna interview with the Governor was a haze of incomprehension for the girl. They had passed through a clearing coloured with red, blue and yellow ghost flowers, which she could not touch or even examine closely, into a room in which a ghost bent over a table making those strange marks on that strange bark or skin, which Meeter Ro-bin-un was always doing and which he said was magic. After waiting a long time, filled with ponderous dread for Trugernanna, they passed through another door and into a small bare room in which another *num*, this one dressed in plain black, sat gazing down at a piece of board. She saw that it was covered with pictures of ghosts and humans. Finally the ghost raised his eyes and she saw another proud one like 'Fader'—but even more so, for whereas Meeter Ro-bin-un bubbled under his stiff exterior, this one radiated a coldness. He was as remote as the chilly ghost islands from whence he had come.

'Your Excellency,' Robinson began, 'I bring with me one of those poor creatures to which I have devoted myself at the expense of my other business—and my wife and children' he added, remembering how his wife had complained of his absence from home. 'But,' he continued, 'no sacrifice is too great. There are many of these people scattered across the island and living in the darkness of heathendom.'

Governor Arthur, though seemingly absent of any emotion, was a Christian and had to agree with the person before him, who was part of his solution to the Aboriginal problem, as was the board in front of him. He stared down at it, then raised his eyes and finally answered Robinson: 'We are all Christians and know our duty, Sir! My intentions are first to pacify them, then to civilise and Christianise them into good subjects of Her Majesty. They are British subjects and thus entitled to the full protection of British law. But first they must be brought to obey that law and to do that they must know what the law is. I have been making, or rather, I have had fashioned an object which might show our dusky brethren that we mean them no harm and that British law applies equally to black and white.'

The Governor passed the board to Robinson. He studied it intently. Arthur explained: 'As they have no knowledge of writing, I think that our intentions may best be transmitted by images.'

'Yes,' he agreed. 'I, myself, on occasion have seen their rude drawings scratched into the bark of trees. They would understand this. Let us put it to the test. At my side stands one of these simple folk: Trugernanna, a princess of her people who, alas, are fast disappearing owing to sickness. Bruny Island appears to be unsuitable as the site for the Institution in which they might be civilised. Another place should be found, and quickly. I trust that the Aborigines' Committee has recommended your plan of placing them in some secure place where they may be taught . . . This female has a lively mind.'

He placed the painted board in Trugernanna's hands and

began to speak to her in his atrocious Bruny. He modelled himself on the real missionaries he had read about in the London Missionary Society pamphlets. He switched to English for Arthur's benefit. 'Trugernanna, you see this, you know what it is and what is drawn there. Look at each picture and tell me what you see.' He glanced at the Governor to check that his attention was on him, then moved his finger from picture to picture. The bottom left illustration portrayed a ghost shooting an Aborigine and being strung up by a soldier identifiable by his red coat. Beside it an Aborigine speared a ghost and was hung by a soldier while a stern-faced man in black looked on. The middle picture on the board had the Governor in full regalia greeting (accepting the surrender of?) a befeathered chief at the head of his tribe. The top illustration showed an Aboriginal man arm-in-arm with a ghost. The *num* clutched the leash of a black dog and the Aborigine clutched the leash of a white dog. Beside the two males stood a human and a ghost toddler holding hands and next to them the two mothers, the white one holding a human baby and the dark one a ghost baby. The Aborigines all wore ghost clothing and obviously lived happily together in a ghost world. Such was Arthur's vision.

Trugernanna looked from figure to figure and added up the messages. Then she looked at Robinson and then at the Governor. What did they want her to say? Finally she blurted out in her broken English: '*Num* with gun kill man. Soldiers come, led by Gub'na, and kill bad ghost. Same thing happens on other side 'cept soldiers killing poor human, like they kill my uncle. Gub'na good man, good man like Meeter Ro-bin-un, want all of us be friends and after that Fader—' she looked trustingly at Robinson, much to his delight—'will teach us to be happy.'

She felt the glee that her words had caused in 'Fader' and knew that she had managed to say the right thing. He had had to impress the Governor that he was the right man for the job and Trugernanna had shown that he was. Now he would get that grant of 200 acres and thus show his wife that he was not wasting his time. The interview continued between the two ghosts. Trugernanna, having performed her part, was all but forgotten. She squatted against the wall and waited, only half understanding what was being said. The *num* were calmly and deliberately settling the future of her people. One piece of news which she caught gave her a bright smile. She could not wait to tell Wooreddy.

II

After successfully concluding his business with the Governor, Robinson strutted, as much as his short legs allowed him, towards Elizabeth Street. His substantial home had been built by the hands of his two assigned convict servants. His once-timid wife had taken to nagging him about staying away. He thought of this with ill-concealed irritation as he stood admiring his smart brick house, one of the best in the town. He had been only a few years in the colony and already was a man of substance. How right he had been to migrate to Van Diemen's Land—yet his wife persisted in wanting to go back to the old country. He grimaced again in irritation. Why, he had had to practically beg her in countless letters to come out and join him. It was no way for a wife to behave, as he had told her time and again. Now she wanted him to stay in Hobarton and not venture away from the town. Well, he knew his course of action and would follow it. When he returned to the homeland, he would return as a man of worth and not as—he grimaced again, but this time in distaste—a mere bricklayer. He felt eyes on him and realised that Trugernanna was waiting for him to move. He entered his abode, deposited the girl with the convict cook (they had not had servants in England) and went into the living room where he found his wife engaged in embroidering a sampler.

After exchanging a cold greeting with her, he told her to see about tea and to give some food to the Aboriginal girl in the kitchen. Then he sank back into his special soft chair (a bargain he had bought from a newly arrived immigrant) and thumbed through the Government Gazette. He admired his name printed therein, notifying the public that he had been

53

appointed as storeman on Bruny Island. He vowed that his name would appear in print again and again, but never more in such a lowly position. His wife poured him a strong cup of tea sweetened with two spoonfuls of sugar, then assumed her seat at the window and continued on with her embroidery. He looked across at her. She was fat and her breath came in little gasps which got on his nerves. Why had he married such a woman? 'Marie,' he called to the stout woman he happened to be married to. She gave a start, and her somewhat vacuous blue eyes flickered to his face and then away. This was another habit which annoyed him.

'Marie,' he said again into the vacuum of her waiting silence. 'God has been good to us since we arrived in Hobarton and we must be thankful for his gifts.' He stopped and the woman slowly nodded. She knew that when he began a conversation so piously in due course he would hurt her. 'Not only have we a thriving brickworks.' His voice lowered, and she waited for both good and bad news. 'Marie, you will be happy to know that already my government position has brought us two hundred acres.'

'Yes George,' the wife replied, waiting for the blow to fall.

'My work on the isle of Bruny has almost come to an end, but the future for me and my charges is still a little unclear. The Aborigines' Committee, that more-than-useless group, have been debating while waiting for the Governor to make their decision. This he will do shortly. I 'ave jus' come from 'im,' he hesitated over his excitement betraying his cockney origin. He spoke on even more slowly. 'The governor his hinclined—' he jerked his head angrily. 'The governor is inclined,' he repeated in a rush, 'to my view. Shortly I will be ordered to proceed into the wilderness to contact the savages living in the forests. If, God willing, I am successful, then all will be well. If not, then it does not matter. I still have the brick business. Marie, in a week or so, I am departing into the primeval wilderness as head of an expedition to contact the Aborigines. Thank the Lord, Marie, this is a great opportunity for us.'

'For us, for us, what about me? Stuck here all alone in this dump. You can't do this to me. Why did I ever come to this place? Why did I?' the wife fairly shrieked in her anguish.

'Marie,' Robinson admonished her. 'It is the will of the Lord.'

Any opposing of wills in the Robinson household always ended with the husband calling on the Lord to back him up. This time Marie hesitated to accept that it was God's will.

'Why in God's name do you want to concern yourself in a business best left to the government? Your concern here is going on good and you are well on the way to becoming a man of substance,' she said in a much better accent than her husband's. 'Then consider my protection in this outlandish town filled with roving criminals. I hardly know a soul apart from a few soldiers' wives and not one of them comes from London. Sir, this colony of ours is a big gaol and no one is safe in it. Why just the other day, the Fords' place just a mile down the road was pillaged by a band of rogues.'

The husband remained unmoved. He deigned to settle the matter once and for all by recourse to his travelling bible (an ominous symbol in itself). He placed it on the table and intoned: 'Let the Lord decide our future direction.' His wife stared at the holy book. She knew that her husband would win, but all the same she continued to stare as he randomly opened the bible, closed his eyes and stabbed out a stubby finger. Then he chanted out in deep satisfaction: '*Matthew, 12, 17–18*. "Esaias the prophet saying, Behold thy servant, whom I have chosen, my beloved, in whom my soul has found its delight. I will put my spirit upon him, and he shall shew forth judgement to the natives." Then he said in his normal voice: 'Now we have the final answer,' and his wife could only nod her head in agreement, while Trugernanna sitting sleepily in a warm kitchen corner next to the door smiled in affirmation.

III

The Aboriginal woman had a different kind of interview with some ghosts before she left Hobarton. A group of female *num*, hearing about the Aboriginal girl, descended on the Robinson household with shrill cries of delight. They saw Trugernanna with her cropped hair and shapeless smock and oohed and aahed over the handsome young savage. Robinson restored her sex with a few curt words. The females were too richly dressed for his puritan taste. His words swung the female ghost minds in another direction. They bore off the passive Trugernanna for tea and cakes, and a complete change of clothing. Robinson could hardly believe his eyes when they deposited the changed Trugernanna back at his house. She was arrayed in all the finery of long past London fashion. A flounced skirt dragged at her legs and her breasts were constricted in a high-buttoned blouse trimmed at throat and sleeves with lace.

She delighted in her new finery and, having taken a few quick lessons from the ladies in deportment, now pranced before 'Fader'. He changed her mood with a frown. Such frivolity should not even be contemplated let alone engaged in. His object was to create respectable Christian men and women free from the immorality besetting European society. Now they had taken one of his charges and led her into that depraved life. Quickly he ordered the female convict servant to divest the girl of such clothing and replace it with a decent smock of Maria Island flax. When she was returned to him, he admired the way she looked. How clean, young and healthy—and he pushed any other thoughts away. She looked as befitted her sex—modest! Now he must take her away from the town lest she be contaminated.

Wooreddy was watching the boat pulling towards the shore. He saw Trugernanna leap overboard and swim to where he was standing. She ran to him eagerly and told him that they would soon leave the island. He laughed in happiness, then laughed again when he heard that they would be travelling along the west coast where he had once lived. That country was still clean, unlike his own where no peace could be found and the link between man and land had been broken for ever. His happiness fled as quickly as it came. His body itched and he began scratching. His wife watched him and felt his sadness. The old ways were dead and the past was only a backdrop to their present and future.

But before they could escape their polluted earth, another one of their people left them. Mangana sat at his fire one night and during that night the smoke of his spirit ascended towards Great Ancestor. Next morning, the loud wails from the few surviving women drew 'Fader' from his ghost-shelter. He came and gazed long in sorrow at the corpse. Once Mangana had been a powerful man, then he had decayed into a lethargy which he could not understand. He sighed and took the opportunity to introduce the practice of Christian burial. He ordered one of the convicts to dig a grave while he went to get his prayer book. Then he got Wooreddy to carry the body to the hole. The man did so, though instead of lowering it gently into the grave, he let it fall with an unChristian thud. Meeter Ro-bin-un harangued them in his bad Bruny that 'this way good: that way bad'. His charges nodded as he began the burial service. They had already decided that Mangana must be cremated in the proper way. They came that night, dug up the body and filled in the hole. Dawn found them on the far side of the island.

Wooreddy, as the only surviving male of the community, had charge of the cremation. He had a problem. The body was stiff and unbendable. After carefully pondering the matter, he finally settled on an unorthodox pyre in the shape of a long rectangle. It was the only possible shape if the bones were not to be broken and, Wooreddy reminded himself, the times themselves were unorthodox. The women collected the timber and he built up the pyre and when it was the correct height laid the corpse on it. In the grey light of early morning, he watched the heat of the orange flames melting down the body. The smoke did not rise beyond the tree tops, a bad omen which might necessitate an extra ceremony; then a gentle gust of a breeze took the smoke up and away from the island and toward the mainland. A good omen for the living and the dead.

They waited until the fire turned into glowing coals. Before leaving Trugernanna gathered some of the ashes into a small leather bag. These would help her in the difficult days ahead.

Wooreddy, from the first, had been disturbed at the way the funeral had gone. It was as awry as the times and potentially dangerous in spite of the good omen at the end. Why had not the daughter of the dead man wailed and lamented in the proper fashion? Even in these times as many as possible of the old ways should be kept up. Frowning, he came into the camp. In the bay a small vessel was furling sails. He saw a boat walking towards the shore.

IV

Next morning the Aborigines were bobbing up and down in the dinghy taking them out to the old ship's longboat extended into some sort of ship bearing a schooner rig. They scrambled up and over the sides and settled down amidships where they might be out of the way. It was no new experience for Trugernanna to be on a *num* watercraft, but Wooreddy had avoided it and now realised his lack of experience. He felt cowed, but still his eyes darted round examining each new object from anchor to the water sloshing at the bottom of the leaky vessel. He looked at the two stubby poles with the crosstrees and crumpled heaps of sail. He watched Robinson standing at the stern in a uniform of his own devising which could be termed vaguely nautical. The ghost shouted a command at the ones in yellow coats to hoist sail. Wooreddy saw his ruddy face turn a deep ochre as one of them laconically replied to the order: 'No 'urry, we're at the mercy of wind and water. The tide'll turn soon.'

Annoyed at showing his ineptitude, Robinson yelled: 'Sir, when I give han horder, I hexpect hit to be hobeyed hat once, an' wit no back chat.'

The convicts smirked at this betrayal of class origins and one of them shot back a 'get stuffed' which had the upwardly mobile bricklayer literally frothing at the mouth. Still, the prisoners had been forced by their oppression to become good judges of character, especially the characters of their masters. Also, some of them had been forced to endure the visits of the Christian Robinson when they had been in confinement, and they were unlikely to forget them.

Robinson, pale with rage, struggled to compose himself before speaking. He had always tried to help such degraded types by bringing to them the message of good cheer; he had often admonished them, but far too often, because their souls were hardened and blackened by many years of foul living, they had greeted his mere appearance with muttered oaths. How unlike his trusting sable friends were these rogues! At last with his mind and, he hoped, his speech safely under control, he said: 'That is no way to address a free settler, no way at all. I could have all of you severely punished for it.'

But the convicts knew that Robinson was itching to be off and would not delay to prefer charges. One continued his defiance. 'I ain't going on a cranky tub like this'un. The bleeding thing'll be on the bottom fore we clear the bay.'

'Trust the Lord and all will be well,' the religious Robinson replied, then added: 'Besides this vessel has lately seen repair . . .'

'An' been repaired with slimy mud and lime plastered over the gaping seams. Salt water'll make short shift of that.'

'No more of this mutiny and insolence,' Robinson puffed, exhausted with the effort of keeping his language and grammar straight as well as his temper under some sort of control. 'My orders must be obeyed and so they will, or by God I'll 'ave you all up 'fore the beak this day. A sound flogging will bring you to your senses. You lot, see to the sails!'

'See to 'em yourself,' the mutineer snarled, feeling secure in his defiance by the solidarity of the other convicts. Then, he shouted: 'You'll 'ave to catch me first,' and before Robinson could react, he leapt into the dinghy and rowed off towards the shore.

'Catch 'im you ruffians,' Robinson screamed, but by then the dinghy lay half-swamped in the shallows and the convict had vanished into the bush.

The Aborigines had stared in amazement, and then in consternation, at the lack of co-operation among the ghosts. They watched on as finally the sullen crew allowed themselves to be persuaded to heave up a sail so that the ship could be worked closer to the beach. They watched as Meeter Ro-bin-un forced those convicts that could swim over the side in pursuit of the fugitive. They swam, then waded through the surf and halted on the sand. At last they straggled off and into the undergrowth — to re-emerge in a suspiciously short time with the absconder. The convicts bailed out the dinghy, squeezed into it and with gunwales awash inched back to the vessel. There, the escapee mock-cringed before Robinson and begged his forgiveness. Robinson, eager to be off and unable to resist a supplicant, forgave the convict as the prodigal son had been forgiven. But he took the opportunity to exhort his crew, promising them tickets-of-leave if they promptly obeyed him. Then he began to explain how they were embarking on a hazardous mission of peace and mercy and so on and so forth until the suffering convicts could take no more and winked and grinned at one another. Finally even these diversions ceased as the enervating boredom of his words overcame all — except for one hardy lad who managed finally to thrust in words to the effect that the tide had turned and now was the time to be off if they wanted to go that day. Robinson swung his exhortation back to the repentant sinner and the end: 'Any other person, sir, would have had you spread-eagled on the triangle by now; but I, I turn the other cheek and well and truly forgive you. In this spirit of forgiveness we set sail on our great adventure.'

Throughout the diatribe, the Aborigines, forgotten in person though not in abstract mercy, had concerned themselves with the ghostly problems. At first Trugernanna had done the rough translation, then one of the strangers Robinson had brought from the mainland took over in a dialect akin to Bruny. Eventually even that trailed off in a general boredom. Wooreddy and the stranger, who had been eyeing and weighing each other before they had been distracted by the ghostly wrangling, now took the opportunity to introduce themselves formally. Wooreddy took the initiative. He removed his shirt to show the marks of his initiations, and the stranger did likewise. They exchanged names and clans, then worked out the relationship in which they stood to each other. They belonged to the same generation and were classificatory brothers.

Ummarrah, who belonged to the Stoney Creek Nation, explained in staccato sentences shot out from the depths of his barrel chest, how he came to be on the ship. He and four others were out on a guerrilla operation and had been captured. They were taken and locked in a ghost shelter (gaol) in the ghost town named 'Richmond'. There they had remained for some weeks until he volunteered to join Robinson's party. As soon as he reached familiar country, he would kiss it goodbye and go on to rejoin what resistance forces remained. Wooreddy described Robinson's character to him and of how he could be used. Ummarrah was sceptical: he knew ghosts and how they even treated one another badly. What hope did humans have to outwit or outfight them? Wooreddy had to agree with him. He liked the short, powerful brother with the cheery face and hard laugh, though he had grave doubts about his ability to survive until the ending of the world. He acted on impulse and had too hard an attitude. Even now he was mocking Ro-bin-un by mimicking the way the ghost pushed his face forward. He told them of another Ro-bert-un and of how that *num* had been different and enjoyed life. He had been with that one, leading his party around in circles as they tried to find and capture humans. Wooreddy noticed how strange words like 'canary', 'police', 'lock-up' and so on peppered his speech. He knew much more about the ghosts too. The good doctor decided to use the short voyage (and to keep his mind off the sea) by learning all he could about the ghosts from Ummarrah. He questioned him about the social structures of the *num*.

Ummarrah put up a hand and scratched at his beard as he thought out a reply. His scratching made Wooreddy realise that he had left his itchy skin back on the contaminated island. He waited for the brother's answer and noticed how thick and luxuriant his long locks were. He appeared to use a brighter red of ochre too! 'It's red powder from the ghosts,' Ummarrah said, noting the direction of his eyes; then he began to reply to the question. 'They have families as we do, but they are not very important to them. Instead they leave such natural groupings to cling together in clans called 'convicts'; 'army'; 'navy', and so on. You can identify which group they belong to by the colour of their coverings. Convicts wear yellow or grey depending on their subsection. They are often mistreated by others. The army wears red 'coats'. They are a little like our elders and are treated with respect as are the 'navy' who wear blue coats and sail the big ships. Then there are the black coats, I do not know their name or their status. They are above the yellow and below the red, but not always. Finally, there are those who are often the subject of our attacks. They are the ones who live in our countries and look after the strange animals they have imported. They seem to have no fixed place in the social structure and mix with the other groups.'

The information perplexed the good doctor. It needed analysing as well as clarifying. A social system built on groupings other than those of kin seemed impossible. If it was indeed so, it raised questions as to their origin and if they reproduced as did humans. It seemed highly unlikely seeing the unimportance of the family group. He questioned Ummarrah further and found out that sometimes a mature male and female with several immature ghosts did live together, but where these immature ghosts came from he did not know, or care for that matter.

He was a man of action, not of theory, and began describing how it felt to ride on a 'horse', then of how he had been shot and bludgeoned when he had been captured. He showed the scar of his bullet wound to Wooreddy, then talked of escape and when he would leave. Until then he would rest and enjoy himself as much as possible. His infectious mood of gaiety lifted the spirits of the good doctor, then he remembered his land and his people. He told Ummarrah of Mangana and of how he had willed himself to death. He described the visitations of the coughing demon and of how many had died. Ummarrah replied that he had been all over Van Diemen's Land, except for the west coast, and everywhere the humans were dying. 'The *num* are many and strong, while everywhere we are becoming weaker and fewer. We will end,' he declared and his rough face twisted in pain. He joined Wooreddy in his sorrow and they remained silent as the sails snapped over them.

Ummarrah had regarded Wooreddy as an old stick in the mud. Bruny Islanders had always had that reputation, he recalled. Now, he realised, except for the man beside him, all that speculation and theory which they had so loved to indulge in had been lost, though perhaps a few disciples who had come to the island to learn and debate the old traditions still lived. He sighed and felt the ship begin to roll gently as it left the sheltered bay to cross the near-open water.

The convict crew pulled at ropes and their master turned the bow towards the line of land across the horizon. Wooreddy moved to the bow and watched it parting the dark depths of the ocean. The sight filled him with horror. His eyes clung to the land evolving into a hardness and distinctness of detail. Fleeing from the sea, his mind thought of the game there and his legs even twitched in anticipation. Ummarrah would have been surprised that such a man of theory could enjoy the feel of his body doing things. Now he thought of the land ahead and not of his home island. Not once had he looked back at it. He was adrift without an anchor, another sea-simile based on new things, but with allies. He wondered how 'Fader' would affect his life. Would he protect him so that he could live on to witness the ending of the world?

V

The small vessel leaned to this side and that as it struggled in to the coast. Robinson pushed back his captain's cap and put a telescope to his eye to search out a landing place. Just like the hero of Trafalgar, he thought, as he held the pose. There was a narrow gap between two low headlands. This he knew with instant fervour was the very place from which to begin his journey of salvation. The convict crew managed to guide the ship between them to a safe anchorage. Robinson landed to walk on the strange earth. Why, perhaps he was the first Christian to touch this part of the coast and one who came to help rather than hurt the natives. With a curt gesture he summoned Wooreddy to his side and in his quaint Bruny sought to find out what language was spoken in this land. The man said that they spoke a cousin dialect of Bruny which he knew. The ghost nodded and thought of how God had changed the common earth language when sinful man had sought to scale the very heights to heaven. This caused him to frown and stare at the members of the so-called child-race, supposedly primitive. He could almost picture them as the primordial parents, though this was absurd. These people had fallen from the heights of civilisation which had begun the construction of the tower of Babel. Why had they fallen so low? Had their ancestors been the very leaders who had inspired the mad folly of attempting to conquer heaven? Suddenly, for an instant, he saw Wooreddy, Ummarrah and the others in a new light. They might be degraded, but they could not be primitive! Then he pushed all conjecture aside. He had come to help them and that was all that really mattered. Resolutely he turned to look at the thick rainforest and his body stiffened with the resolution to mark this land. But the jungle looked as impenetrable as a prison wall—he learnt from Wooreddy that the Aborigines had tracks and one such route led along the seashore. This would enable the land party to keep in touch with the ship slowly sailing along the coast.

While Robinson pondered and the convicts loafed, the Aboriginal men had erected a long, bark shelter while the women went to the end of the headland to check out the rocks for a supply of shellfish. They found plenty and dived into the icy water to collect them. When they returned to camp they found it in an uproar. Robinson shouted at the convicts to set up the tent, to light the fire, to prepare a meal, and the convicts shuffled about without much effect. By the time the ghosts were organising themselves, the Aborigines had finished eating and were lying back smoking. Truger-nanna, who had developed a liking for 'Fader' beyond the necessity of keeping him on their side, took him some abalone. She found him sitting in the front of his tent writing up his thoughts. He nodded his acceptance and continued scribbling down his impressions of the beginning of his great mission of conciliation . . .

Next day the Great Conciliator's voice rose and pushed through the foggy morning air.

Speed Thy servants, Saviour, speed them!
Thou art Lord of winds and waves:
They were bound, but Thou shalt free them;
Now they go to free the slaves.
Be Thou with them:
'Tis Thine arm alone that saves.

Friends, and home, and all forsaking,
Lord, we go at Thy command;
As our stay Thy promise taking,
While we traverse sea and land:
O be with us!
Lead us safely by the hand.

Indeed, they were in a strange, desolate land, but on the Lord's work! He exulted in his new self-imposed title, as he led his little band of pilgrims into the jungle. The cold southern-ocean wind howled in on them. It stretched his voice, thinning it until it faltered forth like the cheeping of a very tiny bird. The huge trees clung to the cliff tops and marched down to the very ocean edge in the few bays. If they stopped short of the sea, tangles of brambles took their place to rip at the legs of the pilgrims. The sullen convicts, burdened under the bulk of the supplies, cursed as they tripped over roots growing horizontally along the ground for the express purpose of impeding their progress. They doubly cursed the unburdened Robinson who rushed on ahead with little thought for his men. He disappeared into the jungle. The band of Aborigines disappeared after him. They cursed and stumbled over more roots.

The drizzling rain made everyone feel irritable. The Aborigines hated the touch of the wet ghost-coverings hindering the free flow of their bodies and dragging at them with clammy folds. 'Fader' would feel sad if they deliberately discarded them, but what could he say if they took them off and lost them? In his possum-skin bag Wooreddy carried a large bottle of whale oil and he shared this with the others. They greased their bodies and felt warmer and much better. They strolled on after Meeter Ro-bin-un and Trugernanna who had elected to accompany him.

Robinson was on a track which circled inland, rising through the wet jungle up into damp stone outcroppings which turned into the rotten teeth of an eroded mountain range. The track twisted upwards to the base of a steep hill and vanished. Not to be deterred he forced himself up, clutching at tiny ledges in the rock. He came to the summit and had nowhere to go but down and down he went. Trugernanna had had enough of such mountaineering and stayed on a wide ledge below the hilltop. The other Aborigines, after abandoning their long spears, finally reached her. They sat and waited for the ghost to come back. Wooreddy pointed out landmarks and traced along the coast the proper track. At last Robinson's head appeared above them and he slid down to flop exhausted from his fruitless struggle with the barren wilderness beyond the hill. When he had recovered his breath, he allowed himself to be led back to the proper route which wound in a series of trails along the coast and through the jungle. It could only be followed by one who knew the country as short-cuts cutting off loops and tracks meandering off into the wilderness complicated the way. 'Fader' had charged off along one such obscure track which ended on the hilltop.

They had left their spears at the junction of the trail and when they stopped to retrieve them, Ummarrah took from his bag a pair of leather thongs and tied them around his ankles. Wooreddy watched him do this. Did he stand in a strong enough relationship to ask about the spell which empowered them? He knew the Bruny spell and would have liked to compare it with that of the Stoney Creek Nation. Ummarrah felt his eyes on him and glanced up with a smile on his rough features. 'My country is as flat as the palm of my hand and it has a big lake in the hollow. There I can run all day and all night, but here I cannot crawl half a day, let alone walk.'

Wooreddy agreed with the roughness of the country and said that he had lived there before. He pointed at his thick thighs. 'The proof of my residency lies in the thickness of my legs. All the local people have them here. They brag that their legs are so strong that if they stamp in anger they split open the ground. The many streams running down to the coast flow in the cracks they caused. Now they are careful not to stamp on the ground for they have too many rivers already.'

'That may be so,' Ummarrah replied diplomatically. 'I can see that here you do need legs, not like sticks, but like tree trunks.'

The convicts came struggling towards them and the expedition was united once more. Robinson stayed at the head of the slow-moving column for a time, then impatiently rushed off. He was followed by Trugernanna and then the Aborigines. The convicts plodded after the blacks. There was no escape, they were too dispirited to wander off into the dismal jungle.

The rainy sky was blackening towards night when the Aborigines caught up with Robinson and Trugernanna. He waited for them at the foot of a vertical rock face where there were caves enough to shelter all the party from the ever-dripping sky. Their firesticks had long since been rained out, but Robinson had his firelighter. They hunted around for dry fuel and Ummarrah found a pile of rotting wood, leaves and bark at the back of one of the caves. 'Fader' took out his flint and steel. Sparks flew and ate into the dry bark-dust. It smouldered, glowed and burst into flame under the breath of Trugernanna. The flames leapt and danced as the convicts staggered into the clearing under the rock face and flopped down weakly on the wet earth. Robinson immediately ordered them to their feet. They were to camp in a cave as far from his charges as possible. The Great Conciliator strongly believed that Aborigines should be segregated from Europeans until they could be raised to a superior stage of Christian civilisation.

The women prepared damper while the beloved tea stewed in the pot. They discussed the day's journey in a dialect which 'Fader' would not know. Wooreddy and Ummarrah laughed as Trugernanna described the headlong rush of the ghost in a headlong rush of words. She had been more economical in her movements and had been able to collect some vegetables along the way. She put these on the fire as she talked, and when they were cooked, instead of giving the first lot to her husband, put them onto one of the shell-like

67

ghost containers and took it to Meeter Ro-bin-un who sat against one wall making the endless lines of marks on the soft white bark. They had watched him doing this before and it held no fascination for them, not even when he told them that one day he would teach them to do it. Perhaps it was his way of making spells that enabled him to rush about like a madman all day and then write most of the night. Some roots had this effect; perhaps the mark-making had the same result.

The succeeding days went in the same way, in the same mad rush which spread the party out into three groups. Always far ahead went 'Fader' and Trugernanna; behind them came the Aborigines and lastly the bunch of convicts. They still carried most of the supplies and managed with their groans and slowness to evade the heartily detested Robinson. They had organised themselves so that they could often stop for a long rest over a pipe or two. They filled these breaks with talking about the journey and how little they cared for it. If one liked sloshing through swamps, padding through dismal jungles, clambering over ugly, battered heaps of rocks masquerading as hills, it was a grand trip, but for anyone else it compared with the chain gang without the chance of scoring any rum. The Aborigines, unencumbered, travelled in their own fashion, resting when the convicts rested. They even began sending the women to the coast to gather fresh seafood for the midday meal.

Only Ummarrah and Robinson looked to the future. Ummarrah wanted to get beyond Macquarie Harbour where he knew the country and could travel safely. He wanted Wooreddy to accompany him and was put out when he refused. The good doctor explained that the *num* were everywhere and one had to accommodate oneself to their presence. Ummarrah had only contempt for this answer—he believed that freedom was everything and survival in a hostile world worth nothing. But he listened as the man explained how the Bruny people had been wiped out and that now he was a stranger everywhere. Ummarrah experienced again the deep sorrow in Wooreddy. He felt the pain of the successive deaths, the loss of his land, the urge to survive, and that last sad cremation before the final leave-taking. He felt and understood, but the times were such that he had to cut himself off from Wooreddy's pain. He too had been affected by the *num* and *Ria Warrawah*, though he did not realize this. Ummarrah leant back letting his body enjoy the shelter of the hut the West Coast people had built as a way station, slowly ate the tail of a crayfish, then, completely at ease, began to describe his last raid. The doctor listened politely while letting his numbness return. Ummarrah knew about his one raid and was contemptuous, though approving. Wooreddy did not realise it, but that one raid saved his reputation as a man in the eyes of Ummarrah. Now in his own dialect, the man of action told of battles in the Northeast. Wooreddy could understand much of what he said. He had heard the stories before, but in this one Ummarrah told of riding with the ghosts against his own people. This was interesting to Wooreddy and he heard more about the ways of the *num* before Ummarrah swung back to the story of another raid.

'We were out one day to annoy the ghosts,' continued Ummarrah, 'to let them know that we were still around. They had built all their huts in the valleys and flat places, but we owned the hills. They could not go into them. From the high places we went down to attack them. But the more huts we burnt out, the more they came. They kept on coming and coming, like flies in summer, like the cold in winter— and no one knew where they were coming from. If we did we might have tried to go to that place and destroy it. That day we went out to get rid of a newly built hut. Ghosts are like the dead logs from which they build their shelters, they hear nothing, not even the wind in the trees, or the sun heating the ground, or the rain growing the plants. We came gliding through the trees and into the clearing which they always make around their shelters. It was summer, the sun glanced off the earth and heated up everything. The boughs hung limp, and the *num*, thinking himself safe, lay limp under a tree. His musket stood against the trunk. It could well have been his last sleep, but what is life without humour? I crept to the tree and took his musket. My comrades gathered around him, bent down and gave a great shout. He opened his eyes, saw our black faces, slowly opened his mouth—and began pissing himself. Unable to control ourselves we burst out laughing. This caused him to spring to his feet. He took a great bound into the air and flashed out of sight. It was so funny that no one thought to send a spear after him.'

Wooreddy grinned as his mind filled with the image of the running *num*. Then Dray, one of the women accompanying the men, said that she did not find it funny and that the men should stop the stupid fighting before they were all shot and the women were left alone. This put an end to Ummarrah's storytelling. In many ways Wooreddy tended to agree with the young woman. She had come with a party from the South West Nation to Bruny Island where the coughing demon attacked them. She had been the sole survivor. This fact interested Wooreddy as much as her rounded hips and strong thighs.

After this it was time to move on, if they were to keep within easy distance of the leader and separated from the convicts. Ten minutes after the Aborigines had left, the convicts reached the fire and settled down to smoke their pipes and cook the crayfish that had been left for them. Far ahead, Robinson hurried on with Trugernanna. A sudden pain made him clutch his stomach and he had to rush to the bushes beside the track and shit. Diarrhoea! He blamed the convicts. They had lost some of the supplies and soaked the rest of the flour when fording one of the many streams. As a result he had had to send two of them to wait on the coast for the ship. They had been gone for three days and all that remained of the provisions were a piece of bacon and some flour. Unknown to the Great Conciliator, who had yet to begin conciliating, the convicts had just finished eating the remainder of the provisions and were even then concocting a story of how one of their number had slipped and almost tumbled to the bottom of a precipice. They had managed to save him, but at the expense of the supplies.

Robinson forced his body on, but ever more slowly. He came to a river too wide and deep to ford. Trugernanna suggested that they build a catamaran to cross it. Her words hit him like a heavy fist. He had not known just how close to exhaustion he had driven himself. He stood there tottering. His body trembled and his stomach spasmed. His legs gave

out and he sank to the ground. Trugernanna rushed to the
river to fill a pot with water. She put it to his lips, then
soaked a rag in it to wipe his face. He covered his flushed
face with the cloth and relaxed while the woman began
building a fire in a spot sheltered by an overhanging bank.
She helped 'Fader' to the place. He flopped down, thanking
the Lord for his faithful, dusky companion. She put some
bulbs in the fire and when they were done, peeled them and
fed the tender flesh to the ghost. While she was feeding him,
the rest of the Aborigines arrived to stand around her in a
silent group. Trugernanna looked up into the hostile face of
Ummarrah and at his hand tugging angrily at his beard. She
felt scared!

He stated flatly: 'The ghosts can never leave our women
alone.' Then he stared at Wooreddy and questioned: 'What
will you do about it? If she was my woman I know what I
would do!' He continued to stare at Wooreddy, and the good
doctor found himself in the position of being forced to
defend something he had never thought of defending
especially in these times. Still it had to be done! He looked
around and saw a heavy piece of wood lying on the ground
some distance away. He walked slowly to it, picked up the
jagged piece of bough, hefted it, then returned to stand near
the side of the sick ghost. He lifted the sharp piece of wood,
held it poised aloft and made a motion to bring it stabbing
down into the chest of the ghost. Trugernanna screamed.
The stick imbedded itself in the ground. Meeter Ro-bin-un,
his face blank from suffering, opened his weary eyes and saw
the people surrounding him. 'My children,' he murmured
to them from some ghost-delirium in which he floated.

The good doctor hated senseless violence and grinned at
the words and at his narrow escape. Killing the ghost would
have meant the loss of a valuable ally; Trugernanna knew
this, but Ummarrah did not. The old ways and customs were
dead or dying and without this underlying stratum things
had little meaning. Ummarrah did not understand this,
though he knew that the times had changed and never would
the old ways prevail again.

The episode was quickly forgotten, even by Ummarrah
who thought that Trugernanna's scream had upset Wooreddy's

aim. The good doctor rose in his estimation, especially when Ummarrah had had time to reflect on what might have happened if the ghost had been killed. Ro-bin-un worked for the government and the government did not forget such things. If they had done the deed and later been captured, things would have gone hard for them.

'Fader' had recovered somewhat from his exhaustion by the time the convicts straggled in. He sat with his back against a tree, and his voice piped out in delirium as he contemplated the flow of water before him. 'Many rivers to cross,' he shrilled out, and the convicts busily erecting the tents tried to think of excuses to move out of earshot. 'Many rivers to cross,' Robinson repeated striving to lower his voice for depth and compassion. 'Though many obstacles are placed in our way, they will be crossed as this river will be crossed. We are on a mission of God, on a holy mission of salvation and nothing the Evil One shall do will deter me from accomplishing this journey through the wilderness laced with serpents and tendrils of fog. These poor heathens must be saved and I will save them. I have been ordained to do this by God Almighty Himself . . .' Robinson lapsed into a religious rapture born of his delirium. The words continued to dribble from his lips. 'I am the Truth and the Light; I am the Way and the Goal; I am here because I have been summoned to be here. I am here because I am here because I am here; you are here because I am here and I am here because you are here and God has caused us all to be here . . .'

'An' we're 'ere 'cos t'em ruddy judges sentenced us t'be 'ere in t's bloody penal colony,' a rough, derisive voice slashed into this fog of words just as he fainted away into a less ecstatic dream. Serpents slithered into his Garden of Eden and threatened his blissful, innocent children with rottenness and degradation. He tried to rise to defend them, but his heavy, inert body lay under the pressure of a strange transparent atmosphere of whitish gas. All that he could manage was to quiver a leg. Then his mouth opened of itself and the gas flowed in. It tasted like gin and had the same kick which sent him back into consciousness. There he ordered the convicts to finish pitching the tents before drifting off into a greyness from which he emerged to find that the late afternoon

72

had turned into late morning. He got to his feet without any weakness, noticed that the convicts were still wrapped in their blankets, flung his arms about for a minute or two to restore circulation, then went to wash all haziness away in the clear, cold waters of the stream. Fully recovered, his querulous voice nagged at the convicts until they left their blankets and got the fire blazing. He ordered them to cook breakfast, then looked around for the Aborigines. They were nowhere in sight. Out hunting, he thought, and turned his attention back to the convicts to find them standing before the fire with nothing cooking on it. His peevish voice urged them on.

'Can't do no cooking, gub'nor, ain't no grub,' a convict finally volunteered.

'But there must be, there must be—what happened to the last of the flour and bacon? Yesterday there was enough for at least three days,' the distraught expedition leader spluttered. Would his expedition and mission come to an inglorious end owing to such a mundane thing as food?

While Robinson faced his dilemma with 'h'-dropping rage, the Aboriginal men tried their luck at hunting. They were hemmed in by impenetrable forest. The women would have to provide the food and they went to the coast. They found that they had already filled their bags with shell and crayfish and were ready to go back to the camp. Unknowingly they had solved Robinson's dilemma.

The Great Conciliator, who still had done no conciliating, welcomed them with delight. The food was quickly on the fires and while it was cooking Wooreddy began to consider his position. They were well into the country of his dead wife, and sooner rather than later he would meet her people. They would be less than happy to find him with another wife and even less so when they saw him bringing a *num* into their country. He shrugged, leaving the future to take care of the future, but all the same he began sharpening his spear. Then he glanced across the river to see a couple on the opposite bank. He said nothing, hoping that they would go away when they saw the party, but Robinson chanced to look up. He shouted in his excitement. Immediately the convicts rushed to the bank to see the objects of their expedition.

73

They saw no one. The couple had melted back into the jungle.

Robinson rushed to-and-fro along the bank in his excitement. 'Quick, quick, in the name of hall that's 'oly, we must get across an' meet 'em.' His voice trailed off as he realized that as yet they had no means of getting to the other side. He remembered that Trugernanna had said that they must build a catamaran. Instantly he ordered the convicts to make one, using the Bruny word, *nunganah*. They stared at him in incomprehension, then one of them asked 'What sort of animal is that?' Pulling himself together, the ghost went to the Aborigines and asked them to make a craft to cross the river. Wooreddy and Ummarrah volunteered to do so. They set about collecting short pieces of bark while Robinson ordered the convicts off to try to shoot game. But they experienced the same problem as the Aborigines before them, and they too made their way to the coast in hope of sighting either the ship following them along the coast, or at least their mates who had gone to her for provisions. The sea was as empty as the land, and they sat in a sheltered spot and smoked the last of their tobacco while they complained of their aches and pains.

The good doctor prided himself on his watercraft-making ability. He was an expert. With Ummarrah helping he quickly had enough sheets of bark to begin rolling them around a stick. They made two rolls and then he left the rolling of the last one to Ummarrah while he went to borrow some rope from 'Fader'. He needed this to tie the rolls together to form the catamaran. Unfortunately, the somewhat inexperienced Ummarrah managed to roll the bark without a central stick, and when they put the craft in the water, the pressure of the current warped the right side. Still, it floated and would hold a load. Robinson sent one of the Aborigines to bring back the convicts before getting gingerly onto the arc-shaped craft. Trugernanna and Dray leapt into the water and pushed it to the other bank. The Aborigines were ferried after 'Fader' who had already disappeared along the trail. At last the convicts arrived to do the packing and to follow it across. By the time they were on the opposite bank, Robinson had returned from a fruitless rush after the local Aborigines.

Still, a little way along the path he had found a number of huts in which they could camp.

His voice, seemingly made stronger by privation, had lost its harping quality and had sunk to run along the ground beneath the trees rather than rising to soar above them. Still, it held that tone of self-assurance which the convicts loathed. Robinson sang:

Awake our souls! Away, our fears!
Let every trembling thought be gone!
Awake, and run the heavenly race,
And put a cheerful courage on.

True 'tis a strait and thorny road,
And mortal spirits tire and faint;
But they forget the mighty God
That feeds the strength of every saint.

O mighty God, Thy matchless power
Is ever new and ever young,
And firm endures, while endless years
Their everlasting circles run.

From Thee, the ever flowing spring,
Our souls shall drink a fresh supply;
While such as trust their native strength
Shall melt away, and droop, and die.

Swift as the eagle cuts the air,
We'll mount aloft to Thine abode;
On wings of love our souls shall fly,
Nor tire along the heavenly road to Mount Zion.

The sentiments might have interested Wooreddy if he had understood the words, but the weary convicts could not even raise a smirk at the stance of the singing leader standing with his hand on his breast, the other outstretched, and his face raised to the heavens. Ummarrah found it fascinating. Later, when he returned to his people, he would lift their spirits by mimicking this strange ghost and his absurd postures. What brought the loudest peals of laughter was when, after singing in such a fashion, he sank to his knees and whined away in the strange keening tone Meeter Ro-bin-un had affected.

That evening, after a day's fruitless chase, the party reached the huts which their leader had described as being a short distance away and set up camp. He then took the opportunity, seeing that they had sighted their quarry, to declaim a particularly inappropriate psalm, 'Bring unto the Lord, O ye mighty, bring young rams unto the Lord; ascribe unto the Lord worship and strength.' 'O Lord, give us some chops from that ram,' intoned a convict's voice from the gathering darkness, wet with rain as always. Robinson glared and continued his chanting while the rain began to fall in huge drops. 'Give the Lord the honour due unto his name: worship the Lord with holy worship.'

He was conducting the service in the largest of the huts and the Aboriginal women had made a fire at the entrance. They cooked vegetables on this while Robinson's voice rose in competition with a sudden rush of wind and hail. The convicts eyed the cooking food, edged closer and snatched most of it off the blazing fire before Robinson descended from the clouds to berate them for losing the supplies. Then he sent them off to a far hut, while he took the one next to the Aborigines. Trugernanna looked after his simple needs and when he slept Ummarrah kept her company. While the camp slept Wooreddy and Dray practised a particularly involved version of *righting the catamaran*.

The next day the search continued, but there was no sign of the local Aborigines, nor was there the day after. The other convicts still had not returned with the supplies and Robinson decided to send a convict accompanied by Ummarrah and Wooreddy ahead to the penal station at Macquarie Harbour. He would continue to try and contact the Aborigines while relying on the women for food. He pulled two red coats (the worse for wear) from a pack and then two pairs of dark trousers. The Aborigines would wear them and look like soldiers from a distance. The army had a reputation for shooting at any Aborigines or loose convicts they saw. If they saw a convict with two Aborigines, the three would not last long enough to identify themselves. He gave McKay, the convict selected, a copy of his orders which requested the Commandant of the station to give him all assistance. In the envelope he enclosed a letter detailing his needs and wants. For himself he requested medicine as he was still feeling poorly and his skin was beginning to break out in great red splotches—much to the amusement of the Aborigines who nicknamed him 'Ballawine', Red Ochre. This name superseded both 'Fader' (though Trugernanna and others continued to use it as it represented his title and kin group) and 'Meeter Ro-bin-un', the latter completely disappearing from their vocabulary.

At the last moment, with one of the snap decisions which eventually drove anyone under his supervision mad, he decided that Trugernanna should go with the men. This left him alone in the wilderness with three convicts supremely indifferent to him and his enterprise. Ballawine checked Trugernanna over to see that she was presentable. For the time being, the woman wore a clean coarse shift of flax. The Great Conciliator, who still had not begun his work of conciliating, bade them godspeed with an extravagant gesture which Ummarrah filed for future mimicry. The stoical McKay hoisted his musket onto his shoulder and marched briskly on his way. Once they were out of sight of the leader of the expedition, they all slackened their pace and the Aborigines took the lead.

They were all hungry and eagerly accepted Trugernanna's suggestion that they make for the coast. 'Aint no 'urry hat hall,' McKay agreed. 'That bastard treats us'un like dung an' hexpects hus hall to run han hobey his hevery horder. A day or two won't 'urt a bloke like 'im. E's got enough still 'bout 'is middle to keep 'im going till wes get backs.'

The men took off their clothing and stashed them in a hollow tree. Trugernanna did the same with her dress. Then they took off for the coast. The men loafed behind and discussed the prospects of hunting.

'This country isn't good for wallaby or kangaroo,' Wooreddy said.

'Nor for possum,' Ummarrah added. 'But there might be an echidna or wombat around.'

'Haven't seen any sign of them. I remember that most

of this country is bad for game.'

'You married a local girl, didn't you? Are you going to drop in on her people?'

'What! and tell them that she died on my island? I don't know about that, but I will have to see them, sooner rather than later. I still don't know how to explain him to them. They don't like ghosts and those who bring ghosts into their country!'

'Never mind all that,' Ummarrah rejoined. 'I'll back you up—' and he began one of his interminable stories.

Wooreddy busied himself looking for signs of game while the man rambled on and on. Sometimes, Wooreddy thought, he almost rivalled Ballawine in tediousness, though he understood what Ummarrah was saying and often only understood individual words in the ghost's long harangues. Not a sign of game, and Wooreddy collected berries as they walked along to the beach. Then he remembered that a track went from that part of the coast towards Macquarie Harbour. Eating the berries, they returned for their clothing. Wooreddy collected Trugernanna's shift. The two men pulled on the jackets and trousers. 'This is how the soldiers walk,' Ummarrah grinned as he began to march, stamping his bare feet hard down upon the ground. Wooreddy copied him and they stamped along the track and onto the beach where they saluted McKay with mock gravity. The convict hardly noticed them—he was too busy watching two large lobsters roasting on the fire.

They gorged themselves on lobster, then snacked on oysters cooked in the shell. The morning lazed away into the afternoon. McKay made no move. Wooreddy had assured him that the track leading off the beach put the penal station only a few hours away and not the days Robinson thought, though a river did lie between. The convict accepted this information without questioning why Robinson had not been told this. If he did think about it, he put it down to the natural propensity of savages to lie and prevaricate on all occasions. In Wooreddy's case, this may have been true; he prevaricated because he could not make up his mind whether it was better roaming around the countryside with a few *num* or being with a lot in one of their settlements. He had finally come to a decision since he would only be among a lot of *num* for a short time before returning to the hapless Ballawine. The attitude of McKay had decided him, too, for with such a person he could make the return journey as long or as short as he wanted.

Finally they made a move. After an hour or so they began to hear 'ghost' sounds. The sharp blows of axes echoed and re-echoed. Every now and again came a thud as another tree toppled to the ground. McKay slowed and showed no inclination to rush and meet his own kind. He had no love for penal stations, chain gangs, harsh discipline and overbearing overseers ever ready to sentence a poor prisoner to the lash. Only the knowledge that he carried letters justifying his present whereabouts made him continue to move on towards the sounds of sawing and chopping. Voices began to be heard with the noises. They came to the edge of a torrent across which they saw a rough clearing in which grey-clad convicts laboured, heaving huge logs towards the river where other convicts worked knee-deep in the cold water, roping the logs together into a large raft. Half a dozen soldiers lazed about a fire.

'Hey,' McKay called across to them.

The soldiers stared across to the opposite bank and saw the red coats of Wooreddy and Ummarrah shining brightly at the edge of the forest gloom. 'What're you doing over there,' they shouted back. 'Did'ja catch him,' they shouted—thinking that they were addressing a couple of soldiers who had been out after an escaped convict.

'We're from Mr Robinson's party coming overland from 'obarton,' McKay shouted. 'I've got letters from Mr Robinson to the Commandant.'

'That would've been a bastard of a walk,' the corporal in charge of the guards replied. A longboat came scurrying up the river to collect the raft and he shouted to it to go to the other bank and pick up McKay and the others.

'See you got some crows with you,' he said as the boat came towards him.

'Yeah, we're going after 'em, to roun' 'em up and put 'em where t'ey can't do hanyone hany 'arm,' McKay answered, suddenly interested in the expedition. He was not just a convict, but one with a mission.

They scrambled out from the boat and Wooreddy and Ummarrah, conscious that they were the subjects of the conversation, saluted while Trugernanna bent in a curtsy.

'Almost human, ain't they,' the soldier said. 'A musket ball'll round them up a lot quicker and better,' he added. 'They're just a bunch of savages, good for nothing, but mischief. If you're going to the settlement best get back on board the boat. It's going to escort the raft. The commandant won't be too happy to see you. Once the convicts hear that you came overland, there won't be any holding them here.'

They got back onto the boat and Trugernanna found herself the object of unwelcome eyes and worse, hands that pinched. She sat between the men and huddled into as small an object as possible. The boat fluttered about the raft being clumsily poled into mid-stream by the convicts. It shot down the river and into the wide, shallow harbour, where the boat took it under tow. Sarah Island was only a short distance away from the river mouth. From a distance it looked overburdened with a high fence or palisade built to provide some protection from the fierce south winds which lashed the coast. The boat crept closer and closer to the docking area. They passed a half-built ship and the raft was swung sideways towards a part of the shore stacked with piles of logs. Wooreddy had never been to a ghost settlement. He was all eyes, ears and feelings. Already he could detect no warmth or human kindness there. The inhabitants were as grey in mind as in body and clothing. The boat tied up at a quay. They went ashore past grey *num* slowly stacking logs under the eyes of a bored soldier whose red coat had faded into a faint pinkish-grey. The prisoners roused themselves to stare at the newcomers and at a female. Trugernanna felt herself shrinking instead of preening herself under the male eyes. They glared with such violence and absence of love that she realised that they had penetrated into one of the lairs of the ghosts and finally found them to be in reality as in theory: unhuman! Wooreddy and Ummarrah felt the same, they wanted to leave this place before its evil afflicted them.

McKay was directed to walk past the two-storeyed dormitory

building to the Superintendent's house which lay beyond a storehouse and some soldiers' cottages. For protection against the wind it stood behind its own high fence and only the split boards of the roof showed above the top. They passed through a gap which served as the gateway, to find themselves in an attempt at a garden. A few stunted English plants survived a few centimetres above the ground and in a damp corner a heap of slimy, orange toadstools thrived. A tall gaunt man, with a nervous tic jerking at the outer corner of his left eye, acknowledged their presence and received them on the verandah. This was the Commandant or Super-intendent—for in truth he was both, being Superintendent of the prison and Commandant of the guard. He heard a short verbal report from McKay, then questioned him about the journey, for it had been thought impossible to reach the station overland from Hobarton. His tic increased as he verified that what he had come to regard as the main, thick and unclimbable, wall of his prison had indeed been crossed. His tic fascinated the Aborigines. Ummarrah had another *num* mannerism to store up for the later entertainment of his people. It reminded them of how some men had a personal spirit through which they divined what was to be. They knew this through various tics and involuntary muscular contractions. Perhaps the commandant had his own personal devil. If so, it was one more proof that they had penetrated into a strong place of the ghosts.

The Superintendent took the letters from McKay and slowly read them, forming each word visibly on his lips. 'This Robinson fellow writes uncommonly unclear,' he muttered, ticcing away while knotting his brow in an effort to decipher each crooked and ill-formed letter. Finally he reached the end and commented: 'What (tic) Hobarton (tic) commands is one thing (tic), is one thing (tic), and what I can do is another thing (he rushed the words in an effort to get more out before the inevitable tic arrived. It came.) Our rations haven't arrived (tic) by (tic) all (tic) rights (tic) they should have (he hesitated, tic, tic, tic), and all I can let you have is a sack of potatoes and another of flour.' The final rush of words escaped without a single tic, but they came at the end, tic, tic, tic, tic, tic. Worse, the final effort to suppress them had only incited them. The whole left side of his face jerked in a flurry of tics, forcing him to retreat hurriedly into the front room. He went to write out the requisition order. McKay watched his head bent over the desk. The Aborigines watched the jerking slow to a soft irregular rhythm bearly noticeable. He got up and presented the order to the convict. 'I expect that that'll do,' he said. 'Hit'll 'aveta,' the convict answered insolently, forgetting that he was addressing someone other than Robinson.

'Get it done immediately and then get out of the station,' the commandant ordered, acknowledging his insolence, but happily aware that the tic had subsided to a slight quiver. He even went to the gap and got the sentry on duty to shout to a passing convict to get him to go to the store for the supplies. He gave him not only the requisition order, but a number. McKay guessed that too many things were going missing from the store and that the Superintendent had instituted a system to prevent the pillage. Eventually, after an hour, the convict returned with the bag of flour. There were no potatoes left. The Superintendent began to tic in consternation and anger. Finally to get McKay and the Aborigines out of his station, and as an apology for giving Robinson only a bag of flour, he went to his own medicine chest and found some tincture of opium and a jar of some sort of ointment. After carefully sealing the lids with strips of paper and signing them, he passed the medicine across to McKay. Before dismissing them, he spoke his apologies: 'Tell (tic) Mr Robinson (tic) that the supply ship (tic, tic, tic) from Hobarton is overdue, overdue as usual, but it should be here in a week or two—' The left side of his face began jerking spasmodically and he had to hide in his room until it subsided. When he returned it was a barely perceptible quiver. 'I expect that he'll want a letter or two sent out on it. I'll order a boat to get you across the harbour.'

McKay still had had hopes of staying the night at the settlement and of scrounging some tobacco. Now he found himself given the shove without even a bite to eat. It made him bitter against the world, though some regulation or other prevented unauthorised personnel from staying within the station. Whatever the reason, they soon found themselves on a longboat speeding over the harbour towards the southern shore. McKay managed to barter some of the flour for a few flakes of tobacco before they were set ashore at a spot Wooreddy had pointed out as being the head of a track. Ummarrah disappeared into the bush and returned with an echidna which they ate with johnny cakes. It was too late to move on that day.

VI

They wandered towards the spot where they had left Ballawine, found his tracks and followed them for part of a day. The weather had improved and so had the game. There seemed little point in following the leader away from the coast into the barren interior towards which his tracks led. They would stay near the coast until he was driven back.

Trugernanna stayed with McKay while Wooreddy took Ummarrah to the village of his dead wife. The good doctor was not greeted with open arms. The people had been monitoring the progress, or lack of progress, of Robinson's expedition, and had become entangled in arguments not only as to the destination, but the object of such haphazard rambling through their country. They had expected the good doctor to visit them eventually, and now that the eventuality had arrived, were in two minds as to how to greet him. The conservative party wanted to denounce him for bringing *num* into their country, the moderates hung back and wanted an explanation, while the extremists were hopelessly split on the issue. The result was that they all stood back and waited for Wooreddy to speak.

He explained firstly the death of his wife, a member of their community; secondly how matters stood on Bruny Island and of how the land had become polluted; thirdly that the whole Bruny Island people as a community had perished and that he was the last surviving male and was alienated from his land and the world. He had no real kinsfolk. Then he realised that they could not comprehend the destruction of a whole community and the severing of the link between individual and earth. The very concept of alienation was beyond them, though they could feel it in Wooreddy, but they put this down to his being too long in the company of ghosts. The good doctor found himself in trouble, not only for not visiting them sooner, but also for not returning a part of the woman to her country. He told them that he had done this and that he had brought along some bones which he had placed in a hollow tree on the west bank of Poynduc. The leaders of the community accepted this as evidence of his good faith and all the parties came together to hear about the outside world and to taste again the wisdom of the good doctor. They had missed the brightness of his mind and the sharpness of his projected feelings. They were only too happy to have a subtle Bruny Island mind amongst them again.

He knew that they had not grasped the concept of alienation. During his journey it had been maturing in his mind and now it was a plant ready to put forth the flowers of discussion. He began laying out a sacred ground of intricate design of logic and supposition. Concepts were tailored to fit into the designs of sentences. The people listened, asked questions and admired—then criticised! But his construction not only took all criticism, but used it creatively in a symbolic ceremony which transmogrified it into part of the overall design. The flowers of discussion indeed had blossomed.

Unknown to the men, the basis of the system rested on Wooreddy's long ago experience as a child. They saw it differently and that it held together on the real premises that the times were changing and that the ghosts roamed the land. These real things had been used by the good doctor to sever the three times. They too began to feel alienated.

The past, which was fixed, had fixed the present and the future, just as the future had fixed the present and the past. All three endured together and had endured since that long-ago time when the seas had risen to capture vast areas of the land. Now that that long-ago past had become the present, the unsettled present filled with events as great as those of that long-ago past, and this made the future hideous with uncertainty. The future then wound back on itself like a serpent with its tail in its mouth. Wooreddy's edifice demolished what they had always believed in, and now they could see that the principle of uncertainty ruled where once there had been certainty. They could trace this principle from the time of the rising of the seas to the first appearance of the strange islands towed by clouds and the coming of the *num*. Behind all these strange things lurked the sea, but Wooreddy did not dwell on that. Strange things had happened, were happening and would happen. The only certain thing was the principle of uncertainty. Suddenly, they too found themselves enduring the ending of the world, and in their consternation, they looked at Wooreddy with bleak eyes until one of their best men, Toomana, asked: 'What shall we do, now?'

Wooreddy gazed long into the fire, remembering how he had once been made *Keeper of the Fire*. He knew that they knew that there were ghosts everywhere and that just a few days walk from their village a powerful ghost settlement had been built which separated the northern and southern portions of the west coast. 'In these times,' he began to speak his thoughts, '*Ria Warrawah* walks the earth and we can do nothing to stop him.' He radiated the sadness and consternation of one destined to endure the ending of the world. 'You can do nothing. Soon you will walk where they tell you to walk and live where they tell you to live. No longer have you and I a choice, perhaps, we never had a choice and our ancestors lived and continued our race to endure this day and the days to come. Now we must become pliable and seek allies and accommodate with fate. Come and meet Ballawine. Make your peace with him. He is as good a *num* as there can be. He won't harm you, or let others harm you.'

The men nodded slowly to what the good doctor said and let it form in their minds. Ummarrah, not to be left out of such a serious and powerful discussion, though he distrusted the intellectual subtleties of the Bruny Island mind, spoke out: 'Other ghosts, they chase you and shoot at you with their muskets which roar with thunder, flash with lightning and kill with pebbles, but this one is different! He can be used!' But then he added, to show that he did not whole-heartedly support Wooreddy's position: 'I am only travelling with him until I reach a part of the land I know, then I will leave and go back to my own country.' He thought for a moment, then had to say with a bitterness which the men thought underlined the truth of Wooreddy's words: 'If I still have a country to return to!'

They continued to deliberate, though it was a foregone conclusion. The *num* landed on their coasts whenever and wherever they wanted. They could do nothing to stop them. Parralaongatek was, as Wooreddy had said, a strong ghost place where they attacked the very trees, shot at any humans foolhardy enough to be seen, and even attacked the earth itself.

'What shall we do?' the strongman, Toomana asked. 'We want to keep our land and remain as a community on it. How can the times be mended and a certainty returned to the world?'

Wooreddy sat, feeling their misery and letting them feel his sadness. He had no real answer or solution. He watched a leaf float from a tree. It tumbled over and over and down and down until a gust of wind reached out and wafted it away. 'First of all you must come and meet this ghost we have, this Ballawine,' he finally said. 'It may not be the only way, it may not be the best thing to do, but it is a beginning.'

The men nodded their heads in agreement, but they would pick their own time and place for the meeting. Wooreddy nodded his head, but then began to outline the way the meeting should be arranged as he knew the psychology of the ghost and the way he liked things to happen. 'Fader' (he used the kin term) wanted always to be in command and had to initiate and carry forward any contact. He would not like it if the people just came into his camp and sat down. No, 'Fader' had to be treated with circumspection and so he told them: 'Wait a few days until I can arrange things to your advantage. Ghosts are funny, and need to be treated with caution. They have their way of doing things, just as we have our own ways. Let him see the smoke of your fires. He will rush in their direction. Let him meet an old man or a woman, perhaps the woman should appear very timid. This will make him feel pity. If things are carefully arranged, he will be very happy at finally meeting you. He will have done it all by himself and will treat you very kindly. Now all that he wants to do is to meet all the people. There is no danger, but if he returns to your land, it may be different.'

After having a meal with the people, Wooreddy and Ummarrah made their way back to McKay and Trugernanna. They were now ready to link up with Robinson.

VII

While Wooreddy plotted with the local people, 'Fader', replenished with supplies by the arrival of the convicts he had sent to the coast for supplies, pushed on in his relentless search for life. His party swung wide of the coast and into the empty jungles of the hinterland. The land was a crumpled piece of paper soaking under the rain. Water flowed along troughs through which Robinson had to wade after finding a ford, for unlike the Aborigines he could neither swim like the women nor make a catamaran like the men. At last, he hesitated in his fruitless mission, then decided to head for the coast where he knew the local people could be found. It had suddenly struck him that he had been exploring rather than trying to contact the natives, that he had wanted to go where no one had ever gone, and now that he had done that he could get on with his job. A job (though with God's help and direction) that he alone could do. But he was reaching a point where he was in no fit state to do anything. His clothing was in tatters. His pants had rotted away up to the knees and he had had to fashion shoes out of pieces of leather tied on with strips of rag. His convicts and lone Aboriginal companion had fared little better. Dray had disliked going into strange country away from the coast. The gloom of the overhanging dripping trees and the dead silence of the bush got to her. She thought *Ria Warrawah* lurked in every brush-choked gorge, and even before Robinson had decided to return to the coast, she had swung the direction of travel towards it. Robinson, suffering from a worrying skin disease and fever, was in no shape to monitor the direction especially when the sun and stars were always hidden behind a dense layer of cloud.

It still took them two days to reach the last ridge beyond which lay the coastal plain with its patches of open moorland. Robinson had again tapped the strength of his faith to take the head of the party. He would have led it around in circles, except for Dray who kept to his side and moved him in the right direction. Every evening Robinson prayed long and tedious prayers that he might find the wretched inhabitants and light the fire of faith in their breasts. God knew that they needed his help, his protection and guidance. The Lord had sent him out to Van Diemen's Land to save them. 'Fader' had been delirious for days. He marched, sunk in God's will. Floating in a golden meditation he entered a clearing and stopped in the middle without realizing that it was a pagan place of significance. Alone in the very centre of the sacred circle he looked around at the rocks arranged in spirals and ovals and thought it was a child's playing ground. He moved on and the convicts trampled across. Dray circled around the sacred area and met him on the far side. She did not tell him that he had trespassed and would have to pay the price.

The day after this incident, Wooreddy, Trugernanna, Ummarrah and McKay walked into his camp to find the suffering 'Fader'. Wooreddy and Trugernanna were swept by compassion and they could not help but compare the ghost with the one that had begun the expedition. Then he had been sleek and rounded in middle-aged plumpness; then he had been clad in a natty uniform of his own design; then he had shown that he felt that in it he had cut a fine figure and radiated authority and distinction; but now, 'Fader' had become as rough as a piece of red ochre. His flesh had all but melted from his bones and the remains of his uniform hung down in filthy rags. His famous high-peaked cap had been lost in some mountain torrent and his unruly red hair glowed like the red kangaroo skin of the Sun Lady.

What brought the tears to their eyes was the skin disease which had crawled all over his body, making it blotched and scratched. Tormented beyond endurance, Ballawine had treated it with his own concoction of gun powder mixed in urine. He had applied this in a thick paste which had been washed away in places by the rain, leaving bare patches of red flaking skin dotted with pustules. Such a sight and such a smell the good doctor had never seen or smelt before. It showed that on occasion, *Ria Warrawah* even attacked his own minions. The current belief had it that the skin disease was spread by *Ria Warrawah* (or an apparition of that force) in the dead of night. He, or it, prowled along through the bush and on coming across a camp reached into the bag hanging at its waist, pulled out handful after handful of reddish dust and tossed it over the sleepers.

Wooreddy decided to investigate this unusual case. He questioned Dray and learnt that 'Fader' had passed through a sacred site resulting in a worsening of the disease overnight; but this had not been the cause of the affliction. He questioned further. The ghost had also desecrated a grave. He had come to a cairn of rocks and burrowed beneath to find the burnt remains of a body. He raked through the ashes with his fingers and collected some pieces of bone which he showed to Dray. She begged him to put them back as they belonged to other people, but the ghost had laughed and tossed them at her. She had avoided harm by carefully picking up the pieces of bone by two twigs, then muttering protective spells all the while had restored them to their place. The ghost had committed sacrilege and was now suffering for it. Wooreddy nodded and they all looked towards Ballawine whom they knew itched and itched—how he itched! When an Aborigine received some of the flung dust and the disease began to spread, it was usual to slash the skin, roll in ashes and afterward string charms over the worst spots. This treatment relieved the disease and eventually cured it. The Aborigines hated it as one of the worse afflictions *Ria Warrawah* could send on them. Now it appeared, or at least it appeared to Wooreddy, that a ghost could receive the dust while trespassing on a sacred site and by disturbing the bones of strange dead. This he had not known before. Perhaps for the simple reason that no human would do such things. He did know that those who committed a heavy offence against sacred law did waste away unless they made amends and purified themselves. Perhaps, Wooreddy thought, ghosts reacted differently from humans. The divine power stored in the strong places and that circulating around the bones of the dead were antipathetic to them. They caused ghost skin to flake and fester just as human skin did. The good doctor stored the facts in his mind and avoided theorising on them. He needed more information. Then he looked at how terribly 'Fader' was suffering and decided that he would cheer him up by 'discovering' the smoke of a campfire. He shouted: 'Look, look, smoke, smoke, "Fader"! There's people in the next bay along!'

'Where, where, for the love of God, where?' the pain-racked Robinson shouted, managing to spring to his feet. He flung his eyes into the rainy sky. He saw no smoke, but his eyes of faith did. 'Quickly, we must go to them. Quickly, at once! At last, they are coming to me,' the sick Robinson exclaimed, as his trembling hands fumbled open his special pack which he had protected through all these days of trials and tribulations. From it he selected the brightest ribbons and the shiniest medals, then, ordering the convicts to stay where they were, he took off with the Aborigines. He charged out onto the beach and scared the daylights out of a small family that had just finished repairing a dome hut. The father and his two sons took a quick look at the evil-smelling demon and retreated into the bush, while the mother and daughter sought safety in the ocean. They swam out to perch on a rock some fifty metres offshore. From there they stared across at the hideous *num*. They had been prepared for the meeting, but not with such an evil-looking ghost.

Robinson calmed down enough to realise his mistake. He took steps to rectify the matter. 'Quickly, Dray, Trugernanna take off your clothing and swim out to those poor females. Tell them that I mean them no harm.' The two women obeyed him, while he breathed a short intense prayer: 'O Lord, please let these poor savage creatures come to me in friendship and peace. Let them feel that I have come to protect them from those evil ones which seek to harm them.'

While the women were swimming out to the rock and Robinson prayed, Wooreddy sauntered into the bush to speak to the males. He found them waiting for him. They explained that although they had volunteered to meet the

90

num, they had not realised just how ugly he would be. Wooreddy tried to put their minds at rest by saying that the ghost looked hideous because he had a skin disease and that under the ointment he had smeared on his skin, he was quite handsome. They were not entirely convinced. 'But apart from his ugliness and bad smell, he even acts like a demon. He ran out of the jungle as if he meant to devour us all! And don't tell us that the *num* doesn't eat humans, they eat each other and who knows what they would do if they caught one of us.'

'But this one is as harmless and warm as the sun,' Wooreddy said. 'Why, he doesn't even carry a gun! He was only excited at seeing you. It's his way. Why, if he wanted to harm you, he would have carried with him a musket or the little guns he carries in his pack! He would have crept up on you and not run onto the beach like a mad thing.'

The father considered the matter, while Wooreddy continued to urge his case. 'My wife and a woman from your own nation are swimming out to your wife and daughter. They will have reached them by now and will be explaining everything to them. Even now they all are swimming back to the land. Come and meet "Fader" with them.' They returned with Wooreddy.

It was as he had said. The women had been persuaded to return to the beach, but when the ghost came towards them, they began to shiver in fright. It was not only his appearance that scared them, they had heard many stories about the depravity of the ghosts and expected to be slaughtered or raped out of hand. How relieved they were to find that the *num* tied bright ribbons around their necks and even appeared to be generally upset at seeing the deep scratch the mother had on her breast. The result of being dashed against the rock by a wave. Then the father and son came back.

Robinson rushed to him with an outstretched hand which made the man think that he was about to be grabbed. He took a step backwards. His hand was held, moved upwards and downwards a few times, then dropped. What did it mean? 'Fader' selected his brightest medal, looped it on a red ribbon, then tied it around the man's neck. He looked down at it. Other people flocked into the cove. Robinson found himself surrounded by about twenty of his 'sable friends'. Tears of joy and gratitude pricked his eyeballs. Against all odds, and only after severe trials, his mission had come to fruition. Now the work of conciliation could begin. He pulled out little looking-glasses and passed them out to the people. They saw an image in the mirror and turned it over to see if the back of the image showed there. But they soon grew tired of the novelty and handed them back to Robinson. Disappointed, he tried to seduce them with scissors. He remembered that on Bruny Island the men had liked to have their locks trimmed. He gave scissors to Ummarrah and Wooreddy and told them to begin cutting the men's hair. He was happy to see that the men flocked around the two barbers. To divert them further, he pulled out his flute and began playing a simple melody. He was overjoyed to find that these savage souls could be soothed by the sweet pan-pipings. Then he attempted to speak to them in what he thought was their own language or a close dialect. They smiled and nodded at his gibberish. He thought that they understood that he was saying he came in peace and that they should remain at peace; that he was to be their father and look after them so that no one would hurt them anymore; that the governor in Hobarton fully agreed with him in every way. He said all of these things and they understood not a single word. They smiled politely and turned to Wooreddy. It was Robinson's turn not to understand a single word. The good doctor was advising them that a good start had been made and that it was time to be off. They agreed, politely took off the assorted ribbons and medals the ghost had decked them with, and left.

Robinson did not believe in force. Also there were too many for him to try and stop, so he let them leave. He had established contact and that was the important first step. Then to complicate matters, Wooreddy declared that they were bad men and would try and kill him. Ummarrah backed him up. Robinson refused to believe this. 'Fudge,' he snapped, but all the same decided to stay on the beach and in the dome-shaped hut for the night.

Next morning with Trugernanna and Wooreddy he raced off after the Aborigines. His enthusiasm conquered any fears he may have had for his safety. Their tracks led along a trail which followed the coast, then they moved away inland towards a near hillock. He wished to climb this to see if he could spy out any traces of smoke. Weakened by his sickness, he had to stop halfway up to get his breath. He sat down, then began getting to his feet. He looked up and saw two of the biggest men he had ever seen and each one held the longest and thickest spear he had ever seen. Worst of all, the long serrated points of the spears were directed at his chest. Paralysed, he neither stood nor sat. Wooreddy and Trugernanna, waiting at the bottom of the hill, saw what was happening. They did not want to lose their ghost and quickly took off their clothes which marked them as being with the *num*, then climbed up to where Robinson was and spoke to the men.

The men were very suspicious. 'How many ghosts are with you?' they asked, still keeping their spears levelled.

'There are no ghosts with us,' Wooreddy replied, not even acknowledging the presence of Robinson.

'If that is so, what is that?' one said, jabbing with his spear towards Robinson.

'That is "Fader",' answered Wooreddy. 'He has come all this way to meet you.'

'That is a ghost,' the other man declared.

'That is "Fader" and you must meet him,' said Wooreddy, unmoved by the apparent contradiction.

The men stared at Robinson, who suddenly regained the use of his body. He smiled and stuck out his hand. Before they had time to react either one way or the other, he had ribbons hanging around their necks and great gaudy medals dangling on their chests. Unable to comprehend such behaviour or motive, they concluded the meeting by nodding their heads and walking off down the other side of the hill. Immediately Robinson thought of capturing such unique specimens. 'They are alone and I have my pistols in my pack. No one will know that I have them,' he said to Wooreddy and Trugernanna.

Wooreddy chose to echo his words: 'Fader, we catch those big two and take them back to Hobarton. The governor will be happy to see such big men and it will prove that part of your mission has been successful.'

Robinson deliberated and the men increased their distance from him. Finally he reluctantly decided to let them go. His aim and the orders of the governor were to contact the Aborigines living along the west coast and to learn their numbers. If he captured those two, it was possible that word would spread all along the coast and that would be the end of his mission. 'No,' he declared to Wooreddy, 'I have come as a friend and I have no intention of capturing or harming any of them. They are God's children and I feel like a father to them. We'll leave them in peace until the time is ripe.' And although Wooreddy and Trugernanna did not know it in detail, the time would soon be ripe for the West Coast Nations.

Wooreddy could accept this because he knew that it was the ending of the world, but he would still feel much of the pain of living through those last days. Now, in these first months of the mission, he thought that the ghost he had allied himself with was good, or at least the best of a bad lot. At this time, this was so. Idealism floated freely in the west coast fogs and it affected Wooreddy so that at times he believed that things might turn out all right. But his enlightenment stopped him from putting too much faith in improbable solutions. The world was ending and the time was one of chaos. Chaos manifested itself more and more, and things would continue to get worse until chaos ruled chaos, until *Ria Warrawah* reclaimed all of the earth and mankind became extinct. He was destined to see that end. He and Trugernanna would survive until there was nothing left to survive for, but Ummarrah was not a survivor and they would see his death.

4

Into Occupied Territory

I

The Aborigines came walking towards the coast. The season
had been good and they were in no hurry to reach a place
with a large food supply. Towards the coast, the people
came, knowing that it was time for seal and that the mutton
birds had arrived. Secure in the unity of the three times and
the known circle of nature, they came to the coast as they
always had come at this time. They still thought that the old
ways stretched, eternal and unchanging. Like a finger the
peninsula pointed towards a near island on which they might
find seal, but they would not cross to it today. The Aborigines
walked along the central ridge of the peninsula until they
reached the track which led down to the sheltered cove in
which they had always camped. A huge pile of shells, arcing
around the mouth of a cave holding a clear spring of water,
testified to the many, many times they had been there. The
people settled in. They spread their kangaroo skins on the
cave floor and were delighted to find on the shore some
oddly-shaped driftwood for their campfires. Already some
of the women were diving into the water prising off with
their wooden chisels the shellfish which clung to the rocks at
each end of the cove. With loaded baskets they swam to the
shore, emptied their loads so that the men and children
might snack, then swam over to a gravelled islet. As always
at this time, the mutton birds had returned to their own
burrows. The women reached down into the holes, grabbed
the birds by the neck and with a swift twist killed them. They
strung them together by the neck on their short digging
sticks, then swam back to the cave. Soon the pungent odour

95

of the fowl began to spread over the cove. They preferred
eating the eggs or the young chicks, but it was best to start off
the season with a feast of the older birds. It was a way of re-
establishing the relationship. They gave strength to the legs
and also helped to bring the birds back each season. Tonight,
as was the custom, they celebrated both their arrival and that
of the birds. It was a greeting as well as an affirmation that
things endured. They would celebrate unto the dawn.

As the night settled more heavily over the land and the
ocean began to swirl up tendrils of fine mist, shadows moved
silently along the cliff top. *Ria Warrawah* stalked the land. He
(or it) should have been driven away by the ceremonies of
the community, but unknown to them the times had changed.
A rough shout, and dirty orange splashes of fire began to
descend upon the people. The dancing dissolved into panic;
the singing into shouts and screams. The muskets continued
to thunder and flash out. The screams and shouts weakened
into moans and finally individual shots ended most of these.
The ghosts grouped at the head of the track and came down.
Some of the people had tried to escape up the path. Their
bodies were tossed casually into the sea. The ghosts cleared
the area of humans and human remains. The wounded, the
dead and the young were flung into the ocean. The kangaroo
skins and utensils were gathered up and the fires kicked out.
Soon the only sound was that of boots rasping on the rock
floor of the cave, then the alien words: 'That's the last of that
lot.' Scuffings and scrapings faded away into the underlying
sigh of the sea. The cove was vacant except for bloodstains.
The few survivors, mainly women who had escaped by diving
into the sea, crawled ashore to find not even a fire to warm
their shuddering bodies. They huddled together right at the
back of the cave until in the dawn light they saw the first
bodies beginning to be washed against the shore. The sea
was taunting them. They wailed out their fear and loss. In
just a few dark hours their whole community had been
destroyed. Only a few individuals were left to roam over the
land like phantoms.

Wooreddy listened to the account of the massacre in the
matter-of-fact ghost language. Since he had been with
Ballawine, he had set himself the task of learning the language.

Now he could understand almost everything he heard. But dressed in his ghost clothing and listening to the ghost language, he felt distant from the events, from that terrible loss of community. His numbness protected him. He knew that such things had happened and were likely to continue to happen until there were few if any humans remaining. Since they had left the west coast, after contacting most of the people there and marking them for future reference, life had begun to lose all value. The same apprehension he had felt in the penal station at Macquarie Harbour he felt everywhere. Where the ghosts ruled, human life was constantly under threat, and familiar things were banished. Strange animals roamed and even strange grass replaced the old. Trees were chopped down in huge numbers, others were circled and left to die, and the furrows from 'wheels' scarred the earth. This land was stranger than Bruny Island and more polluted. And what could the good doctor do but accept it in all its horror? This was what the ghosts had wrought — and Robinson listened to the account of this and other massacres and ground his teeth in horror and dismay.

Recovered from the trials of the west coast and in a new uniform (carried on the last voyage of his vessel before it was wrecked on the coast), a slimmer but self-important Great Conciliator questioned the convict-shepherd before him.

'You took part in the crime?'

'I was protecting the flock. They took some of 'em away, drove 'em over the rocks, that they did. We was protecting the sheep,' declared the shepherd doggedly, taking an instant dislike to Robinson.

'How many of these poor defenceless creatures did you murder?'

'Not me, mate, not me. I didn't say anything like 'at, 'at I didn't. I didn't do in not one of those crows. Why I ain't even got a musket,' the shepherd said triumphantly, as if that settled the matter.

'How many did you say were killed?'

'I didn't say, maybe thirty or so, can't be sure though. It was as dark as one of their skins that night.' He realised his error and his mouth clamped shut in a tight line.

'So thirty or more were ruthlessly done away with?'

The shepherd concentrated on scratching his thin, sandy hair. Robinson thought he looked like some sort of hog. 'So thirty or so were done away with, were they?'

The hog nodded his head and fluttered his straw-coloured eyelashes down over his little piggy eyes. He could no more keep his mouth shut than pigs could fly. He blathered out: ''Bout that. But we was only protecting the sheep. Terrible 'ell we gets from the overseer if we don't.'

'And what did you do with the bodies?'

Might as well get hung for two as for one, the shepherd thought. He was rather proud of his deed. It had been one of the most exciting things he had done in his life. 'Well, after it was all hover, we thought that some folks might not like it hovermuch if it should get about. What with that governor away down in 'Obarton making his proclamations and what all. They went in where they drove hover the sheep.'

'Did you shoot any of the women?'

'Not one of them, governor, not one of them women were shot. It's the blokes that hare the bad'uns, not the female ones. Why, I've been with one or two meself, and . . .' He stopped. Befuddled by what he had revealed he looked more like a sly pig than ever. Robinson could not even dislike such vermin. He continued to do his job.

'Don't you know that these poor inoffensive creatures are under the protection of the British government and British law — the same law which sentenced you to transportation to Van Diemen's Land and which, sir, if I have my way, will sentence you to a good flogging or better still a good hanging which you richly deserve? You are an animal, sir, an animal!'

'But they were killing the sheep. I was only doing me job.'

'The killing of a few sheep is not cause enough for the slaughter of over thirty men, women and children. Sir, I know the story, it is common knowledge in these parts, and it will not go unpunished! You should have notified your master and he would have taken the proper measures . . .'

''E would 'ave tol' hus to do the same. 'E don't like the crows heither. Says the sheep can't stan' the smell of 'em.'

'You are not justified, and nor is your master, in using arms against the Aborigines of V.D.L. unless it is to protect your life. And how do you know that these people were the culprits?'

'T'ey were, t'at's why,' the shepherd replied defiantly. Such a lot of fuss over the killing of a few crows.

'All blackfellows look the same. Even I, who have been travelling with a group, still find it difficult to identify one from another at a distance. Those people which you and your cohorts so wantonly killed, those people, sir, were innocent!'

'Yes, sir,' the shepherd replied without conviction or care. What did it matter to him! They were just a bloody pack of crows, better off dead. He decided to agree with what the governor said no matter how silly it was. That was the best way of handling him. And no one had been hanged for killing a crow yet.

Robinson had finished with his questions. He stared through the man at that lonely cove. He heard the volleys of shots and the screams of agony from the wounded. With tears in his eyes, he gruffly bade the convict to be gone. With such types being allotted to the Van Diemen's Land Company, no wonder the Aborigines were shot down whenever and wherever they showed themselves. The wretched people had a right to their land, didn't they? No, they no longer had such a right. They had to be collected together and taken to a place of safety. This was the only solution and he would begin emphasising it in his dispatches to Governor Arthur.

He continued to ponder and agonise over the wretched inhabitants of the island and the crimes committed against them—and too often by those who prided themselves on being considered 'Christian'! The Aborigines must be protected at all costs! His eyes met those of Wooreddy, and he thought a flash of commiseration and acknowledgement at what he was doing passed between them. The civilised and the savage briefly shared the same feelings of pain and outrage—but the good doctor was not sharing anything with the ghost. He was thinking about when they would cross to the offshore islands in the *num* boat and although he had been many times on the ocean, he still dreaded the prospect. The ocean belonged to *Ria Warrawah*, the source of all evil. But he had to go as he had to obey the *num* in many things. For a long moment, he wished that he had left with Ummarrah, then disagreed with his wish. He did not want to spend his time skulking in some patch of scrub fearful of being found and killed out of hand. He had heard the *num* talking among themselves. They were murdering the humans all over the island.

II

Wooreddy continued trekking through the occupied region. Nowhere had the local Aborigines been able to find a place of refuge. Each spot was a place of slaughter. Where the boat waited for them, four ghosts had been killed while trying to kidnap women. They had jumped from their boat and rushed towards the people firing their muskets and expecting them to flee. The men counter-charged. Only one ghost escaped with his life. He took refuge up a tree and shot at any one that came within range of his pistols. Finally a woman took pity on him and helped him to escape to the beach. She was rewarded by having the male child she carried ripped from her arms and dashed against a boulder. The ghost laughed as he did this. More *num* came crawling across the sea to his rescue. Then they stood offshore and when the Aborigines came onto the beach, they opened up to teach them a lesson with a few well-directed volleys of musket fire.

The soles of the good doctor's feet cringed as they touched the sand. The particles felt like dried specks of blood. He, Trugernanna and Ballawine got into the whaleboat and the crew sent it scudding across the sea in the direction of one of the larger islands off the point. They rowed along the east side of West Hunter Island and finally landed on a long, wide sandy beach where a small stream of fresh water trickled over the sand and into the sea. Leaving the boat crew behind, Robinson rushed off across the island to the cove where the ghosts called 'sealers' had set up a camp. No one was there and he took the opportunity to poke into everything. Wooreddy too examined what took his interest. He looked into the half dozen huts constructed in the ghost fashion with four square walls and a peaked roof. He was surprised to find that behind each hut some land had been fenced off on which grew ghost plants in rows. One whole hut was piled high with kangaroo skins and Wooreddy knew he would find few kangaroos on the island. The Great Conciliator began listing the sealers' possessions and while he was doing this the man left to try a little hunting. He passed through the coastal screen of trees and reached a central plain which would have been an ideal area for game, if there had been any! No fresh tracks and only a few old ones. He came to the opposite coast and looked across to where some rocky islets squawked with bird life. At least they had not killed the birds yet, he thought.

He walked back to the boat, arriving there at the same time as Ballawine and Trugernanna. They were now to sail across to Robbin's Island. Again they pulled into a broad, curving bay and landed to walk along the beach. Wooreddy felt a mood of happiness rise in him. Autumn was coming and the clouds were separating to reveal the vivid blue of the sky. The white sand of the beach glittered in the sunlight and the grey rocks protruded from the sparkling jade of a now quiescent sea. Inland, the land rose covered with the grey-green of a forest in which the white trunks of dead trees could be seen. Pelicans waddled along the beach, making Trugernanna grin, for they had the same gait as Wooreddy. Then she gave a short yelp of delight as she reached an area covered with the small shells from which she could make necklaces. She could exchange them with the *num* for tobacco. She gathered about a bushel and daringly made her husband carry them. He was so bemused by the request and the dumping of the loaded bag in his hands, that he made no protest. They tramped inland from the bay and found no fresh tracks of men or animals. The Aborigines began to feel alarmed at being on such a barren island and muttered protection spells.

Ballawine rushed here and there at his usual scampering pace, which made Wooreddy wonder if he did not have some of those circles called 'wheels' under the soles of his boots. Strangely, he never appeared to enjoy lazing about taking things easy, or even in standing still and admiring the scenery. He was always rushing this way and that way in a fashion which the Aborigines could not understand. They might hurry to a warm meal, a festival or after game, but always with a goal in mind. And he was never aware of discomfort, and they had even seen him thrust himself into the heart of a thicket which reduced his clothing to ribbons. His haste and uncaringness for others made him an object of wonder to them. To others, it was often a mark of self-respect to disobey and hinder him. The Aborigines had tried to adapt to his ways, but often on finding things too rough and rude, they disappeared into the bush to achieve some serenity. Hunting was always the excuse and as the ghost was always finding himself short of supplies, he accepted this. Then, his whole future was bound up with the Aborigines and he took care not to alienate the few he had conciliated.

They circled back to the shore and climbed over the rocks at the base of a point to find themselves at the edge of the wide sweeping bay in which they had landed. A few kilometres along the beach, they could see the waiting boat. Perching on the last large rock, they also saw that extensive mudflats stretched below them. Robinson lagging behind, his boots had slipped where their bare feet had gripped, came up and barely hesitated before jumping down. The others followed, gingerly, feeling out each step in an ooze which went past their knees. From past experience they edged closer to and then into the shallows where the water had compacted the mud into some solidity. Wooreddy disliked even this much of the sea and was glad that after a kilometre the mud began to harden and they could walk out of the water. They were on firm ground before they reached the boat, and after washing in the stream, they tumbled into it. The boat angled out and into a swirling current which threatened to capsize it. One side sank, the other rose to sink in turn, and the craft shuddered with a twisting motion which made Wooreddy think that his last moments were upon him. No catamaran could have lived in such a current. At last, he felt the boat settle. They were through and heading towards the base of a thumb-shaped headland where, so they had been informed, was another sealers' camp.

The crew ran the boat through the surf and skidded it

102

right into the joint where the thumb met the palm of the hand. There several caves had been excavated from a high clay bank. Their arrival was greeted by a swarm of dogs, all yelping teeth and snarling snouts. Robinson fended the brutes off with an oar until an Aboriginal woman came out of a shelter with a whip and chased them away. Trugernanna shouted out in delighted surprise. It was her eldest sister. Long ago she had seen her kidnapped, or inveigled into a boat. The slim girl and the heavy woman fell into each other's arms crying and laughing at the same time, then Moorina, her sister, dragged her off to meet the other women. Robinson took the opportunity to make a rough count of the huge pile of kangaroo skins the sealers were drying.

Trugernanna chatted away, explaining how 'Fader' was a good ghost that wanted to help all of them and that he was going around meeting everyone. Moorina, her eldest sister, wanted to hear all the news from home. Trugernanna began describing how the coughing demon had attacked the people and killed most of them. The news made the women cry. It was a terrible feeling to be alone in the world. Then Trugernanna cheered them by telling them that she had been married and that her husband was with her. She pointed at the taciturn doctor who was examining the shelters. The caves had been lined with poles and sheets of bark. He wondered if they were waterproof and peered at the ceiling and saw water stains. They did leak, but not very much! He heard Trugernanna bragging to her sister about how good a hunter he was, then complain that he had been previously married to a foreign woman who had spoilt him. 'You know what they're like,' she added, then went on, 'She made him so conceited. He thinks these great big thoughts which weigh down his head so that he can never look up at the sky.' Then she went on to say that she had no children and that this was a good thing in those unsettled times. Moorina told her that she was 'married' to a *num* who treated her well, but he was often away and when he returned always expected to find that the kangaroo pile had grown in his absence. She added that she had had two children, but they had drowned.

'So young to be taken by *Ria Warrawah*!' Trugernanna exclaimed—and the two sisters hugged each other again.

Moorina quickly recovered from her sadness and said with a shrug, 'These things happen all the time.'

The others nodded in agreement. Trugernanna did not know whether to agree or disagree, and so she changed the subject to ask about her other sister, Lowernunhe, who had been kidnapped with her. Elder Sister replied that she had gone sailing off with another sealer and might be gone for days or months. 'No telling with those fellows,' she said. 'They get in their boats and off they go to the edge of the world. To think that once I thought Van Diemen's Land and a few off-shore islands were just about all there was. Why, I've been far to the west and all along the coast are people living just like us. Well she's gone off with him, and might return now or never,' Moorina concluded with a fatalism which scared Trugernanna. Times were bad and making the people worse. It was the fault of the ghosts and their ceaseless killing and changing of things. 'And he makes us wear these things which trip us up because ghost females can't show their bodies. Why you can't even run in it,' she said, commenting on one of the changes which directly affected her.

'And they make us wear these things most of the time too,' the other women replied, pointing to their sailor caps and rough frock-like garments made from kangaroo skins. 'Still, they're not that bad. They keep us warm.'

'Yes,' the others agreed. 'It may not be for the best, but it could be worse.'

Again that fatalism which alarmed Trugernanna. She had to comment on it. 'It is the times,' she said tactfully. 'The old days are going. We've just been to some of the islands and found no animals there at all. Even in some parts of the mainland, there are only *num* sheep and cattle.'

'Everything going, going, gone—they have taken everything,' the women replied in unison. A sudden sadness darkened their mood as they contemplated a bleak future.

Robinson had moved closely to the women during their conversation in order to monitor it. He could not understand much, only individual words and an occasional sentence. When they began talking about their clothing, he looked at Trugernanna and then the other women. They were much stouter and had let their hair grow. It poked out from

104

beneath their caps in tight curls. Trugernanna with her cropped hair still looked as slim and vulnerable as a youth.

A whale boat came into sight heading directly for the settlement. It ran through the surf with such a speed that its impetus carried it right up onto the beach. The four ghosts in it scrambled out, heaved the boat around until it lay lengthwise across the front of the central cave, then saw Robinson and came to him. The Great Conciliator was very good at greeting people. He gave each of them a hearty handshake and introduced himself. He soon found out that one of them, a New Zealander named John White who had considerable status among the sealers, owned two of the Aboriginal women present. He called them Jack and Marie. Another one, Bob Drew owned the other two women. The other two sealers were Dave Kelly and Paddy O'Neil. Trugernanna recognised the latter as the ghost that had raped her. Hatred flashed in her eyes. She had vowed to pay him back one day and she would! He had been brutal and she had never forgotten his pale blue eyes, the rattish face and the white hair now thinning on his pointy head. He looked at her and she almost spat in his face. She saw that he did not recognise her and vowed that he would know who she was when she was tearing out his kidney.

The sealers had heard all about Robinson and his business. His progress had been followed since he had arrived at Cape Grim and began visiting the off-shore islands. They invited him to stay the night in one of the empty shelters, only the middle one being in use, then told him that a group of Aborigines had passed by just the other day. This Robinson refused to believe. He thought it a ruse to get him away and so accepted their offer. He even allowed one of the women to take his socks to wash them while he settled back in the central cave to have a yarn with the sealers.

The women continued to talk to Trugernanna while they did their chores. They told her that the shepherds of the Van Diemen's Land Company were a bad lot, always trying to entice the women into their huts, and if the Aboriginal men objected they were fired on. Elder Sister said: 'If the local people hear the sound of a gun being discharged, they exclaim, 'Nau Hammoi', which is Ria Warrawah in their language, then leave the area as fast as they can. Is it any wonder that we stay here with our ghosts? Only one of us had the guts to run off. That was Walyer—she was married to that Paddy creature. He decided that she spent too much time with her baby and did not collect enough skins, so he took the baby and drowned it in the ocean. She went and got his gun, shot at him, but missed. Then she took to the bush, vowing that she would kill all the ghosts she met. When she hears that you are travelling with one of them, there'll be trouble.'

Trugernanna told about her own experience with the Paddy ghost and said that she shared in the feeling of Walyer. 'If I have a chance like she had, I won't muff it. After I get through with him, he won't rape another woman or kill a baby,' she said with such vehemence that it startled the others who had learnt to live with such things. They tried to calm her down and muttering angrily she began to help them with their chores.

Meanwhile, Wooreddy sat as quiet as a mouse beside Robinson. In the next cave where they had been ordered to go, the boat crew complained bitterly, saying that being on a chaingang was better than serving under Robinson. But by suppertime their master had been thawed out enough by the hospitality for him to allow them into the main dugout to eat. The meal of fried kangaroo cutlets and fish was followed by a few tots of rum which mellowed the Great Conciliator even more. Then the women, including Trugernanna, took off their clothing and began to dance and sing. This infuriated him, though he kept his peace for the time being. What a lecture he would give her! It might be the thing for these savage sealer women to do—after all they had but advanced from savagery to barbarism—but he was teaching the arts of civilisation to this girl . . . He tried to keep his eyes off the bouncing breasts and stamping thighs while he planned a course of action. With an effort, he wrenched his mind from such distractions and decided to hold a religious service next morning at which he would lecture them on their infamy. He spent the rest of the evening planning his sermon, ignoring the vulgarity in front of him.

Next morning, with Wooreddy clad in white trousers and

a red jacket, Robinson posed at the side of the whale boat. Near him sat Trugernanna and before him stood the four rough sealers and their rougher womenfolk. Beyond them the red clay bank rose to support the roots of trees, and in the distance jagged mountains pierced the sky. Such a sylvan scene filled the Great Conciliator's heart with delight. He began to speak. His voice entering into the rhythm of the sea eating at the land, eternally eating away at the land, eating great chunks of it—Wooreddy called his mind back from the sea to listen to Ballawine's strong voice echoing out. He noticed that the ghost's skin disease had cleared up and that he looked healthier than he had ever seen him. This strong, confident 'Fader' exhorted his congregation:

'Examine yourselves, whether ye be in the faith, prove by your labour. And what is your labour? it should be the teaching of the message of Jesus Christ to those unfortunate enough to be born heathens in this land. It is our duty and our labour to see that the gospel is made known to them. Today, I have the honour to preach the living message in this place. God has chosen me to give his message and perhaps for the very first time in all of time, Christian words are echoing over this desolate beach . . .'

And so he went on and the congregation began to yawn. After a tedious hour his sermon began to grind towards an end: 'Now his message and glad tidings are being blown this way and that way throughout all this land. Let us pray that these poor savages may be brought to know him. Now let us pray, to the one, true God, that peace and justice may descend upon this new Christian country!'

He bowed his head, said a hurried prayer, then began to judge the quality of his sermon. He thought that it had been appropriate—now for the business of government! 'Many complaints have reached the government and His Excellency, Lieutenant-Governor George Arthur in Hobarton, that you so-called sealers have been and are continuing to mistreat the subjects of His Majesty, namely these poor Aboriginal people.' He stopped to let his words sink in, and they did! The Great Conciliator was losing friends quickly. He continued to lay down the law to his audience. 'The Government's stated aim and moral duty is to teach these children of the forest and eventually make them into good British subjects. From this day forth, I, in the name of the Government, order you to stop molesting these innocent people in any and all ways. If it comes to my attention that they continue to suffer ill-treatment at your hands, I will not rest until I see you in a court of justice. You have been warned!'

He finished, and the sealers looked at one another, then stared off at the distant mountains. They did not know it, but Robinson lacked the authority to order them to do or not do anything. Still, he considered that he had the moral authority and the next time when he met Arthur he would receive the secular one too. He was so carried away, that he began anew to scold them, this time on their dogs. His voice was beginning to lose its strength and regain its old querulous tone. 'And as for your dogs. I have been over the Hunter group of islands and find that the kangaroo population is almost nil. I have heard that the islands used to abound in these animals. You have destroyed them for the sake of their skins. Your dogs are allowed to roam free without let or hindrance. The Government has passed a new regulation that all dogs not registered must be destroyed. This is the law and must be obeyed, and I will see that it is obeyed! Reform yourselves, you are pests to your fellows. Begin anew and seek the new life that awaits you.' He stopped, highly pleased with himself, but the sealers scowled and said nothing. They knew that he would be away soon and that that would be the end of the matter. If not, they would not be here next time he came calling.

III

The Robinson expedition had to return the boat to the Van Diemen's Land Company and continue on land. Wooreddy began to tire of the journey and the breakneck pace. New things and places appealed to him, but he was passing over the land at too fast a rate to enjoy and discover things about it. It still felt dead and filled with dread. They

108

had come across no recent traces of the local people and Trugernanna said that they had all been killed. It might be so, but as they had done on the west coast, they would contact any people, first and without letting Ballawine know.

They kept to the coast, going along to Emu Bay, and then onto Blackman's Point where rocks and boulders were heaped up in such a way that Wooreddy identified it as a place of religious significance. Great Ancestor had sat down there and left his marks behind, but without the local people he could not be sure of this. He still felt that the land had been soiled by the blood of its owners. They walked along a beach and came across the proof to his feeling. One of the convicts had heard the story and gleefully related it to Robinson. Two women had been walking along the beach when they saw a party of ghosts coming toward them. They were unafraid and kept on walking. Then the muskets began firing. One of the women carried a baby and she could not run into the ocean for shelter. The ghosts surrounded her and she put the baby between her legs and crouched over it to protect it. A ball smashed through her body. Before she could fall a *num* raced in with an axe and dealt her a heavy blow on the back of the neck. The baby screamed, lying in the warm blood of its mother. Then the axe descended on it too. The other woman was dragged exhausted from the sea. She was tortured and killed. The horrified Robinson allowed himself to be taken to where a dry gully came down to the beach. There lay two skeletons. The little one had disappeared.

In such a way the ghosts and humans shared the land. Wooreddy moaned softly as he heard of this and other killings. McKay had once worked for the Van Diemen's Land Company which had received title to large areas of land. Not only the Aborigines, but also the animals and plants were nuisances to be killed off or uprooted. They were to be replaced by ghosts, cattle, sheep and clover. McKay was the expert on the company and its policies. He regaled Robinson with such exaggerated stories of cruelty that the good *num* flung up his hands at the folly of his fellows and wept. Most, if not all, of the bloody deeds had been done along the coast and Wooreddy breathed a sigh of relief as Robinson turned the expedition inland to escape the pollution which even he smelt. The good doctor felt a weight lift from his heart. Along that coast the ocean had seemed to batter and thunder away at not only the earth but also human life. It had succeeded in making the Aborigines evacuate the fertile coastal region for the uplands. But how long would they be safe there? Even now this ghost was seeking them out.

They travelled through a thick jungle. Towers of giant gum trees with a scattering of beeches rose above the cabbage tops of the ferns and the brushes of the wattle. The brush pressed in and entangled them on all sides. If it had not been for the path, they would not have been able to proceed, and even the path was rapidly becoming overgrown. Wooreddy was amazed that inhabited country could be in such bad repair. He remembered his own parklike island with many clearings free of brush and paths the width of tracks. Then he remembered the bad times and how his country too had begun to deteriorate in this way. Now it would be like this. Suddenly he began sobbing wildly and had to hide at the side of the path. Hidden in the tangle of ferns and wattle, he sobbed out his loneliness. All that he had known and loved was no more. His country was dead; his people were dead, and his family was no more. Now he was alone until the world ended and nothing existed, not even his loneliness. Then his blessed numbness arrived to smother all in a fog. He was a survivor and that was enough! He wiped away the tears and ran after the party. They were moving into a range of hills and the beech trees began to outnumber the stringy bark. The path began to descend into a wide valley in which the last outstation of the Van Diemen's Land Company stood. Robinson halted his small band as Wooreddy hurried up. He went forward to meet the overseer, a Mr Willis, who appeared a cut above the other company employees he had met. This only meant that he had a good accent and appealed to the snob in Robinson. Again he was pleasantly surprised to find that the overseer eagerly listened to and backed up almost every one of his pronouncements on various subjects. At last he had found a congenial spook in Mr Willis, an English gentleman forced by circumstances to make himself absent from England for a time. Robinson fawned on such people. They could belong to a rich and important family, and who knew what might come from such a chance meeting?

While his party camped out in the frosty cold, The Great Conciliator spent an agreeable evening inside the overseer's house discussing his conciliating and how he would solve the Aboriginal problem once and for all. His host informed him of the military operations which were planned against them. He seemed more or less to favour them, and Robinson immediately leapt to the attack: 'Sir, I beg to inform you that no formal military operation can root out the savages from their hidden fastnesses. They can squirm to the centre of the most impenetrable thicket . . .'

'We'll burn them out,' Mr Willis said determinedly, as if finally beginning to assert an opinion contrary to Robinson's.

'But that is not all they can do, sir,' exclaimed The Great Conciliator rising to defend his charges, and his job! 'They can slip past any alert picket and no cordon can hold them. Sir, the country won't permit the success of such an operation—only my methods are correct and proper. And on this, sir, I assure you, I have the ear of the Governor. In fact I have it from a source next to His Excellency that he too agrees that the operation will not succeed. It is to serve another purpose entirely.'

'It is?' Mr Willis questioned, leaning closer to catch a piece of gossip from Hobarton.

'As you know, what with the fall in wool prices and one thing or another, most of which come from the stupid control exerted on us by London, there has lately been a great downturn in business. Our Excellency has conceived this scheme to help the colony. The government will be buying supplies and equipment and those employed in military service will have to be fed. There is another thing, sir, which is not generally known, but there have been signs of unrest among the convicts. Some kind of plot was discovered last month, and so it is expedient to raise a force to go against the blacks at this time. It will be in effect a show of arms to quell any unrest from the other quarter.'

'But His Excellency has not the highest reputation amongst the free settlers?'

111

'Free settlers, sir! Those ex-convicts such as Bent and his crowd know only a part of it. What if the convicts, those thousands and thousands of prisoners, go on the rampage? Sir, it could be the end of this colony, it could be the end of all of us. There has even been talk of some of them getting to the blacks and teaching them the use of firearms. I have to tell you that the contacting of the savage denizens of the forest is but part of my work. His 'Excellency has given me the job of discovering, once and for all, if there really are escapees living among the natives and directing their attacks against the British government represented by His Excellency George Arthur. So far, sir, I am happy to tell you in strict confidence that I have found that only the sealers have had an arrangement with the blacks, but now, owing to their cruelty, most natives shun them.'

Mr Willis looked at Robinson with new interest. He was a peculiar one and a cut above the ordinary self-seeking fellows he had been forced to associate with since coming to the colony. The gentleman, languishing in the depths of the Van Diemen's Land wilderness, raised his glass of rum in homage to his guest. Then The Great Conciliator called in some of his sable friends to entertain his host with their primitive ceremonies. The scene was perfect and appealed to the romantic in the gentleman. Here in the wilderness far from all the comforts of civilisation, sitting in a rude habitation they were entertained by the primeval natives. Such a pleasurable moment and one to be treasured in later years. Robinson felt himself to be the fearless missionary he longed to be, but, alas, found unprofitable.

Next morning, Robinson, still playing a role, moved briskly from the clearing at the head of his little band of pioneers and savages. He felt the admiring eyes of the overseer follow him into the forest. They marched along into the afternoon and began to pass through whole areas which had been burnt free of undergrowth. It was still inhabited and kept in repair.

'People have been through here,' Wooreddy informed Ballawine who could not read sign too well. He did not tell him that they had been in the area recently. He pointed out a tall tree up the trunk of which notches had been made a metre apart. 'They went after a possum there,' he commented, leaving out the fact that it had been only a day or so before.

The Great Conciliator doubled his pace and rushed the whole party along the track, rested a few hours at sunset, waited until the moon rose and continued throughout the night. He ignored any complaints of tiredness and was ignorant that the track had turned towards the coast. Such was Ballawine's pace that by dawn they found themselves at the end of a great split which had let the ocean far into the land. Wooreddy shuddered at such a strong and cruel attack by *Ria Warrawah*.

They walked along the eastern edge of the split and morning found them on a sandy beach. Here the Aborigines squatted down and refused to go further. Robinson too was approaching total exhaustion and was inclined to agree with them. He saw the bow of a whale boat projecting from the sand. He thought it would make a good shelter against the western wind which was gusting and flinging sand about. He ordered it dug out. Surprisingly it looked almost whole. Wooreddy began digging with his hands and found himself holding a skull. He gave a yelp of fright and Robinson chided him for his superstition. In reply to this the Aborigines left the beach and the convicts followed them. Robinson ordered them back, but they kept on going. They scrambled over a rocky headland heaped with boulders and disappeared.

They reached a small clearing on a rise above the water. In it was a shelter made from driftwood. By the time the leader of the expedition approached ready to scold them, a fire was blazing at one side of which a damper was cooking. The convicts had laid out the shelter as his quarters and Trugernanna came to him with a mug of hot tea. She took him to the shelter and showed him where she had decorated it with yellow flowers which would help him to sleep and have pleasant dreams. Robinson was agreeably surprised. It was the very first time that the whole party had gone out of their way to make him comfortable. He sat down in his quarters and sipped on the tea, smiling at the silly super-stitions of these simple people. The scent of the flowers made him drowsy. He smiled, feeling the beauty of the spot sweep over him. A few metres to one side a stream ended in a pool of still water, not quite reaching the sea beyond. Across the split a mountain ridge floated, a twin to the one behind him. Both ridges descended into the sea, became reefs and ended in weathered piles of rocks.

Wooreddy too was looking at the scenery. He felt that the piles of rocks were children of the Great Ancestor rock which guarded Bruny Island from the sea. Like it, they too stood firm against the wiles of *Ria Warrawah*. He heard the snores of Ballawine and they drove all thought from his mind. He stretched out to sleep.

He woke to Robinson's querulous voice issuing orders. The hut was being pulled down and the pieces being arranged to make a raft to cross to the other side of the inlet. Eventually it was made, and they crossed to walk along in the late afternoon sun to where the land turned and straightened against the full force of the ocean. Behind the coast large black swans swam in the shallow lagoons and Wooreddy examined the wide patches of reeds where they built their nests, but there were no eggs. He pointed out some tracks and said that they were the tracks of the same group of the night before, but that they were very old. Unfortunately for Wooreddy, they found a freshly killed kangaroo cached in the branches of a tree and the place where they decided to camp that night had been lately used. Robinson felt the warm ashes of the recent fire and looked at Wooreddy who immediately shouted that they were just behind the local people and would surely catch up to them next morning. The Great Conciliator accepted this. He was so excited that he could not sleep.

During the night the sound of a barking dog and human voices came floating toward the camp. Instantly Robinson leapt to his feet and shook Wooreddy awake. He whispered for him to get ready to follow. The good doctor said that it was too dark and that they should wait for morning. Ballawine refused to listen and they took off after the local group. They moved in silence and Wooreddy left in stricter silence. He was off to meet the Aborigines and find out who they were.

114

IV

Swiftly Wooreddy made his way through the forest along a path running parallel to the one taken by Ballawine. He had taken off his clothing for greater ease and stashed them in the branches of a tree for later retrieval. His bare feet made no sound on the beaten earth. The path circled around the long wall of a fallen tree to make a clearing—and at the base of the trunk, where the roots rayed into the air and in the natural hole, glowed a fire. Half a dozen figures sprang up as he neared. The good doctor found himself facing muskets, not spears; he instantly surmised that this was Walyer's band, and the thought flashed through his mind that the group had passed beyond the theological argument of whether humans should use ghost weapons or not.

A hard-eyed woman, with a kangaroo skin wrapped around her waist in the new fashion, stalked to him and prodded him in the belly with the barrel of her musket. Suddenly a loud shout shattered the security—*Narrawa pallawah Wooreddy*—and Ummarrah rushed up to hug the good doctor. Instantly the tense atmosphere dissipated. Ummarrah was in good standing and accepted as almost a member of the guerrilla band. If he knew the stranger, then he must be all right and Ummarrah had made himself responsible for his good behaviour. They all went back to the hidden fire where food was cooking in the *num* style. Ummarrah gave the good doctor a mug of kangaroo stew and said: 'We keep odd hours and travel day or night. So you are here,' he added staring into his face.

'You left us just after Macquarie Harbour,' Wooreddy replied, using the *num* name instead of *Pairralaongatek*. 'How did you find the journey along to here?'

Ummarrah's beefy, good-natured face darkened with his mood as he recalled the journey. 'Everywhere I found the people dying or being killed like flies. I talked with all the communities I could find. Few of them are confident enough to attack the *num*. They hide in the jungles and are too afraid to light a fire to warm themselves. The only strong people left are the ones you lived with in the South West, but after your ghost gets through with them they will be ghosts. He is just as bad as the rest,' he exclaimed, turning to the others and saying: 'Let this man give you his version of the mission this ghost, that I have told you about, is on. You know what I think about this Meeter Ro-bin-un, now you can have another opinion. I think that he is dangerous and if after you hear him out, you also consider him dangerous, I say that we kill him immediately! Has that ghost killed any humans, yet?' he suddenly shot at Wooreddy.

The good doctor, conscious that he might be fighting for his life as well as that of the ghost, became very cautious. This was the third change of atmosphere since he had entered the clearing and these people were dangerous, though fair! 'No,' he said truthfully. 'He has hurt no one and does not plan to hurt anyone. He only wants to meet all of us and talk a little. He wants to know if we are desirous of being taken to a rich land where we may live at ease and in comfort. We can exchange our lands here for that promised land. Over there the *num* will never be able to war on us. If we accept, he will take us there and teach us new things and new ways of living.'

'I don't believe you,' the hard-eyed Walyer snapped. 'The only land those bastards will give us is the Islands of the Dead!'

Wooreddy looked at the woman in her late twenties who stood while the men sat—but not through custom. She was firm bodied and still kept her hair short in the old fashion. He had not met such a woman before, just as he had not met such a group of people. 'At the moment,' he began his carefully thought out answer, 'we are on our way to the north-eastern part of the island to see what it is like. We may even cross the great sea to find the perfect land. And when we have found this land, we shall tell everyone, and they will travel to it and it shall be theirs for ever. There we shall be given enough flour, tea, sugar, mutton and tobacco until we can grow our own.

Walyer clutched at the hope of a new land. Her ties to her old community and land had been broken for a dozen years and she was tired of fighting and running and fighting and running. She desperately wanted a refuge, a place of her

116

own. Her needs made her weak and her weakness made her angry. She hissed out: 'I would go anywhere to escape the sight of a ghost. They have separated us from our own land, we can no longer call it ours. I would go—'

The cynical Ummarrah broke in without apology: 'It is but a ghost trick. They will never rest until we are all dead. They will give us nothing but death. When have they been generous to a single person? They get you in their power and that is the end. We must be on our guard and fight against this ghost and his pernicious lies.'

But Walyer had been given hope and she, in turn, interjected. An argument began. Wooreddy stood forgotten and could reflect on this band of Aborigines he had heard about. Walyer led a group of men, including Ummarrah, collected from the remnants of the communities which had once owned this land. They had not shared a common language and had had to evolve a dialect made up from all sources including English. When Wooreddy had approached their camp, they had moved with a deadly precision; and even now while the two argued, they were on the alert for danger. Ummarrah, himself, had chucked off the hearty, not very bright, image he had projected whilst with Ballawine, and, though still impetuous, appeared to speak with more thought. He now declared in his strong voice: 'They have no authority to make us go where they want us to. This is our land and we have always been here. We have numbered the trees and the very blades of grass. Great Ancestor together with his family made everything. Emu Ancestor made my land and if I were there I could take you over it and show you where he walked. They can never take away our land. I will retreat into the mountains. They will never find me there.'

But they had taken the land; they all knew this, but tried to avoid the sadness. Instead Walyer attacked Ummarrah's plan of moving back into the mountains. 'There isn't much to eat up there,' she stated with a little too much satisfaction. 'What do you plan to live on? You would have to descend into the valleys for food and they would see you. They would track you back to your hideout and kill you. We are supposed to be defending our country, not leaving it, and retreating to your mountain fastness is just the same as going

117

to the place the *num* want us to go to. I think it would be a good idea to meet this ghost and find out what they are thinking of doing.'

The good doctor noticed how many *num* words they spoke and suddenly realised that more and more *num* words had also entered his vocabulary. 'Yes, there does not seem to be much of a choice,' he spoke into the silence. 'Things are so different now, right down to the words we speak. You can stay in these parts until you are found and killed, or run to the mountains where you will probably die of starvation. The way I see it, is that the only logical thing to do is to go and see the ghost we call Ballawine, and hear what he has to say. In that way you will be able to come to a correct decision. Just think, a place of our own where we can be ourselves again.'

Walyer had been won over, and she said in her demanding voice: 'And what about those of us who have killed some of the ghosts? They are quick to take revenge—' Wooreddy had an answer for everything, which was suspect to those who had ears to hear. The old mistrust Ummarrah had felt for him, resurfaced.

'Ballawine says that none shall suffer for those acts done in self-defence. In his words *we are more sinned against than sinning.*' He used the English sentence and they all understood. The times had indeed changed.

'He is out to prevent injury to us and he will see to it that not one of us comes to harm,' he finished.

Walyer said in a softer voice: 'Perhaps I will go and see this Ballawine. If I do not like what he says I will leave. I have been among the ghosts before and they did not hold me.'

Wooreddy smiled at his victory. 'But we must plan the time and the way of the meeting. I know this ghost well and he likes things done in a certain way. Make it hard for him to catch up with you. Let's work out our plan of action.'

Ummarrah protested about the duplicity and even the very idea of meeting with the ghost, but he was in the minority and the others sat with Wooreddy and worked out how the meeting would be effected. Then he left to rejoin Robinson's party.

It was morning before he rejoined the party and just as Aboriginal voices were heard ahead. Instantly Robinson became all whispers. He ordered everyone to halt and not to make a sound. He signalled Wooreddy to come forward and then for him, along with Trugernanna, to take off his clothing and go ahead with him in an attempt to contact the strangers. To effect a cordial meeting he took with him a small packet of trinkets. They rushed off and reached the clearing where Wooreddy had just been.

In the full light of day, he saw that there were two huts pressed against the side of the huge fallen trunk. They went and looked inside. He pointed out some line drawings of kangaroo and some symbols to Ballawine without telling him that a sign had been left behind telling him to continue along the track, but slowly. He showed Robinson the construction of the hut and how the front had been walled in, then pointed at a heap of wood shavings which he said showed that the Aborigines had been sharpening their spears in readiness to attack the pursuing party. He did not reveal to Robinson the place where the Aborigines had stored their muskets. Trugernanna said that five men had gone off along the track and with them was one woman and she showed Robinson the smaller footprints. Before Wooreddy could signal to her, she added that the party possibly was that of Walyer and that they should look around the clearing to see if they had hidden anything. The good doctor was horrified at his wife's suggestion. He must have a talk to her in the near future about how much they were to tell the ghost.

Fortunately, Trugernanna caught Wooreddy's look, and with the smoothness of a possum glided from the clearing. Robinson and Wooreddy followed her. They rushed on for two kilometres, then the forest began to thin. Ahead was open country, and they saw the backs of two men just ascending a rise. Four more figures came into view and went over the rise and out of sight.

Robinson increased his pace to a trot. He breasted the rise and stopped. Nearby he could hear the sound of Aboriginal voices. His smile died as he realised that the voices came from behind him, that the Aborigines had circled around and were between him and the party of convicts. Worse, the convicts were armed and if they came up and fired on the Aborigines all would be lost.

'They behind us,' Wooreddy said to the alarmed Ballawine.

'Those villains will come up and open fire on them,' moaned the ghost. 'I know they will. All my work will be ruined. I must formulate some plan. Let's go back. Hurry.'

They retraced their steps and arrived back at the camp site to find it occupied. A fire was blazing and Aborigines were roasting a kangaroo. Walyer and Wooreddy exchanged glances and Trugernanna suddenly smiled knowingly. But Ummarrah had left the party to go his own way. The ghost beamed and began to distribute trinkets. He was overjoyed, for they were not that far from Launceston and he had heard that the Governor would soon be there. If only he could get these six there. They would be proof that his way could work. And was not the woman, the savage Walyer! She would be a feather in his cap.'

V

Strangely, Walyer and her men elected to stay with Robinson. Together they made their way through the rolling hills towards the Tamar Estuary and Launceston. The woman confided to Wooreddy the reason why she stayed. She was tired of running and hiding, of inconsequential encounters with an enemy which vastly outnumbered them, and being in a fight with no chance of winning. She wanted rest and an easing of the pain of isolation and loneliness that affected her like a disease. Then, although she tried to hide it, Walyer was a sick woman. Though she looked and acted strong, the coughing demon had attacked her. She hid a racking cough as best she could. Walyer took Wooreddy as a lover. She found a comfort in his diffidence which demanded nothing permanent from a relationship. She found a certain peace and a slight happiness in him. Like newly-weds they ran off to be by themselves in some romantic sun-drenched place. There they lay in each others' arms and shared their sadnesses. The party was short of supplies as usual and had to rely on the hunting of the Aborigines. Robinson accepted as fact that the couple were out after game. He was not unduly worried as he had told Wooreddy to keep with her and see that she did not run off.

Wooreddy enjoyed Walyer's firm body as much as she enjoyed his. Somehow, both found a tenderness which they had thought lost. He even hunted for her and both shared a single campfire when with the expedition. Robinson accepted the arrangements even to the extent of explaining to Trugernanna that it was important to get the woman to Launceston. He went out of his way to be nice to her and even discussed the future he was planning for her and her people. They were to be taken to a place where they could be happy and at ease. This was what Wooreddy had told them, then he added that there they would learn to be civilised, and she did not know what he meant. She asked Wooreddy about it and neither did he. He asked 'Fader' and received a complicated explanation which he did not understand. Both remained in the dark as they came closer to the estuary and Robinson fussed around them. He did not want to lose a single one when so close to the Governor.

None too soon for The Great Conciliator, they reached the shores of the estuary where he arranged for a boat to take them across to George Town. Safely there, the gleeful Robinson set up camp outside the town. Early next morning he bustled his charges into the boat for the final stretch to Launceston. He took with him a garrulous fellow called 'Punch', not out of kindness, but because he could hear from him all the gossip of the district. What he heard he could shape into a report and forward to the Governor who wanted to know everything that was going on throughout the colony, including rumours and speculation. 'Punch' was an old hand in the district and knew everything that had happened from the very first landing in 1804. As they sailed along close to the eastern shore, he pointed out places that had been cleansed of the 'crows'.

'See that lagoon, that long piece of water just over there, well there it was that a mob of horsemen came galloping along the far shore looking for a bunch of cattle that had gone astray. It was one of the first mobs to graze on that shore, and there weren't too many in those days. They saw this lot of crows on that there neck of land and with a whoop and a hollow took off after them. The crows saw them *nums* (that's what they call us) coming and took off away from the estuary. They splashed through the near end of that lagoon and found themselves up against that bit of a cliff with the white face, that one with the dead tree on top of it. Well, they got them up against that and they could go no further. That was the end of that lot. Good for us too, mate, that's what I say. The less of them blighters around the better for the sheep and cattle.'

'Poor, poor, defenceless creatures,' Robinson sighed in disapproval.

'Then see that swampy place at the foot of that hillock,' began the imperturbable 'Punch'. 'They drove another half dozen into the quicksand there. What I don't know about this part of the country isn't worth knowing. There was quite a few crows here when they put us down, now they're as scarce as kangaroos. They took to spearing the cattle and sheep, and had to be given a lesson. They needed one too! Then all the land was taken up and we couldn't have them trespassing on the farms. After that I suppose there just wasn't any place left for him and they had to go.'

'Punch' droned out the words through the bent pipe of his nose. Wooreddy listened to the pitch in fascination. Then the weedy honky-nosed ghost became aware of his intense interest and nervously began darting glances here, there and everywhere except at the good doctor. At last, unable to bear the unwinking gaze any longer, he shot a glance towards the Aborigine and changed his drone to a honk: 'Jacky, you been sitting there all quiet. No more spearing cattle, eh! You no do those bad things, no bloody more, right!'

Wooreddy switched his eyes to the water flowing past the hull and slowly answered: 'They came like thieves when least expected. They took our land; they took our women, and they take our lives.'

Robinson broke into the conversation because he did not like Aborigines and settlers conversing together. He alone knew what was good for them and he alone could feel the

122

pain of the sufferings they had endured at the hands of persons like the one in the boat. 'Sir,' he said to the ruffian. 'They have had their loved ones torn from their very arms. They have seen their children clubbed to death in front of their very eyes. Is it any wonder that they seek revenge? Even the Blessed Book declares: "Eye for eye, tooth for tooth", and these folk are but following that injunction.'

'That may be,' rejoined "Punch," 'but you'll find blessed few people agreeing with you in these parts. They settled the trouble in this district long ago and they're going to settle it in the same ways elsewheres. Why, the whole area is in an uproar with the military operation getting underway. That'll be the final solution, that will. It's what we did here and it worked. Your crows are the first I've seen this year.'

Robinson seized on his words to find out about the military operations and how they were regarded by the local settlers. The Governor would welcome this information. He asked 'Punch' if he was going to go, and received the reply: 'It's me rheumatism, it plays up something awful in the cold. I can't go, but I can tell you that it'll be a right old show and'll scare the crows right away from the settled districts.'

'It may or may not,' The Great Conciliator stated firmly, suddenly aware that the black problem might be solved by other means, and means which excluded him! 'It will not succeed, sir,' he stated again, more to reassure himself than to cast doubt on the operation.

With a stiff breeze blowing straight up the estuary the whaleboat made good time. A schooner tacked across their bows a good kilometre away, then came back to pass across their stern. They flapped to a halt as the vessel's sails took the wind, but only for a moment and they were away again. The weather had been fine for a week now. The sky was blue and the breeze nippy and playful. The Great Conciliator felt glad to be alive, and after telling himself over and over again that the military operation was bound to fail, put it out of his mind. He watched the shores flowing past and noticed how the land had been divided up into lots some of which were beginning to show the neatness of long-settled farms.

Trugernanna, Wooreddy, Walyer and the others watched the big smoke of Launceston smudging the southern edge of the sky. It told them that dozens and dozens of *num* lived there. The boat sailed closer and closer. They could make out the square ghost houses arranged in rows, many rows, and some of the buildings were two-storeyed. Walyer's men began murmuring at being led into the camp of the enemy, but she quietened them. Finally the boat swung to the quay and they climbed out onto the wooden platform and walked on dry land. The Aborigines were overawed by the size of the town and allowed Robinson to lead them along the main street. He had hoped for some sort of welcome, but the town was almost deserted. Most of the able-bodied males had gone off to man the cordon which was to advance and drive the Aborigines east onto Tasman's peninsula where they could be run to earth. The few people on the street shook their fists at the Aborigines in Robinson's little band and wished them dead.

They marched past the double-storeyed Cornwall Hotel, bare of the drinkers who had flocked after a keg of rum to their allotted places in the cordon, and onto a square paddock holding a number of buildings of government design. A low cottage was both the office and home of the Commandant of Launceston. He had managed to avoid field service in a military manoeuvre he regarded as asinine. Major Abbott looked from his office window and saw the gallant Robinson and his band of convicts and savages marching towards him. He stared at the travel-stained Robinson and saw trouble, then he counted the Aborigines and computed the amount the government would have to pay out. It was £5 for every adult and £2 for the rare child. This person, whoever he might be, had nine of them and that meant £45. But where was he to put them? There was only the gaol, though really that was no place for them.

The Great Conciliator marched into the Major's office and stood waiting to be welcomed, while the Major looked up from his desk and waited for the person to state his business. He would tell him to deliver the Aborigines to the gaol compound. After an overdrawn silence, he at last asked the fellow: 'Sir, what service may I perform for you?'

The Great Conciliator ignored the sarcasm and replied: 'Major Abbott, the Commandant of the Launceston Station,

I presume, Major, I have just completed a hazardous circum-navigation of the island and have safely passed through the wilderness. I am on a mission of conciliation for the Lieutenant-Governor and I have come to receive my orders. Have they arrived here yet?'

'No,' the Major said flatly, then spoke on: 'There are no orders for you here and it appears that your mission is at an end.' He looked dourly at the fellow standing before him. It was strange that no mention of him had been in the dispatches he had lately received from the Governor. The Governor was a stickler for detail and omitted nothing without a purpose. Was this one of his tricks to see if he would act out of line or not? He knew Arthur had never liked him and would like to hand his job over to one of his cronies. The best way to deal with the situation was to do nothing, as the Governor would be in Launceston soon. Having made up his mind, he stared at the fellow and said: 'Sir, there are no orders here for you. Take your blacks to the prison compound. You are entitled to bounty money, totalling £45.'

Robinson's face purpled. He refused to be dismissed like one of the major's assigned servants. He would protest to the Governor about this, this upstart! 'Major,' he spluttered, 'I, major, I am amazed, positively amazed at your attitude. I protest, protest strongly this treatment. I, as you should know, have been on a mission of conciliation expressly ordered by His Excellency, the Governor of this Colony, sir! I have been on a mission of mercy and have not even heard of this, this so-called bounty — but if the government set it, it must be proper. If I had known before, I might have brought in much more, many more — but I refused to do so,' he hastily added as he saw the drift of his words. 'I do not do it for money, my reward is not here . . .' And so on and so forth while he watched the major counting out the sovereigns of glittering gold. He stopped his spiel when the counting stopped. The major handed them to him and ordered him to take the Aborigines to the gaol compound. This brought another outburst until he remembered the large Cornwall Hotel they had marched past. He could do with a warm bed and convivial company after all these long weeks on the road. A night in the gaol would not hurt his charges and would keep them from wandering off. And so he marched his 'sable friends' off to prison.

When he arrived there next morning, he found that the savage amazon, Walyer, the pride of his collection, had collapsed. He thought the others took it well as he strode off to see the major. He had found out in the bar last night that the Governor was due in the neighbourhood. In reality, all the Aborigines were in mourning for Walyer who was on the verge of death. Wooreddy was listless with despair; Trugernanna had cried herself tearless, and Walyer's men, suddenly finding themselves leaderless and locked up, were completely demoralised. On top of this they felt betrayed and abandoned by the ghost who had told them over and over again that he would protect them like a father.

But they had not been abandoned. They had worth to Robinson. He learnt that the Major was with the Governor in the barracks at Royal Park and hurried there to meet him. He handed over his dispatches and complimented the Governor on the successful beginning of his military operation. Arthur handed the reports to his secretary and on hearing that Robinson had captured some Aborigines, including the famous *amazon*, Walyer, decided to go immediately to the gaol to see them. He completely ignored the hapless Major, who, he thought, should be in the field leading his troops, and ordered horses. He flung his body onto one of the animals, told Robinson to get on the other, then galloped off. The Major derived some consolation from seeing Robinson bouncing on his mount like a sack of potatoes.

At the prison gates, he left his horse and briskly walked through. At last Robinson had found a rival in pace. He brushed aside all comment from the superintendent and proceeded towards the cells. The superintendent ran after him and said that the Aborigines had been put in an exercise yard. He marched there and his blue eyes pierced out from beneath his frowning brows at each in turn. Then he pushed words out through his tightly pursed lips: 'Do any of you speak English?'

'Yes, Governor,' answered Wooreddy from his position at the head of the prostrate woman. He had been trying to get a little water to trickle down her swollen throat.

Arthur's eyes missed nothing. The woman was very sick. He would see to it as soon as he spoke to these people: 'On this occasion,' he began, 'of my first meeting you, I extend the hand of friendship. You are guests here and not prisoners. You are free to go whenever you wish.' He ignored the locked door. The Governor was a bad speaker and might have rambled on for some time, if Wooreddy had not broken in: 'Our friend is very sick.' Walyer had just fainted away in his arms.

Instantly the Governor became all Christian concern. 'Get a doctor,' he rapped at his secretary, who had just entered after galloping to catch up with him. Then he looked at Wooreddy, who seemed intelligent, and asked him if Robinson could contact all the Aborigines so that the government might know how many they had to help.

Wooreddy, sick with worry, said 'yes' and the Governor nodded. He had judged Robinson the man for the job. Immediately, he decided to take him to a private place for an interview. He stated his desire and the superintendent offered his office. He marched his stiff, black-clad body there. Robinson marched beside him. Arthur, though burdened down with the details of his military operation, which he had invented for the edification of the Colonial Office in faraway London, and for the advancement of his career, was pleased at the way things were going. Panic had spread like a bush fire and attacks by the natives had been reported from many places, some of which, he had ascertained, had been the work of whites in blackface—but all these in turn justified the operation. In his mind's eye he saw the dispositions of the troops (real troops, not the ill-disciplined rabble he had had to use), and saw them advance in perfect formation to drive the hordes of naked savages before them to be penned up on Tasman's peninsula—but such a perfection, he was perfectly aware, existed only in his imagination and, to a certain extent, in the dispatches he sent to London. In reality, the line would fail, so now he would prepare his second offensive, even though his heart lay in the field.

Robinson stood, somewhat impatiently, and waited for the Governor to at least look at him. Finally Arthur returned his mind to the room and told him to sit. Robinson did so and immediately began to speak: 'Your Excellency, I have come to give you a verbal report on the condition of the Aborigines of Van Diemen's Land. I have managed, at great peril to myself, to contact those Aborigines living along the West Coast. I detail their population in my written report. I am happy to inform you that there were no whites living with them. No Aborigine even mentioned that there had been any with them in the past. Those persons, termed sealers, have had some intercourse with the natives, but this had now ceased. The reason you will find in my fourth report. Your Excellency, since I arrived in this settled area, I have been busy canvassing public opinion, the settlers' attitude to government and the military operation under way—'

Then he detailed all that he had been able to find out last night before swinging back to the basic problem of the blacks. He emphasised that it could be solved by his method of conciliation. He told of the massacres that he had heard about, and the hard features of the Governor struggled to take on an expression of sorrow. His Excellency was a Christian and hated the sufferings so casually inflicted by his fellow Christians. Robinson, seeing that the Governor had so reacted, spoke about the poor Aborigines locked up in gaol, and all because he had not the authority to prevent it! 'Your Excellency, I have no letters of authority to requisition help, when I need it, from such persons as the Commandant of Launceston who, I thought, would have been taking a much larger part in the operations seeing that he holds a military title—and I have no authority to compel persons to obey the law in regard to the Aborigines. How can I prevent them from being mistreated, when I have not the means for doing so?'

Arthur liked Robinson's words mainly because he disliked the Major and the ex-bricklayer posed no threat to him. He readily promised to send him letters of authority and to make him a justice of the peace. Thus, His Excellency bought a henchman cheaply.

Robinson thanked the Governor profusely. Thanked him so much in fact that Arthur began to suspect him of duplicity. His sea-blue eyes pierced out searching for signs of it in the face before him. He found only self-seeking, and relaxing, said: 'Mr Robinson, this problem must be solved. I am beginning my second term as Governor of this colony and would not like to have it drag out to the end of my tenure. I am relying on you!'

'Your Excellency, I will do it! My methods have now been field-tested. We shall save these poor savages and place them in a refuge where they can no longer harm others, or be harmed by others. With your permission and under your orders, I shall start immediately for the north-east corner of the island and then explore the off-shore islands to see if one will be suitable to hold them. Naturally I will contact and conciliate any Aborigines living in that area and collect them together at a suitable place . . .'

'Go, sir, go, and may God go with you. I have the utmost faith in you. I have read that Great Island is large enough to let them live a life in some degree similar to the one which they now live.'

'Your Excellency, they must be civilised; they must be Christianised,' Robinson exclaimed aghast.

'I was about to make that observation, sir,' Arthur said in obvious annoyance. He wanted the interview to be at an end, but Robinson continued to speak.

'It is our Christian duty, Your Excellency, and I am ready to begin collecting the natives for transportation to a suitable place of instruction and training. There are some with me already . . .'

The Governor frowned at a slight problem. He pursed his lips and thought awhile before replying: 'As much as I would like to begin immediately to remove the natives from the main island, I find that impossible. I must await the outcome of the military operation. The cordon has already begun moving towards Tasman's peninsula. In a week or so, it will have reached the neck and sealed it as a cork in the neck of a bottle. Then I must send mounted parties onto the peninsula to see what we have caught. This will take another few days. I think that in two weeks everything shall be ready. By that time you should have surveyed the island and also collected together a sizeable group of Aborigines. And then my operation may well turn out to be a success,' he said with feeling.

'It may, Your Excellency, and I pray for its success for it will lessen my own work. There is one more thing, about the bounty money, do I receive it?'

'You do and if you are successful, as I know you will be, you will be further rewarded.'

The interview was at an end, but the Governor had got over his irritation and ordered Robinson to stay for tea. While he sipped it, Arthur unrolled a huge map and painstakingly pointed out the positions of the detachments of troops and the routes by which they would converge on the peninsula. Robinson agreed with everything he said. The Governor was in two minds about the operation: the colonel in him wanted success, the politician schemed to use either for future advancement. Robinson knew the territory and thought the manoeuvre had little chance of succeeding. The cordons would break up between the hills and valleys, leaving gaps through which the enemy could slip. But he told Arthur nothing of this, and they parted each pleased with the other.

The Great Conciliator having done some conciliating, went to rescue his blacks from the prison yard. He found Walyer dead, but this did not lessen his feeling of triumph. Now he was entering the field with definite orders and authority. Staring down at the dead woman, he promised himself that he would lead the last of the savages through the streets of Hobarton in a victory parade.

His mind filled with the spectacle as he looked down upon the simple children of nature grouped about their fallen comrade. He comforted them in their grief. 'Do not worry,' he softly said. 'We shall take up her body and carry it and lay her down in some simple grave in a peaceful rustic grove. Perhaps I shall even inscribe some verse on the trunk of a tree as a suitable epitaph.'

> They came, remnant of a bygone race,
> Surviving Mourners of a Nation's dead;
> Proscribed inheritors of rights which trace
> Their claims coeval with the world!
> They tread upon their nation's tomb!
>
> They came like straggling leaves together blown,
> The last memorial of the foliage past;
> The living bough upon the tree o'erthrown,
> When branch and trunk lie dead.

5

They Put Them in Captivity

I

Penderloin swung a slow blow at Toomana's chin. He gracefully sidestepped and flicked out a fist to blood his nose. A
heavy right followed and Penderloin was down for the count.
A dirty, drunken soldier wandered past with a secret leer in
his mind. Wooreddy looked away from the filth and across a
bare paddock to the distant inland hills. Perhaps he would
go there? He took a few steps in one direction, stopped, took
a few more, then stopped in confusion. He was in exactly the
same spot. He had nothing to do, or even to think for that
matter. Perhaps he would go hunting, perhaps not. The
women were boiling up some potatoes and turnips and these
mixed with some salt junk would be enough to fill his
stomach.

Wooreddy continued to stand, sagging, in the middle of
the establishment. To one side of him some of the convicts
were slowly piling up the logs they had managed with great
difficulty to drag down from the hills. They resented having
to work and resented the Aborigines for not working. 'Bloody
crows,' they sneered, as they exchanged their tobacco ration
for a half hour's pleasure or not. Wooreddy's dull eyes
drifted as uncaringly over the convicts as they regarded his
near presence. Just down from him, they briefly settled on
the cleared site of the chapel, which was supposed to be
built to teach them some of the white fellow's religion. His
mind swung back to the old days, not so long ago, but now
seemingly an eternity in the past, when they had regarded
those with white skins as ghosts. Now they were only men,
evil men perhaps, but humans for all that. His eyes jumped

to the military barracks on the other side of the track and the gaol in which they put you when they wanted too. His eyes avoided the distant cemetery, that ever-growing patch of sheltered ground, and went to the row of wattle and daub huts, low and ungainly in their squat squareness, and dirty with the smells of too long occupancy. How he wished to be away from this place! But did it matter if he was away from this place? Where could he go? This was their promised land! He sighed, and eyed the commandant's house. The brig was due and the commandant was busy packing up to leave on her. At last his mind had wandered to a decision. He would go to the beach and see if the ship had come.

The good doctor put his hand under the dirty shirt he wore and scratched an armpit, then he scratched under his pants. He had never got used to wearing clothes. He decided to wander off the direct track so that he could take off the foul-smelling skins and be free of stink. For everything smelt of too long an occupancy, of being in one place for too long a time! The whole settlement should be moved again. It had been shifted from Swan Island to Gun Carriage Island, to a point on Great Island (now renamed Flinders), and from there to the coast and then from the coast inland to the present position. Now it should be moved again, but the ghosts, he corrected himself, the white men seemed to be settling down for a long time. Perhaps it was time to try and sing them into shifting to another place, but would the old spells work seeing that everything else was decaying and fading so rapidly?

Wooreddy shuddered as he pulled off the alien clothing. At least he still had his long locks, but there was no more ballawine (red ochre) to smear over them. He smiled as he repeated the word, ballawine, for he remembered the good old days of travelling over the island. Now he was locked up and nothing ever happened. To rid himself of the despair and of the evil stink still clinging to him, he began gathering some green branches. When he had collected a pile, he scooped a hole in the ground and kindled a fire in it. He piled the branches over the hole. They were not from the correct species, but would have to do. The smoke began billowing up and he lay across the boughs, staying there

132

until the flamelets flickered through the green leaves to burn his skin. His mood lightened, he sprang to his feet and continued on his way to the bay.

The brig *Tamar* sailed at a fast clip over the sullen green waters of Bass Strait. Dark clouds scudded over the ship. It looked as if a storm were blowing up, but they would be at anchor before then, safe and secure between Green Island and the longer coast of Flinders. Robinson had explored the Furneaux group of islands over a year ago, but with his excellent memory he could picture the site of the Aboriginal settlement. After catching the last of the Aborigines, he had enjoyed a long rest at home supervising his brickmaking business, before accepting the post of 'Commandant' (he savoured the title and repeated under his breath, 'Commandant Robinson') of Flinders Island Aboriginal Establishment from Governor Arthur who had promised that it would lead to bigger and better things. 'You see,' he had said in a voice devoid of its usual sharpness, 'some Quaker missionaries visited the island and were unimpressed with it. It seems that it is in a bad way, and God knows you are the man to set it to rights. And once you have got the establishment organised and functioning as it should, I shall see to it that you are offered a much more congenial post, one suited to your talents.'

Robinson had accepted Arthur's offer with alacrity, for to tell the truth he was bored at home and missed his old roaming life. He told his wife that God had again thrust work upon him and he must be off. This was the truth, for he did feel responsible for the people he had sent off to Flinders Island and felt that he must see to their comfort.

As soon as the ship dropped anchor, the commandant began to give orders, much to the disgust of the officers and crew. The captain told him stiffly: 'Sir, I must inform you yet again that you have no authority on this ship. It would be better for you to go ashore and exert it on your convict servants. I wish to be out of here as soon as the storm abates.'

In the sheltered anchorage the storm was hardly felt and Robinson was put into a boat at once. Wooreddy stared at the dark-clad figure standing in the bow of the approaching boat and leaning eagerly forward to peer at the shore. It awakened a memory, and he pointed it out to Trugernanna who stood near him with the rest of the Aborigines who had come to meet the ship. It was the only exciting thing that happened on the island. Trugernanna stared at the portly figure, and suddenly screamed in delight: 'Fader!'

Wooreddy began laughing in joy. Their old ghost leader had come back to look after them, to save them and lead them to the promised land. He shouted out the old name of 'Meeter Ro-bin-un' and frantically waved. The rest of the hundred-odd survivors of the original exiles also recognised the person who had promised them paradise. Now he had returned to them. They rushed forward and dragged the boat up onto the land. The longed-for hero stepped down, then immediately began ordering the soldiers in charge of the convicts to see to it that the scoundrels safely unloaded the supplies he had brought with him. Then he realised that they did not know who he was. 'Commandant George Augustus Robinson,' he stated pompously, 'especially appointed by Lieutenant-Governor George Arthur to relieve the present commandant. Where is he? He should have been here with the rest of the establishment. Haven't you been informed?'

He was told that the old commandant (or rather the acting commandant) was packing his things, so he had to go and present his credentials to Mr Nicholls at the commandant's cottage. This took only a few minutes, then he came out to meet again his charges. Tears of happiness trickled down the cheeks of the Aborigines as they clutched at his hand. He beckoned to Wooreddy and Trugernanna to accompany him on his first inspection. It was just like the old days.

They steered him in the direction of the lonely cemetery with its multitude of graves. European flowers flowed over the mounds in purple profusion and the spaces between them had been kept free of weeds. Robinson smiled, finding the scene idyllic. He was still smiling when the rest of the Aborigines appeared walking behind the shrouded corpse of one of their comrades. At their head strode Mr Clark, the Catechist, with bible in hand. Robinson thrilled. His departed sable friend was enjoying a Christian burial. At least that side had not been neglected, though he would have to take

134

a hand in the religious instruction himself. The Catechist, Mr Clark could handle such things as birth and death.

Cheerily he left the cemetery and approached the site of the projected chapel. When informed of this by Mr Clark, who had rushed through the burial service to come after the new commandant, Robinson said: 'It shall be finished within the month. There are convicts enough for the job.' Then he walked off to the low row of squalid huts in which the Aborigines lived. They had left them dirty in the hope that the white people would move the settlement to a new site. Robinson was shocked and put it down to the mismanagement of his predecessor. 'All this will be changed. It is still early afternoon, by evening these huts will be clean!' The rest of the Aborigines had been following along behind; he turned back to them and, using his excellent memory, singled out women by name. 'Larrentong, Tonack, Lanney, Dinah and the rest of you women will clean out the huts.' They stared at him with big eyes, and in explanation he seized a leafy branch and began sweeping the floor of a hut with it. They got the idea and laughingly began cleaning out all the huts. The new commandant watched awhile, then went on to his cottage which he got Wooreddy and Trugernanna to clean. They were to be his servants and his assigned convicts could teach them their duties. Then he hurried off to check on the stores being unloaded and after that to organise a banquet for the evening. The storm had long since blown over and as it was December, the sun was drinking up the moisture and steaming the air with fever.

After that he met the entire military detachment which consisted of a corporal in charge of five privates. The corporal introduced himself by saying that the military were not under the control of a civilian, then thanked him for the invitation to attend the entertainments planned for the evening. In such a God-forsaken place anything was welcome except fever. Next the new commandant met the civilians stationed at Wybalenna, as the establishment was called. These consisted of the storekeeper, who, Robinson had already discovered, was very lax in keeping his records up to date; the Catechist, a congenial person with a flowing black beard and a meekness of manner that made him agreeable to

135

everyone except the Aborigines; a coxswain, an ex-convict and thus completely unimportant, and lastly, a medical man who had been recommended by the Governor as being a good doctor though inclined to suffer obscure ailments requiring massive dosages of laudanum. Three of their wives were there and they greeted the new commandant with requests about the health of Mrs Robinson. He announced that she was well and would soon be joining him, then he told all of them that tonight they were to symbolise their mission of service by waiting on their charges at table. He sent the ladies off to his own kitchen to prepare the food, while some of the convicts began setting up rude tables. The Aborigines would sit at them like good Englishmen. He sent the storeman off to round up the blacks.

The new commandant had inspected the store, to find it empty, but Arthur had supplied him with supplies of all kinds, and he had occupied himself with cataloguing them during the voyage. Now he opened the bale containing clothing he had personally chosen. He handed out heavy pants, short jackets and flannel shirts without collars. The Aboriginal men were allowed to select their own boots from a row of identical ones which were guarded by a convict who had already purloined a pair. The women were under the charge of the Catechist's wife who had been called from the kitchen to minister to them. They received from her heavy shoes and thick stockings, rough smock-like dresses and, wonder of wonders, linen knickers donated by His Excellency's wife herself. Before donning the new clothing they washed at a communal trough set apart from that of the men. Then, dressed in their new finery, they hobbled and dragged themselves to where the men were getting their hair cut. Poor Wooreddy had lost his pride and glory, and much of his last vestiges of pride had vanished with his locks.

They watched while the new commandant opened a package. He ordered them to file past and he pulled a red cap over each shorn pate. Now a changed lot of savages, they were marched to where the feast was to be served to them. Robinson exhibited his charges. They sat stiff and unmoving at the rude tables on the rude benches while inside they quaked. Then the white people came bearing gifts. Chunks

136

of boiled mutton were put before them, but they had to wait. Commandant G. A. Robinson came to the head of the table to exhort them.

'Only this day,' he began, and the sun began streaking long rays of golden light which strangely reddened the land. The golden disc began sinking away from the dark sky, as his voice continued on: 'Only this day,' he repeated as the sun disappeared below the horizon, 'I have arrived and I have come here to set things right for you. Your good friend, the Governor is concerned about you. I, your new commandant, am concerned about you, as I always have been concerned about you, as each of you know! I promised you a home where you could live safely and this is your home.' He swept his hand around at the darkness and the Aborigines stifled a collective moan. 'It shall become a paradise through hard work,' he declared in ringing tones. 'Under my direction you shall rise up to learn new skills and decent ways of life. I and my staff are here only to serve you, and we are showing this now. Just remember and follow their example and you will become better and more like them each day . . .'

He went on and on while Wooreddy watched the steam from his chunk of mutton diminish in the cold air. Finally grace was recited and he chewed on meat that had become like a piece of stiff skin. He enjoyed the following course of rice and plum duff. Robinson had planned a further surprise for them after the meal, but owing to the darkness, it would have to wait for morning. He had heard that a predecessor had taught them the rudiments of the game of cricket and that they had seemed to have liked it. He determined that he would divide the Aborigines into two teams and thus they could learn the art of co-operation in friendly competition. Unknown to the new commandant, the Aborigines had already divided into groups. The Ben Lomond and Big River people were at loggerheads, blaming each other for having given in so easily. The people from the west coast tried to hold onto the traditional ways and often mediated between the two other groups. They were the umpires. The other Aborigines joined whichever faction they preferred, or drifted from one to another. Thus, the following morning, Robinson was agreeably surprised to find that the Aborigines

137

easily separated into two teams. The west coast people held aloof, remembering that the ghost had always stirred things up and often blundered into trouble easily avoided with a little foresight.

The pitch was laid out and the wickets pushed in at each end. Commandant Robinson volunteered to be the umpire. He organised the field, putting men in the positions he could remember, then selected a man to bowl the first over. The man ran up to the wicket and flung the ball at the head of the batsman who dodged nimbly. The Aborigines had adapted their form of personal combat to the game. The batter fended off the ball with his bat, but had to be reminded to run by Robinson. On the last ball of the over, the batter received a direct hit in the middle of the chest. In retaliation he picked up the ball and hurled it back at the bowler. The fielders picked up rocks and pelted the two batsmen. The rest of the batting team rushed in to help their men, spectators joined in, and it was on. A distraught Robinson stood aghast at such a display of savagery. It would take time to bring them to civilised ways, and sighing he picked up his heavy walking stick and physically separated the combatants. A good time had been had by all except the commandant.

The portly gentleman, who now never ever dropped his aitches, lined up the miscreants. He stood before them in his best Arthurian mode. He might have been the puritanical governor berating a group of idle convicts. He stood, stern and plump in dark clothing and began to berate the Aborigines in his querulous voice: 'Just now we witnessed a disgraceful sight. My sable friends, I am here to work for your benefit and it is not easy to stay in such a place. I stay here for you, and if I leave a bad man will come to take my place. You must obey me, you must listen to me, you must not fight any more.' Then he changed the subject as he decided to begin immediately the work of civilising. 'I order you not to fight any more, and I order you not to take off your clothing and dance away the night. Dancing is evil and worse than fighting, just as is taking off your clothing unless to wash yourselves. I have heard that night after night you have been wont to make an undignified din. I order you to stop this, but you will lose nothing for I will replace your savage wailings with singing of a grander nature. Now that we are agreeable to change, I will mark this great change by giving you noble names. I have been up for most of the night working in your interests. Now to signify your rebirth you will be Christened anew.'

He marched his short, plump body to the end of the line and stared into the face of Wooreddy. 'You were the first to follow me,' he murmured and then declared: 'I name you Count Alpha!'

'Count Alpha, good, Commandant Robinson, good,' fawned Wooreddy. In his numbness he did not care if he was renamed Mister Brown. Robinson crossed to the female line, and to Trugernanna who stood demure in her decent and warm clothing. 'You, the most beautiful princess of all your race, I name you Lalla Rookh! From now on you are Lalla Rookh!' And he went to each person in turn and renamed them. They had to repeat their names until he was satisfied that they had the proper accent. No one objected, except for one soldier onlooker who had just finished drinking his weekly ration of rum: 'Christ, what 'e think of next! Poor bloody buggers.' The commandant glared at him and commanded him to go. He went, taking away all protest.

After the naming Robinson took out the list of chores he had worked out through the night. The men went to the large paddock to plant turnips under the direction of a convict, while he took the women back to their still clean huts where he handed out needlework for them to do. Then he went to the Catechist's house to get his wife to supervise them. He got to talking with the bucolic Mr Clark and decided that he would test the Christian knowledge of his charges. Mr Clark was amenable to his suggestion. He too wanted to live as peaceful a life as possible.

The commandant went to the chapel site and saw with satisfaction that a gang of convicts was already labouring there. It was a warm day and he went to bring the females to sit under a tree while they awaited the arrival of the Catechist. He stared across at the paddock where the men were supposed to be working. Only a few backs were bent in labour. He sighed: time would solve these problems and bring them around to more civilised modes of behaviour.

Mr Clark rushed up from burying another Aborigine, but only a child, to ask if he was ready to start: 'Commandant, I have not neglected my spiritual labours. And you shall see just how far I have progressed,' he added somewhat sardonically.

'We shall see, Chaplain, we shall see,' Robinson answered heartily in the tone so much loathed by those subordinate to him. 'Bring Mr Dickenson, the storekeeper, and the medical man, Dr Walsh. The state of their religious knowledge is vastly important, and His Excellency will be desirous of receiving a full and complete account on the subject. I trust, Chaplain, that it will be up to our expectation.'

Fortunately for Mr Clark, the Aborigines had discovered that a sealer's boat, which had put in down at Adelaide Bay, wanted to employ some of them for mutton-birding. Wooreddy and Trugernanna were among those that went along with the less diligent and more rebellious pupils of the Catechist. Thus, Mr Clark was able to muster his best and most docile students. The commandant was pleased to find that they still remembered their new names and, what was more, could spell them. He selected Isaac, Neptune, Washington, Albert and Leonidas to be examined. The others must wait for another day.

The examining committee stared at the Aborigines. They sat quietly hiding their nervousness under an unnatural rigidity of body and expression. Robinson, to put them at ease, said: 'This gathering is only to test the extent of your knowledge in the Christian religion. Do you understand?'

Leonidas chose to answer, 'Yes, commandant' and for his pain was selected to be the first examinee. The Catechist came forward with a smile. He knew his Aborigine! 'Recite the Lord's prayer for me, Jemmy, I mean Leonidas!'

Leonidas did so without a mistake. Robinson beamed with approval while Clark sighed in relief before picking Washington to answer some theological questions. He explained to Robinson how he had had difficulty in making understood to his pupils advanced concepts and that the knowledge he had managed to impart was fairly rudimentary.

He began: 'What is the devil?'

'The father of lies.'

140

'Do you like the devil?'

'No.'

'Do you like God?'

'Yes.' And so on . . .

Finally the impatient Robinson, having enough for his report and enough of the banality, dismissed the men. The Catechist's wife came forward with those women she had managed to locate.

While this was going on, the other Aborigines were getting into the sealers' boat. Wooreddy felt his misery lighten a fraction at the prospect of getting away from the establishment and its atmosphere of ennui which dragged them down into inertia and gloom. If things went well and they collected a lot of mutton birds, the sealers might take them over to Cape Barren Island and later bring them back. Wooreddy pondered at length, but did not consider that the commandant, having finished his examination, was aghast to find that so many Aborigines had left the settlement. He received the excuse of hunting and accepted it for the last time. He intended to tighten up discipline and stop them from roaming here and there.

Trugernanna stared at the face of one of the sealers and recognised the rat-like mask of Paddy. It had been long ago and many things had happened to her, but those weasel-like movements and that raspish voice still moved her with hatred. The sealers sailed off with a dozen Aborigines in the boat and put ashore at Gun Carriage Island, where an old man, George Robbins, had a cottage and garden.

Trugernanna felt an unaccustomed glow of happiness— her sister, Lowernunhe, lived with the ghost and had had a son by him. George Robbins received them with plates of hot mutton stew—he also ran a few sheep on the island—and an invitation to camp near his house. He said that there was a huge rookery occupying the western end of the island and it was easy to reach. Because only feathers were taken from the birds, they needed a huge amount to make any money—only a few pence per pound were paid for feathers in Launceston. When the sealers heard that thousands and thousands of birds were roosting there, they nodded and went off to see for themselves. It was only a short walk from the cottage and as they passed through his field, they remarked that the crop wasn't going too well.

'Barley, that's what I'm planting next year,' Robbins mused. 'Used to plant potatoes before and got a good crop. Someone swapped a bag of wheat for a bag of spuds. Decided to plant it to see if it came up right. It didn't,' he said scornfully, jerking a thumb at the miserable straw. Trugernanna walked hand-in-hand with her sister. She really felt glad to be with her and even to be on the island. The settlement was really getting her down, and suddenly she felt herself trembling violently. Her sister had to hug her back into some sense of balance.

'That Robinson may be better than the other one,' Lowernunhe said.

'But it doesn't matter, so many people are dying or dead. They just up and fall down. It scares me, and worse we have to stay there. You're lucky you live with that *num* and are free to do what you like.'

'Yeah, and he's too old to hinder me, too,' Lowernunhe replied with a grin. 'I wish you could come and live with us, but the government won't allow it. Worse, they even tried to get me away from my man and lock me up in that death place. They won't get me there, no!'

Trugernanna said that she wanted to get away, and her sister wrinkled her brow in thought: 'The only way you can get away is to get some bloke in a boat to come along. But you couldn't stay in the islands. The soldiers at your place are there to keep us in check. They come patrolling around here every now and again. But if I could find a bloke who was going across to Port Phillip, you could go there. There's not so many ghosts there and—'

'And none of us either,' Trugernanna broke in bitterly. How could she go off all by herself? She needed her people around her! 'No,' she said. 'I can't just go off and leave them. If they die, then I die; if they suffer, I suffer and that's that.'

The sealers were so overcome by the multitude of birds that they immediately set to work. Trugernanna emptied her mind and thrust her short stick down hole after hole. When it prodded a warm body, she reached down a hand, grabbed the bird by the neck and tugged it out. A quick twist ended its life. The bird corpses began piling up. When they reached beyond a few thousand, they were carried off to a sheltered place to be plucked. Old George did not want any dead carcases stinking up his island and they were hurled into a great cleft in the earth. The stench of rotting flesh rising up showed that it had been used for such a purpose before. The two sealers stayed on the island for a week and by then they had more than enough feathers for a trip to Launceston. They lingered another day, and were having dinner at Old George's place, when a whale boat came swinging into the cove. It beached and from it came a wrathful commandant to confront those who had lured his people from him.

'This won't do; this won't do at all,' he fumed at everyone. 'You know I have the power, sirs, of getting you thrown off these islands. The natives are not to be interfered with. They are not to be enticed away!'

It was the old Robinson, and the sealers were suitably unimpressed, especially as one of them was James Munro, a special constable who had some influence in a section of Hobarton society that had no love for the government or its policies.

He replied firmly to Robinson: 'Sir, I am a special constable, and these men have done no wrong. If you consider them guilty of wrong doing, lodge a complaint with me and I shall see into the matter.'

The cultivated accents of the special constable put Robinson off his stride, but he recovered in a moment. 'These natives have absconded from the government establishment on Flinders Island. I am the commandant of that station and a justice of the peace. It is my duty to look after my charges and I am doing just that.

Old George put in his penny's worth: 'Commandant, the man before you did not object to them doing a bit of mutton-birding. He thought it a good idea, gave them notions of industry and such like—'

'It may be, it may be, it may be what he did, but I am the person in charge now and the final judge in these matters. If they want the natives to work for them, they must make application to me. Apart from this, there is the matter of intemperance and indecorous behaviour. Just look there, that disgusting old man lives with that native female, and there stands the result of their union, that boy there, a mixture of both races. What will happen to such hybrids? They show us our own immorality. The Governor will hear of this and, moreover, of the special constable aiding and abetting these villians.'

'Oh, go to Hell,' Constable Munro said suddenly. 'That child is a happy little bugger, and his mother and father are happy too. No trouble between them at all. It's sorts like you that have harmed the race. We live on these islands in our own way, then you come along to hound, not only us, but these poor women who have taken refuge with us. If they are held against their will, let them say so. Here is one of them, ask her! Do you think that she will elect to go to that hell-hole you call a station to die there in a few days?'

Robinson looked at Lowernunhe and softened his expression and voice. 'Leave these evil men,' he murmured, 'leave them and come to my establishment where you will learn to be happy.'

'I will never go there. That place you call Wybalenna, Blackfellow's Home, is Meracklenna, The Home of Death, and I will not go there.'

'So hardened, so hardened and led astray by villians', began Robinson sorrowfully, as the two sealers began loading bales of feathers into their boat. He continued as they got aboard and began rowing out of the cove. George Augustus Robinson stopped speaking and stowed his sullen Aborigines into his boat. It had been both a victory and a defeat for him, and on the way back he sought ways in which the establishment might be made a good place. Firstly, he would work out a daily programme of work and instruction which would keep his charges too busy to run off; secondly he would set up a market to teach them the use of money; and thirdly, why, he would start a newspaper! What could it be called? Perhaps, *The Aboriginal and Flinders Island Chronicle*? That had a ring to it and would serve to promote Christianity, civilisation and culture, not only among the Aborigines but even among the sealers. Now, if he could only get the death-rate down. How could he do this? His programme of work

144

and learning together with cleanliness and Christian morality
would solve the problem!

II

FLINDERS ISLAND WEEKLY CHRONICLE
The brig Tamar *arrived this morning at Green Island. I cannot
tell perhaps we might hear it by and by. When the ship boat comes
to the settlement we will hear the news from Hobarton. Let us hope
it will be good news and that something may be done for us poor
people. We are dying away. The Bible says some or all shall be
saved, but I am afraid that none of us will be alive by and by. There
is nothing but sick men amongst us. Let the black fellows pray to the
King to get us away from this place.*

Wooreddy huddled on the hard bench halfway down the
side reserved for the men. He had managed to have a seat
right against the whitewashed wall and was safely away from
the supervising eyes of the Catechist prowling the central
aisle. He held the sheet of paper low in his trembling hands,
he was getting over an attack of the coughing demon, and
stared at the letters forming words and sentences that stood
at attention in line like the red-coated soldiers. He had
watched Macy, a young Aborigine, copy it out from a draft
supplied by Robinson and had heard him repeat each word
and sentence as he wrote them. Thus he had a good idea of
what the lines of writing meant, and could even puzzle out
many of the words. He stared down at the black marks and
his eyes went right through them to the twenty-nine people
that had recently died, leaving the sick behind to suffer and
to recover listlessly. Death was the central fact of their lives—
the steady placing of bodies into the cold ground in the
Christian way. No more smoke to waft a spirit warmly on its
way as in the olden days. He knew the new rituals just as he
knew the old, not from the lips of the old, but from attending
funeral after funeral after funeral—twenty-nine of them
stretching back to more deaths. Softly, he chanted the words
of the burial service as he imagined himself dead and being
put into a hole.

'Man that is born of woman hath but a short time to live, and is full of misery. He cometh up, and is cut down, like a flower; he fleeth as it were a shadow, and never continueth in one stay. . . . In the midst of life we are in death: of whom may we seek for succour, but of thee, O Lord, who for our sins art justly displeased.'

It had been many months since he had thought of Great Ancestor. Now he thought of him and wondered if they had displeased him in some way. He, alone, knew how they were suffering. He, alone, and everyone of his people, Wooreddy amended . . . and his mind lapsed into despair. The commandant's voice wavered through the chapel hopelessly. Even he had been attacked by the coughing demon and was recovering as listessly as the rest.

'We have lately suffered many trials and tribulations and barely can find the strength to carry on. Somehow we must. We must cast away our despair and find again that happiness and energetic drive that our Christian faith gives us. I still hold in my mind the vision of the nine-year-old son of Wymurrick, I mean Washington, who was recently taken from us, sitting at a table and endeavouring to teach Wooreddy, I mean Count Alpha, the letters of the Alphabet. What a beautiful sight: a little child teaching the mature man. It is these sights that give us the strength to not only continue but to work on, as best we can, so that we can show ourselves worthy of Him, Our Creator, and to show such signs of our progress towards civilisation that the Governor will release us from this terrible place. How far you have come since that time, a year ago, when I first came to minister to you. Then you were still wont to throw yourselves into the savage dance. Now, no more! Now, very seldom do you rush from the settlement to haunt the sylvan glades in which once you delighted to wander. Not only have we reaped our first crop of barley, but are about to plant a second. You that once did not reap, now sow. You are indeed changing for the better, but many of you slip and some even fall back into savagery.' He paused to gather his strength before continuing. 'Our sister, Emma, has caused contention in the settlement. If she does not want a life of connubial happiness, she should remain celibate. If she does not want to be celibate, she

146

should remain married to one man, as a good Christian woman should. The other women should keep their humble dwellings clean and tidy. Cling to the family hearth and don't go wandering off into the bush to do what is improper. This wicked wandering has been the cause of your suffering, which put an end to it. Learn from it. Some of you people wander about the settlement like stray dogs, even though you are weak from the disease. God does not like that, and you will not become better. He does not like you to do such things and bad people go to hell. They are the devil's children! So women mind your own home. Do not keep going and staying in others' houses. Keep your blankets clean. Get you husband to carry plenty of wood there so that the family fire will be blazing strongly to dry out the dampness in the walls. Keep your clothing dry and see to it that your husband does not go around in damp clothing. You women, model yourself on my wife or on the good wife of Mr Clark, our Catechist. Stay with God and—' He was attacked by a fit of coughing and Mr Clark brought the service to an end by croaking a hymn.

He had recovered by the time it ended and the people began filing from the chapel. Robinson's words, those that had been understood, had induced further despair. They were responsible for their own state. Listlessly they straggled towards their one room apartments. The commandant stood talking to the Catechist, gathering his strength for the weekly inspection and giving the Aborigines enough time to put the finishing touches to the neatness of their quarters. After ten minutes, he slowly went through the gap in the palisade surrounding the chapel and out into the open space across which the L-shaped terrace holding the apartments of the Aborigines waited for his inspection. But he was without his usual dash and stopped halfway across to rest. He looked to his right and along another palisade fence edging the road he had built. His eyes followed it down to where his own restful house awaited his tired body. His wife had got over her sickness and should now be supervising the convict cook in preparing the Sunday dinner. He put all idea out of his mind about going straight home, and went to the first apartment occupied by Count Alpha and his wife, Lalla Rookh.

The stone walls might be cold, but if they obeyed him and kept a fire burning the dampness was kept down. Still, they had to watch out lest the thatch of the roof might ignite. Lalla Rookh, in her heavy drab clothing and bright cherry cap, awaited him at the door. He passed into the single room and cast an eye around. On the shelf to the right of the fireplace stood two plates and mugs, and on the one to the left were a small bag of flour and a piece of pork wrapped in a rather grubby rag.

'Very ship-shape,' he commented, fighting the urge to go home and take to his bed. He stared unseeingly at the clean blankets in the sleeping place. 'Very good, Alpha,' he told Wooreddy, and suddenly broke into a fit of coughing. He had to sit down at their table and wait for it to be over. Trugernanna or Lalla Rookh tried to squeeze some sort of dubious pleasure from these weekly inspections, and when he had recovered, she insisted on his seeing the damp clothes hanging on a clothes line she had erected herself. But this was not all, she suddenly revealed her *pièce de résistance*! Under the lattice window in a small patch of ground she had planted some seeds and these were now pushing up little shoots. These gave Robinson a boost. They were learning to do things on their own. Soon Lalla Rookh would be growing her own vegetables. Activated by the progress, his mind began composing a paragraph of his next report to Hobart. He even felt strong enough to begin it after dinner. 'The females attend to the domestic duties, keeping their little family parlours clean and laundering their clothing. They cultivate one large garden in common which is very successful. I append the types of vegetables raised together with their measures. I am extremely happy to communicate that one of the females, aided by her husband, has on her very own initiative begun a little garden. Unfortunately the only drawback is the great mortality amongst them and they are still recovering from the ravages of a pneumonic malady. This was due, I am sure, to the general unhealthiness of the site, and were the people removed to a more salubrious place, they would form a contented and useful community.'

Extremely satisfied with Count Alpha's and Lalla Rookh's home, Robinson cast a perfunctory eye over the rest of the apartments and then took himself home. Wooreddy and Trugernanna had been taken into his household as under-servants, and were careful to do enough work to keep them-selves there. They were the eyes and ears of the Aboriginal community and what happened or was said in the Com-mandant's house was communicated in the nightly meetings which were held when the masters were asleep and out of the way.

Robinson settled down to an old copy of the *Government Gazette* detailing his exploit of single-handedly bringing in the savage inhabitants of Van Diemen's Land. He smiled as he remembered those days, then patted his paunch. So weak and so out of condition! But what could you expect sitting on a small island month after month worrying over petty administrative details? How he wished he was out again with his savage band travelling over the land! No wonder the Aborigines were dying off on Flinders Island. The assigned servant came in to summon him to the dining table a few metres away. His wife was already seated and he noted with distaste how well her ill complexion fitted in with her fat and bloated figure. He tried to find the girl he had married beneath the middle-aged spread, and failed! Then he pictured how Lalla Rookh had looked just a few years ago. A child of nature, naked and free in her savage state. Even she, he saw, as she entered the room carrying a tureen of soup which she plonked down in the middle of the table without the grace of a true English servant, was becoming obese. His wife spooned out the liquid. It was an obscure boiling down of salt beef and ill-prepared turnips, swedes and potatoes. The beginning of a typical meal, and one which he hated. The rough meals of shellfish and grilled slices of kangaroo of his journeys seemed vastly superior to them, and then the Cornwall Inn in Launceston had always put on a good spread. Those were the days—he sighed and recalled the time Lalla Rookh, then Trugernanna, had saved him from certain death.

It was on his return to the west coast to collect together the people there. Among his attackers had been the woman who had, when he first contacted them, swum out to a rock off a beach and clung there in fear of him. He had had to send Trugernanna out to her. She had been a good-looking woman, but she was dead now, as was her husband, Maywerik. Eventually he had got them to the Macquarie Harbour Penal Station for transportation to Flinders Island and they had perished there with many more of their people. The husband had known both Trugernanna and Wooreddy as children— strangely neither of them had warned him that he might be attacked.

He had just crossed the Arthur River on a raft of drift-wood when the natives were seen approaching. The men reached him and he gave them presents as was his wont on first contact. He passed out knives and handkerchiefs, and some bread and plums. They appeared friendly and he relaxed as they brought their women up and began to set up camp. He camped with them. After the evening meal, the Aborigines began to dance, and they danced on until he decided to retire. Some of them watched him as he divested himself of articles of clothing. They ran their fingers over his velveteen jacket and identified it as a bullock skin, then they pointed at the old blue coat Wooreddy wore and said that it was a wombat skin.

The night passed without incident, but he awoke to find the strangers sharpening their spears. Wooreddy rubbed the sleep from his eyes and felt for his weapon. It was gone. The Aborigine looked at him and he reassured him that nothing would happen. Still, he sent him off to talk to them and find out what was afoot.

Wooreddy returned to say that the Aborigines were planning to kill him. Immediately, with a snap that he had since lost, he had leapt to his feet and began to pull on his clothing, then packed his knapsack. Ready, he called those Aborigines travelling with him to move off. This caused the strangers to get to their feet. They raised their spears. There was a sudden shout and the thudding of feet as his own Aborigines broke and rushed off into the jungle. Never had one of those people ever been prepared to lay down his life for him, he realised, as in panic he jumped to one side and between two shielding trees. Then he was out of the camp and racing along a path back towards the river. He caught up with Trugernanna making her way in the same direction. She went slowly as if their lives were not in danger. He urged her to hurry, then suddenly realised that the trail ended in the angle of the river and they would be trapped there. He could not swim. Trugernanna knew this and told him to hide himself in the jungle. She pointed out a briar-like thicket which would have ripped his skin to shreds if he had tried to worm his way into the midst of it. What could he do? 'They've killed all the others,' the woman told him, and as if in proof a frightful scream echoed from behind him. Stupidly, this flung him into a frenzy. He scrambled down the steep bank and into the water. It was too deep and he could not cross. How to escape? He looked up to the top of the bank and saw the head of an Aborigine. They were closing in for the kill! Panic gave him the strength to heave a huge log into the water. It sank. He found another and dragged it into the water. It sank under his weight. Another one! It too sank under him. He lashed both of them together with his belt expecting all the time to feel the sharp pain of a spear piercing his side. Just as he thrust himself into deep water, one long shaft did come hurtling toward him. It hit the water near him and skidded across to the far bank. Now he faced another fear. The swift current threatened to sweep him away. He heard the cry of his faithful Aboriginal companion, then a splashing behind him. The logs began to be propelled toward safety. His dusky companion had come to his rescue.

Now he forgot the stodginess of his Sunday dinner in memories of that time and in the wild beauty of the woman who had saved him. She was indeed a figure of romance and worthy of the name he had bestowed on her: Lalla Rookh! He sighed for those days of adventure. He was trapped on a lonely, desolate island with a dreary drab of a wife. How long ago was it since he had sent in that application—the government moved so slowly on such matters . . . Then he realised that his wife had been talking at him for some time and he had not heard a single word. He watched her swollen lips (everything seemed bloated about her) form fat words. 'Yes, dear,' he said in her direction.

'How anyone can live in such a miserable place is beyond me, it is! You were much better off in Hobarton. You had a thriving business there, you know you did. And what did you do, you threw it all away for this miserable place of

151

exile. You did, you did,' she moaned, her face quivering.

'Marie, must I remind you yet again, that I was there a mere nobody, and now I am the Commandant of a government station, that is something!' The shrill tone of his voice became even more pronounced, 'and, dear wife, much better than being a bricklayer!'

'That Governor, you admire so much, that cold fish, only gave you this position because he couldn't find another fool to take it on. The other bloke resigned . . .'

'Marie, must I remind you yet again, that this is not just a job to me. It is a work of great merit and of everlasting reward. We are helping these poor souls to become good Christians.'

'Helping them, helping them — helping them to their graves, that's all you're doing,' his wife almost screamed. She too had become too conscious of sickness and death. 'An' it'll be the death of me too, this awful place. I feel it in my bones. That Governor fellow of yours, that high and mighty Governor sent us out here to die, both black and white. He wants us out of the way.'

'Marie, I make allowances; you have been ill, you are ill. Only now are you on the way to recovery. Try to curb your tongue!'

'An' that's not all. I was better off in Hobarton, happier too! Had a girl to do the cooking and cleaning. Good girls too! Here I have two ruffians who steal all the food and spoil the rest. And I have to teach that Lalla Rookh, that little friend of yours, how to be a good maid. She'll never make a maid, just as that Alpha won't make a cook's helper. It ain't in them. All they can do is die and good riddance too, I say. They're the lucky ones. This island is an island of the dead and the sooner we're all dead, the better off we'll be.'

Wooreddy could hear everything by standing just inside the kitchen door. Her words made him remember that the people living in the north-east corner of Van Diemen's Land believed that these islands were the fabled Islands of the Dead, that it was to these very islands that the souls first went after death. Such places were forbidden zones to the living and so they had proved to be. 'But was this the real reason for the many deaths?' Wooreddy asked himself, hesitating to put faith in what Robinson called 'savage superstitution'.

'An' I have to try and teach them women needlework and suchlike things,' Robinson's wife continued to moan. 'They're all thumbs, they are, and can't even learn to stop pricking themselves. They don't want to learn and I can't say I blame them, what with being imprisoned in this place of pestilence.'

'Marie, Marie, control yourself and have faith in me. We have been here but one short year. You are doing good work and I thank you for it,' he said, hoping to pacify her. 'Do not think that I do not concern myself with your ailments and dislike of this ghastly place. Of course, I do, and let me tell you that I do not intend that we should live out the rest of our lives on such a desolate island, just as I do not intend that we should stay on in such a miserable colony. These are but steps in our advancement. Have patience and before you know it, we will be sailing out of here. Only a few months ago, I received a letter from the Governor to the effect that a new colony was being made on the southern coast of New Holland. Marie, there is an appointment open for an officer who will bear the title 'Protector of the Aborigines'. If the income is sufficient, I will accept it. The projected new colony is to be made up of respectable men and women — perhaps it will prove a suitable place to settle in?'

'Just another wild place, just like this one. Haven't you had enough of them by now? I should have stayed in London. I've never got used to these wild places. Why don't we go home where we belong?' the woman cried, her face red and twitching.

'Because I have not yet been made eligible to receive a pension when I retire from government service, and my assets are insufficient to allow me to live in any degree of comfort. Marie, I have outgrown my humble origins, and will never return to the bricklaying trade. Marie, I beg of you to have patience. A little longer and I promise you that we will be off the island. On the next ship I intend to go to Hobarton to negotiate the terms for my acceptance of the post in the new colony. But I must also try to save these people I have devoted my life to. I want to have them transferred to the new colony. They will be of great help in affecting a friendly relationship with the local Aborigines. Then as the new colony is to be without the aid of convict labour, they will readily find employment as servants or farm labourers. This is what we have been training them toward at this establishment, and I must go and convince the authorities that they have advanced far enough in the arts of civilisation to work for their daily bread. My earlier reports will help in this regard, and the very mortality of our charges will be an aid, not a hindrance. How can those in authority turn a blind eye to the many deaths that have occurred here? They cannot, and if the remuneration is sufficient, we shall soon leave this island!'

Wooreddy heard the last words with a joy he had not felt for a long time. They were to be taken from the island! Their protector was not going to abandon them. He ran off to tell his wife and she rushed off to tell the others. A strength born from hope flowed over the settlement and some of the people began singing:

My mate hunts the kangaroo and wallaby —
Here he cannot — there are no kangaroo or wallaby!

The emu runs in the forest with her little chicks;
The kangaroo runs in the plains with her little joey;
The possums hang in the trees with their young —
Here the forest is sterile and there are no babies;
Here there are no rivers, only the streams of our tears;
Here we sit on the hilltops watching our far-off mountains;
We want to go home; we want to go home:
We are going home, Our Protector is sending us home.

The plaintive words ending on a joyous surge of joy filtered into the commandant's house as he sat putting the finished touches to what he hoped would be his last report. He felt the joy and took it as an omen of success.

III

G. A. Robinson enjoyed leave-takings as much as he enjoyed arrivals. He arranged them to satisfy his taste for the melodramatic whenever he had enough control. This day as he walked the road leading to the ship and the next stage of the journey to the Governor at Hobarton, he was satisfied with the actions and emotions of his charges. They flocked about him as he walked along the road he had built, towards the bay where the ship lay at anchor. On his right, Lalla Rookh clutched his hand and gazed up into his face, while on his left her taciturn husband waddled along in his curious gait. He was pleased to note tears in the eyes of the women and men. 'How they loved him,' he thought, little realising that the Aborigines were pinning their last few hopes on him. If he did not get them off the island they would all die there.

The Great Conciliator was not inclined to guess what really was in the minds of his charges, and the present scene reminded him of his greatest triumph when, at the head of the last of the Van Diemen's Land savages, he had marched through the streets of Hobarton in a grand parade. Everyone loved a parade, he most of all.

Dressed in his neatly pressed, somewhat naval-style uniform which he had ordered sent from home, brown and tough from deprivations suffered in the wilds, the Great Conciliator came on with his little white dog bounding at his feet. Nearby, and close to his side, though a little behind, as was befitting, came his faithful companions, Wooreddy and Trugernanna. Behind them came the remnants of the Oyster Bay and Big River people. They came on with spears and waddies, in their primeval condition, truly a terrible sight. These were the remains of the people who had fought the invaders for over twenty years. White women looked and delicately shuddered at some half-naked black man, then cast their eyes to their saviour—Robinson came out of his dream staring directly at an apparition from the past: an Aborigine, with his long red-greased locks drifting about his smiling face. His right hand held a long spear, while the left clutched a blanket about his body. Under it he was clearly naked. The Commandant of the Flinders Island Establishment smiled at the man, a welcome addition to his dwindling charges, and was happier to see that he came with a wife and two healthy children.

'Welcome, Ummarrah, welcome, welcome,' The Great

155

Conciliator said, detaching himself from the grip of Lalla Rookh and stepping forward with his hand outstretched in the old fashion. 'They told me that you had perished when the last of the West Coast people were put into the station at Macquarie Harbour to await transportation here. I remember the last time I saw you you were north of that harbour, then you left our expedition to return to your own people, eh? Things were different then, but those times are over. I welcome you, and your brothers and sisters will welcome you too!' Suddenly a wild idea hit Robinson. It caused him to ask: 'Are there any more of you left in the jungle?'

'No Meeter Ro-bin-un,' Ummarrah replied in a voice directly from the past.

The tiny flame of hope died, though the news was good, for it showed that he had indeed done his job properly. 'Too bad, too bad, Ummarrah,' he said somewhat sadly, and turned away to instruct the convicts in stowing his luggage. Then with an exaggerated wave to his charges, he climbed, ungainly with middle age and overweight, into the boat. He sat down in the stern with an audible thump.

Ummarrah turned his eyes away from Wooreddy and the rest to survey his new home. From the bay it did look very pleasant, with a flat coastal plain rising to a central mountain peak. It might be agreeable, he thought with a trace of optimism, then turned and under the cap and bald head recognised the good doctor. 'Wooreddy,' he cried and rushed to him and gave him a mighty hug.

In return, Count Alpha managed a faint Flinders-Island smile. 'Wooreddy,' Ummarrah cried again in his strong voice, then stared at the man in a puzzled consternation which moved from man to man and woman to woman. 'Hey,' he declared in ringing tones, 'what has happened to the old doctor, has he lost his cleverness? Why have you cut your hair like a woman, and why do women wear their hair like unkempt men?' He shook his own locks vigorously and they swung out about his face. They were much longer and more matted than ever. Still it was an old style and no longer in fashion. Then Wooreddy remembered his own glory, his ochre-smeared locks—part of the visible sign of his manhood. He thought of them and added sadness to his sadness.

'Well, we'll fix that! In time they'll grow back,' Ummarrah declared, taking part of the sadness onto his own shoulders. He took a bag from his wife, opened it, and Wooreddy saw that it was filled with the best grade of ochre. 'From Warnita,' Ummarrah stated. 'And it looks as if every one of you will need some. What has happened here? Is there no ochre to be found in our promised land? I know *num* lie, but it is difficult to know to what depth.' His expression saddened. Already the Flinders Island depression was affecting him. 'No-one is left on the mainland. I lived around Cradle Mountain until the loneliness ate into my bones and I could stand it no longer. I left my mountain and wandered as far as the west coast. I remembered that the people had been strong there. Not one of them remained. I found only a few of their huts rotting back into the jungle. Even their roads were disappearing and not even the ghosts lived there. The land lay in ruins and I went down towards the south east and even looked across at your home island, Wooreddy. Everywhere the smoke of the *num*, nowhere the smoke of humans. What could I do? I was sick of being alone. I went near a ghost town and they caught me. I told them that I wanted to be here with the rest of my people and so they sent me. Great Ancestor, you look a miserable lot!'

The Aborigines drifted towards the settlement. They had all the time in the world. Ummarrah sauntered with Wooreddy. He had to adjust his pace to that of the lethargic other. Trugernanna kept the wife walking slowly behind as she told her about the island and how bad it was. Ummarrah felt himself settling into a dark pit of depression as the pace slowed even more. Wooreddy had to rest. But his nature was such that he refused to stay there. 'Things may be bad,' he almost shouted at the unresponsive doctor. 'This may be a bad country, it may be a place of death and not of life, but we've got to make the most of it, especially now. You say that that ghost has gone off to plead to the Governor that you be taken off this island and that he has taken a paper with him. We must wait and see what happens, that is all that we can do. I know that he is a one for getting things done, that Meeter Ro-bin-un! Look how he got all of you here. He'll get us off in the same way. We have but to wait and what

157

shall we do while we are waiting?'

His words aroused no response in the apathetic Wooreddy, but he refused to be downhearted. When they at last came to the establishment, he insisted that the good doctor show him around the place. 'It smells of people living on one spot for too long,' he commented. 'No wonder you all get sick. And where is the ceremonial ground? You must have one in the bush somewhere.'

'When we first came we had hopes and there were still youths to be made men. We made a ground and then the commandant told us not to dance at night. We agreed in our way and tried to continue, but he stopped our food until we really gave up our ceremonies. If he caught anyone even talking about them, he was put in gaol. Our ground used to be where that field is. He made us dig it up. He said that we were Christians and if we wanted to sing we had to sing in that chapel shelter there. We sing there every evening, and that is now our ceremony.'

'But if you don't continue the old ceremonies they will die out,' Ummarrah said. He did not yet know that his two children were the only ones in the settlement. 'Ceremonies make us strong and keep us strong. 'We have to begin holding them again. Are you sure that this was the only ground? Was not another prepared further away?'

Wooreddy slowly nodded. He had forgotten about it. 'Let's go and eat, then I will take you to one which was made, but hardly ever used. I forgot about it.'

They went to Wooreddy's apartment where Trugernanna was showing Dray (Ummarrah's wife) how to boil up a stew. She was happy to meet her old friend again and wanted the happiness to last. She even managed a joke about Ummarrah's locks during the meal. After she took Dray off to meet the other women, while Wooreddy and Ummarrah went off on men's business.

Wooreddy was feeling an upsurge of interest he had not felt for some time. He felt ashamed for his slackness and as they walked on, he pointed out the grass trees that were not found on the main island. He went to one and broke his way right into the heart of the brittle crest to pull out the soft flesh, which they ate. They found some pigface and sucked

158

out the red juice until they reached the ceremonial ground. It had been hidden well away from the settlement, inland in a slight dip in the rising ground below the central mountain-peak of the island. A circle had been hacked out of the ti-tree, but since it had been abandoned small shrubs had overgrown the clearing. The two men set to work and after a few hours the ground was clear enough for ceremonies. Stamping feet would soon harden the soft earth. Then for that night's events they collected dry branches from the many dead trees. Death had attacked the very plants on this island. They piled these up at the places for the fires and then, as it was still light, they decided to try their skill at hunting. Great Ancestor favoured them, for in an hour they succeeded in spearing four large wallabies. They did not know it, but since Robinson had forbidden hunting the animals were increasing. These they placed up into the branch of a tree well out of the reach of any wild dogs, though most of these had been shot, by order of the Commandant, by the soldiers of the establishment. With everything ready, they went back to the settlement to spread the word about the ceremony.

Ummarrah's timely arrival and energy had quickened the establishment just as the discipline had immediately slackened when the commandant got into his boat. The men heard the news and waited for the night. As soon as their guardians were asleep, they slipped off through the darkness and past the sentries which Robinson had insisted on mounting. After the horror they had suffered and seen, darkness held no terrors for them and they hurried toward the ceremony ground.

Fires blazed in the four quarters to illuminate the circles. Another blazed in the middle of the eastern edge and at this sat Ummarrah. He got to his feet and directed operations. They freed themselves of their mission clothing and began painting their bodies with the white chalk they had taken from Robinson's school house. They outlined their man-hood scars in red so that they stood out to show their degrees of initiation. No women or children were present. Next they smeared red ochre grease over their cropped heads. What shame they felt when they compared their bald heads with

159

Ummarrah's luxuriant locks which writhed about his face like tamed serpents! Ummarrah had requested the good doctor to be master of ceremonies, but before he began, the man began the proceedings with a song outlining his exploits.

Pappela rayna'ngonyna, pappela rayan'ngonyna,
pappela rayna'ngonyna!
Toka mengha leah, toka mengha leah—
Lugha mengha leah, lugla mengha leah,
lugha mengha leah!

Nena taypa rayna poonya, nena taypa rayna poonya,
nena taypa rayna poonya!
Nena nawra pewyllah, pallah nawra pewyllah,
Pellawah, pellawah!
Nena nawra pewyllah, pallah nawra pewyllah,
Pellawah, pellawah!

Next the master of ceremonies began slowly thumping the palm of his hand upon the ground. The rhythm worked its way into everyone and they too began thumping the earth. It belonged to a ceremony of the bird clan to which Wooreddy had rights. Ummarrah, also a birdman, was entitled to lead the dancing. Wooreddy began to sing:

The pigeon sits in the cider tree;
He sits in the cider tree sorting the seeds;
Letting the best fall one by one into the hollow,
Into the hollow, filling the hollow, waiting for
The rain, the rain to come, to come to touch the seeds.

Ummarrah imitated the pigeon pecking at the seeds and letting them fall into the hollow. The rain began to fall, the hollow began to fill, echoed in the stamping of the feet, the moving of the hands. The birds drank and sang, then danced! From the darkness a stranger bird shuffled into the circle of light to give a 'caw, caw!'

With the flapping of wings, with a flapping of wings,
The crow lands, lands and hops toward the nectar:

160

Look out, look out—drive him off—there!
In the paper-bark tree he lurks close to the ground
Sitting and waiting, ready to steal!

The men danced in a line, one after the other. The order changed, two men danced abreast with Ummarrah. The dancers sprang and hopped, then stopped! They turned to face Ummarrah. They each bent and flapped a wing-like arm. They leapt sideways, then stopped. They leapt the other way. The dance leader faced them. 'Kaw, kraw,' they stopped and waited. A large, grey bird swooped gracefully down.

Pacific gull, Pacific gull flying just out of the reach of
   Ria Warrawah,
Watch out, Pacific gull flying, watch out or be trapped,
   be trapped by
The hands of *Ria Warrawah*. Don't dive, fly up; don't
   skim, fly up,
Reach the sun, let your wings take it beyond reach of
   the waves.

The men, holding a long length of twine, whirled and swooped imitating the flight of the gull above the sea. Towards the end of the segment, Ummarrah danced to a fire and took up a burning brand. A Red Robin fluttered out to sip at the nectar before the pigeon could prevent it. All the dancers rushed in.

Red Robin calls out as he flies from his mountain home,
   from
His mountain home touched by the ice-flame, not the
   fire-flame. He
Calls out as he comes flying, coming to drink the nectar.
   They
Seek to stop him, seek to drive him away, as he comes
   flying. The crow
Watches, watches from the paper-bark tree, he calls to
   the clouds.

161

But the cloud brings rain and the rain falls, the cloud
Brings rain and the rain falls, falls into the hollow,
Filling the hollow, overflowing the hollow. The storm
    cloud
Laughs, the storm cloud shrieks, filling the hollow,
Overflowing the hollow, hissing as it overflows the hollow,
As the nectar flows away, as the nectar becomes water.

The thighs of the dancers quivered as their feet struck the
earth again and again. They tapped their fingers on pieces
of bark making the pitter-patter of the gentler rain. Darkness
swept over the earth and from the stormy darkness came
stalking the ghosts that have no home. The slaves of *Ria
Warrawah* came forth from the darkness. With skins the colour
of bark ash they lurched into the circle, stumbling around
seemingly blind. Ummarrah did not lead them. He sat at the
side of Wooreddy ready to take over the singing. The good
doctor would lead this part of the ceremony.

Ummarrah's voice sounded out a low, dirge-like chant.

The ghosts sigh, the ghosts sigh, hear their sighing, they
    sigh
Longing for the proper road, longing for the nectar to
    give them
The vision of that way. They walk, they cry longing for
    that drink,
Longing and crying for that drink, they shamble out of
    the darkness
Longing and crying for that drink, but the way is not for
    them,
They cry and sigh and find no way. Chant the magic
    words, sing them
Away, chant the magic words, sing them away from us,
    sing them away.

Rain falls, the ghosts came, the crow he brings the rain,
The crow he takes the rain, he takes the ghosts to the gull
Flying over the sea, flying low and dropping them down,
Dropping them down, let us give the crow his share.
He leaves his perch, the sun empties the hollow,

162

He sits in the cider tree sorting the seeds, feeding
The hollow, feeding it and causing the sap to flow, to
Fill the hollow with sweet nectar, dropping in the seeds,
Making the nectar even sweeter, let us drink and eat!

This was the end of the bird ceremony. The wallabies had
been baking in earth ovens and were ready to be eaten. The
men separated into their clans and went to their fires. While
eating they would decide on the next ceremony. Then from
the distance came the sound of singing.

Ne popila raina pogana:
Ne popila raina pogana:
Ne popila raina pogana—

Thu me gunnea, thoga me gunnea!

Naina thaipa raina pogana
Naara paara poivella paara—

Ballaboo, balloo, hoo; ballaboo, balloo hoo hoo!

A strong female voice wailed out a verse which was repeated
in unison by many female voices. Ummarrah recognised
that of his wife. The women had also been conducting a
ceremony and were now calling for the men to come and
join them. Another lament began. Trugernanna led the
singing. Wooreddy swung into a version replying to the
verses. The men began dancing and echoing the chorus.

The women sit thinking of their men folk:
They stand thinking of their men—
While we dance thinking of our women,
Thinking of our beautiful women—
While they dance thinking of their
Handsome men, handsome men—
Handsome men thinking of beautiful women.

The eyelashes flutter together—
Breast to breast together—

Heart to heart together—
Fluttering, seeking, finding—
Dance, men, dance you to me—
Sing, women, sing me to you:
We come, we are coming—
You come, you are coming—
Hallahoo, hallahoo ho ho:
Hallahoo, hallahoo ho ho!

At the end of the song, the men picked up the food and left for the women's ceremony ground which they could enter only on invitation. At other times it was a deadly female area to be carefully avoided and not even to be talked about. But tonight the men had been sung there and had to go. If they did not, they risked incurring the enmity not only of the women, but also of the secret forces which they could control. And so with feelings of trepidation the men entered female territory to begin the mixed ceremonies which would give strength to both halves of the new community.

IV

While the Aborigines were trying to forge new links and unite the tribal remnants into some sort of community, Robinson plotted his way towards Hobarton. He was a man of substance and owned some hundreds of acres. Still, he wanted to gain a government pension so that he could return home and live as a gentleman of leisure. To achieve this he had to stay on in government service, but he did not want to spend more time as Commandant of the Flinders Island Aboriginal Institute, though he loved hearing that word: *commandant*!

The brig made an uneventful voyage down the east coast and eased into Hobarton Harbour without delay. As the commandant looked upon the small, neat city nestling at the base of the flat-topped Mount Wellington, it came to him, with the rush of certainty that an evangelist feels, that it was time to sell up and move on. During his stay in Hobarton, he would arrange for the ultimate disposal of his property — the land on Bruny Island and the three houses in Elizabeth Street with the brickyard beside them. He recalled that time over a decade ago when he had watched the approaching scruffy town with different feelings, with the feelings to better himself there, and he had, just as Governor Arthur had changed a town of huts into a compact city of some fine buildings. He glanced towards the shore, feeling again that it was time to move on. Van Diemen's Land had become too settled, he wanted to feel the thrill of wandering through the savage wilderness once again before he settled down at home.

The ship's boat set him and his convict servant ashore on the crowded jetty. A proper wharf had been planned, but had as yet not been constructed, and so he had to endure being jostled while organising his servant to carry the luggage. Free from the turmoil, he again was struck by how much the place had grown over the years. A row of fine buildings, built from the local sandstone (it had cost him a contract or two for bricks when he cared about such things), stood facing the harbour and it was these that gave the city such a neat appearance when seen from the sea. Passing a fine two-storeyed building, he stopped and decided to put up there. The 'Commercial Tavern' had lodgings above a first-class bar in which he could listen to all the gossip of the town. Making himself known to the proprietor, he arranged for a room and leaving his servant to unpack, continued towards Government House. Macquarie Street had been paved in his absence. He walked past the Commissariat Office and Store and along the rails of a fence, then through a gateway guarded by two red-coated sentries, and through shrubbery and flower-beds to the front office where His Excellency's secretary received him. He had to wait while the secretary consulted the Governor before finalising an appointment. It was for ten the following morning.

Next morning, Robinson was ushered into the presence of the Lieutenant-Governor. Since he had psychically washed his hands of the colony, he was noticing each and every detail. His Excellency had changed since their last meeting a year ago. The lines running from the corners of his mouth had deepened to give him a perpetually sour look, in harmony with the perpetual frown on his forehead. His Excellency bent his head to finish off the sentence he had been writing when Robinson entered the room. The commandant noted that he had a bad case of dandruff. His Excellency pressed his pen down, then looked up over his spectacles. The once-sharp eyes might have faded, but the stern look remained. Robinson had tried to model himself on this person and had failed. He was too rotund, too frivolous and impetuous to be able to become a reasonable copy of this cold fish whose position he envied and yet could never realistically aspire to. Arthur was the boss, Arthur had selected him to look after Aborigines, and he had looked after Aborigines. Now he wanted a better deal, to continue looking after Aborigines, but in the new colony of South Australia, and he complicated matters by wishing to take the Aborigines from Flinders Island with him. This London frowned upon. Where was the profit, and they refused! Still they could always use a person of Robinson's experience. Arthur was to offer him another position.

His Excellency began a little hesitantly, not knowing if Robinson would be agreeable to the offer. 'Sir, I am afraid that the delays in our correspondence between Flinders Island and Hobarton, and Hobarton and London, have meant that the position of Protector of Aborigines in the new colony of South Australia is no longer available. The expedition to settle the new lands has left England already and unless you specifically want to take up the position by proceeding directly, if possible, to Spencer Gulf, I am afraid that some other area will have to be found for your expertise . . .' He stopped to gauge the effect of his words.

Robinson had not been all that interested in the position at Spencer Gulf. The projected colony had been discussed in detail in the inns of Launceston and the opinion was that colonies set up directly from London had little to offer a local man. In Launceston, the important new colony was going to be Port Phillip and it was to be set up, not from London, but directly from Van Diemen's Land. Launceston was not far from Flinders Island, and Robinson had been to and from that port since he had become commandant. He knew the men engaged in the project. One was John Batman, a strange sort of person who had competed with him in trying to bring in the blacks, and the other was Mr Fawkner, a publican. He, and a group of like-minded businessmen were outfitting a schooner to sail to Port Phillip and set up a settlement. All in all, that would be the place to be in, and not some London-organised colony at Spencer Gulf.

Governor George Arthur did not know what to make of Robinson's silence: did it mean that he wanted the job, or did it not? 'If you still want the position,' he said to break the silence, 'it may be possible to put you on a small vessel which is about to sail to the Swan River settlement far to the west. It could, I believe, put into Spencer Gulf and set you down there. But there are your charges on Flinders Island—'

'Your Excellency,' Robinson hurriedly replied, 'I could not think of abandoning them, especially now that they are almost civilised. The only problem is the high death rate, but this, I believe, is falling. There are now young, healthy children at the establishment. I believe that Spencer Gulf is not the place for my charges and that if I am to be given a new posting on the New Holland landmass, it would be better if it was closer to Flinders Island.'

Arthur nodded: 'There is some problem in allowing your charges to roam free on the mainland. They have been guilty of crimes that are not easily forgotten by the people, not only of Van Diemen's Land, but also of New South Wales. The questions are: are they civilised enough, and do they want to accompany you there?'

The commandant produced what he considered to be his trump card. It proved not only the willingness of his charges to go to Port Phillip, but their attainment of such a degree of civilisation that they were capable of framing a petition to the authorities. Robinson, in his eagerness, had overlooked the fact that Port Phillip had only recently been settled by Batman and Fawkner and this unofficially. The Governor knew of it, but ignored it as it was out of his jurisdiction.

Arthur took the sheet of paper and examined it carefully. He saw that the Aborigines had signed their names with an X symbol. If he had been the commandant he would have schooled them better, or at least coached them to write their names. Still, that was just an oversight and would pass while he was governor, though he was long overdue for recall. He put the thought from his mind and read the document.

FLINDERS ISLAND

12 AUGUST.

We, the undersigned Aboriginal Natives of Van Diemen's Land and now residing on Flinders Island, testify, on behalf of ourselves and families, that we are not only willing but perfectly desirous to accompany the Commandant, G. A. Robinson, to port Phillip, from whom we do not wish to be separated:

ALEXANDER his x mark		HANNIBAL his x mark	
ALPHONSO	"	JOSEPH	"
ARTHUR	"	JAMES	"
ALPHA	"	LEONIDAS	"
ARCHILLES	"	NAPOLEON	"
ANDREW	"	NEPTUNE	"
AJAX	"	NOEMY	"
ALFRED	"	PETER PINDAR	"
BUONAPARTE	"	PHILLIP	"
EDWARD	"	ROBERT	"
EUGENE	"	ROBINSON GEORGE	"
FREDERICK	"	TIPPOO SAIB	"
KING GEORGE	"	THOMAS	"
HENRY	"	WASHINGTON	"

Arthur was renowned for his lack of humour and it was proved again on this occasion. Not a strain of a smile intruded on his rock-hard features. He read the petition through twice, then a third time, noting drily that it had the style of a Robinson report or letter and left it on his desk for future filing.

'It seems,' he said, 'that your charges are at least as anxious as you yourself are to leave Flinders Island; but as to the matter of Port Phillip, I am afraid that not only does it lay outside my jurisdiction, but that the recent settlement there is illegal, though I doubt that the Home Government can do much to unsettle it. It also appears that the Government in

London has finally put together a consistent Aboriginal policy which they intend to reinforce—thus, it is extremely likely that with the proper recommendations you will be enabled to take up a worthy position there. I am, sir, willing to give you those letters as well as writing to London. I know that the new Governor of New South Wales, Sir George Gipps has received instructions in how to deal with the native inhabitants, and I am sure that a Chief Protector of Aborigines will soon be appointed there. You, sir, are the one to fill that position! I suggest that you sail to Sydney and lay your case before Governor Gipps. I assure you, sir, that it will be but a formality and the position will be yours, or at least a similar one.'

Robinson accepted what he regarded as his just due, but ungratefully. The Governor had not even mentioned the application he had put in for an increase in salary as well as being considered for a pension. He hoped that the Port Phillip position would prove to be plum enough, and so he thanked the Governor absent-mindedly as he pondered on the possibilities—then he remembered his charges and said: 'Your Excellency, will it be possible for me to take all my charges across to the mainland? Shall their wishes be honoured?'

Arthur looked down at the petition, then up and past Robinson. 'Sir, I do not know. You must take up the matter with Governor Gipps. I think that some, if not all, will be allowed to go with you as personal servants. There is a way, if you can think of it, and that should always be a legal one,' the moralist drily remarked, remembering his long term of governance, his personal fortune and profitable investments.

'Thank you, Your Excellency!'

'Mr Robinson, thank you for your services to me in my term of office here. I hope that you receive a position worthy of your talents. I shall draft the letters and get them to you immediately. My secretary shall arrange your passage to Sydney on the next available boat, at government expense of course.' Then, unusual for the man, he got to his feet and saw Robinson to the door. Such solicitude gave him pause, but it was answered when as he stepped into Macquarie Street a bill was thrust into his hand.

169

SUPPLEMENT.

GOVERNOR GEO. ARTHUR

Is Ordered

H O M E !

LORD GLENELG closes his Despatch as follows :—" I have felt it my duty, to advise his Majesty, that you should be IMMEDIATELY RECALLED ; and I have to convey to you, his Majesty's commands, that, on receipt of this Despatch, you will, with as little delay as possible, repair to this Office.　　　　　("Signed)　　GLENELG."

TO-MORROW OUGHT TO BE A DAY OF GENERAL

THANKSGIVING !

For the deliverance from the iron-hand of GOVERNOR ARTHUR. We have now a prospect of breathing. The accursed gang of blood-suckers will be destroyed, Boys will be seen no more upon Police Benches, to insult Respectable Men. Perjury will cease to be countenanced, and a gang of Felons will be no longer permitted to violate the

LAWS OF CIVILIZED SOCIETY.

COLONISTS,

The dismissal of Arthur from the Governorship of unhappy TASMANIA, is a BLESSING, that will be felt by the worthy, and be duly appreciated. The Impounding Law, which was made to benefit the great Members of Council, will be abolished. The Turkey and Perdan Act will meet with the same fate ; and the Acts of abomination practised by the hirelings, and secret emissaries of the Government, upon the People, will no longer be countenanced.

REJOICE!

FOR THE DAY OF

Retribution

HAS

ARRIVED.

RELFE's HOBART TOWN.

6

The Ending of the World

I

It was not very often now that the Commandant reverted to his aspect of Great Conciliator. Officially, 'The Chief Protector of Aborigines' he rarely thought that he had too much ambition. This was one of those rare times. He sat at a small table on a stool in the small, single room of a hut, which he had dignified with the name of 'office', in the Aboriginal encampment at Purran. It had been thrown up at his order, and was the only European construction in an area which, he had to admit, was a beautiful spot—but too close to the temptation of the white settlement for his charges. It would have to be removed, or rather they would have to be removed to a place better suited to their advancement. Then, perhaps, he could have the land assigned to him in recompense for leaving his comfortable post on Flinders Island for this newly settled district. Thank God, he had managed to have a cottage erected near the punt plying across the Yarra Yarra before his wife had arrived from Wybalenna. He really could not blame the poor woman for her complaints. The climate of the island had wrecked her health—but he thought she should make some effort to manage the home rather than letting the convict servants do as they pleased, not to mention the natives he had brought with him. They needed a firm hand! Wooreddy, or rather, Count Alpha and his wife, Lalla Rookh would make good servants with a little supervision. If only his wife took an interest in his work!

He looked down at the very first report, which he was completing after a few weeks in the field. His superior was Governor Gipps in faraway Sydney. There was another person who seemed to lack both interest in, and knowledge of, his work. This person was completely different from Arthur; he had issued no instructions and expected the Chief Protector not only to supervise thousands of Aborigines scattered over thousands of square kilometres, but also to prevent clashes between them and those Europeans that had taken up selections on their land. He sighed, then smiled at a piece of gossip he had heard at 'The Shakespeare'—the only decent public house in the settlement. When Gipps was an officer on the Spanish Peninsula he had been called 'Dirty Gipps'. Come to think about it, there had been a slight odour of uncleanliness about him when he had been interviewed—not the uncleanliness of the unwashed, but of something else? Oh well, the Governor was far away, and now he was letting him know, that is if he wanted to know, that the assistant protectors had just gone off to their posts except for Parker, whom he was keeping with him as a secretary for the time being. Shortly, he would be making an extended tour to contact some of the natives of Port Phillip and he hoped that Ummarrah (should he give him an European name?) would prove his worth in this. He looked through the doorway at the bright sunlight streaming in and remembered how sad the people had looked when he and the others had left Wybalenna! It had been so moving and a fitting end to his work there. He doubted that he would ever return to Flinders Island and that lonely little station, though he might go back to Van Diemen's Land (what were some of the settlers there beginning to call it—ah, yes, Tasmania after its alleged Dutch discoverer) to collect some of the possessions he had left in storage there. His eyes shifted to a black bust of Alpha standing on top of a cupboard, the only other article of furniture in the room. It was a fine piece of work, executed on commission by a rehabilitated convict whose name he had forgotten. He got to his feet and admired the image just as three Aboriginal women came and hesitated at the door. He turned his eyes on them, noting with satisfaction that they had covered their nakedness with the blankets which he had issued.

Still knowing nothing of the language, The Chief Protector gestured them into the room. After a long hesitation, they edged through the doorway to line up against the wall in front of the table. Space prevented them from doing anything else. Suddenly their eyes fell on the bust of Alpha and they grew very still. The first one who had entered the room turned to her two companions and said in a faint voice: 'Bendi-an boort-an tollerom malee, baboop! (Mother, they have cut his body in half and smoked the top part)'. They turned to the doorway only to find that Robinson had anticipated their reaction and stood there.

Waiting for the worst they began sobbing, and were agreeably surprised to have coloured ribbons thrust into their hands. Maree, the bravest among them, even stood still and let the stranger tie one loosely around her neck. She did not complain or pull away as he took her hand and tugged her towards the bust. By this time she had noticed that it was made of some sort of stone and had told the others, 'mooja'. They repeated this word as they watched Robinson put Maree's hand on the chest of the image. Then they too squeezed around the table to feel it, marvelling at the smoothness and life-likeness. The women laughed at how they had been tricked, and Maree began to explain how the men carved images on trees, but seeing that he did not understand her she stopped. They tested out their few English words on him, learnt more including 'friend', then left with a few pounds of flour. Robinson sat on his stool and finished off his report with a final flourish. He went to the doorway and looked at the sun. It was past midday. He would walk home, have his lunch, then go over on the punt to hand the report to Mr Latrobe, the Superintendent of Port Phillip. For an instant, he was overcome by an unreasoning jealousy. Only an accident of birth kept him from ever holding such a post. It would have been the logical step from being commandant of an island to Superintendent of a new settlement—but all that he had been given was the post of Chief Protector of Aborigines. He pushed such heretical thoughts away and decided to inform the Superintendent that he had planned to hold a festival for both black and white. There the Aborigines would perform their quaint ceremonies and show their traditional arts and crafts and he, in turn, would give them a banquet.

He left his office and stooped to lock the door. It was a formality purely and simply. The weak wattle and daub walls could not withstand any sort of assault, even a man leaning against them. He turned around to marvel again at the world he was in — so different from the conditions he had found in Van Diemen's Land. Here the people were whole and living their own way of life. The scene gave him a feeling of contentment, and he knew that he was in the wilderness for more than merely securing his future. It was what he had dreamt about in the grimy air of London — to wander in strange places among strange peoples. And so here he was! Perhaps here he might even find what he had been seeking: an end to the restlessness that drove him on and on.

He shrugged and put aside the thoughts. He had a job to do. He walked towards the camp, noticing the difference between it and those he had seen in Van Diemen's Land. Here each clan camped together in a certain order, not only of families, but of sex and age groups. Each family had their own shelter and fire, but so did the young unmarried people. The boys and girls tended to form into gangs and do everything together. But the girls had their own long bark shelter and so did the boys. Robinson walked past the small lean-to in which an old couple lived slightly apart from the others. He wondered why, as he went to where he might find the head man, Waau, or Crow.

It was like some small village. At some fires women were cooking and two gangs of boys were hurling reeds at each other in mock fury. A group of men sat under a spreading tree discussing something in low voices. High-pitched voices shouted out from the bush and a crowd of women, who had been out gathering vegetables, entered in a scrawling heap of contention. Robinson marched through the arguing women and came to where Waau sat engaged in pressure flaking a spear head. Robinson waited, as he had learnt to do in Van Diemen's Land, until the man raised his head and gave a slight nod, then he squatted across from him and waited again.

The heavy-set man, with the thick, black beard and hair

174

knotted behind his head in a European female fashion, continued working in silence. The sounds of the camp surrounded them. The women had settled their squabble and had gone off in the direction of the creek. The warm sun shone down through the gum trees, giving the ground the look of a brown head with a few thinning grass hairs. Robinson squatted and wondered if these people had knowledge of the Supreme Being. Part of his life was committed to carrying the words of the gospels to such poor heathen. He had done this in Van Diemen's Land and would do it here—but later. He wanted to know more about the people so that in his projected book he could contrast their customs to those of the people he had worked for . . .

Waau spoke in English without raising his head: 'Everyone will come tomorrow. I have arranged it.'

'Are you sure?' The Chief Protector insisted. 'Did you tell them that after they have danced and shown us the use of their weapons, they will be given plenty of food?'

Crow nodded, as he reached to the side and pulled toward him a spear shaft. 'Everything is arranged. We will put on one of our ceremonies. Some of us will throw spears at a target. I will demonstrate the art of boomerang throwing. They appear to like that.'

'Very good,' Robinson said heartily, pulling from his pocket a small pouch of tobacco and laying it before the man. 'If everything comes off well, I'll give you some more tobacco.'

Crow left off fitting the point to the shaft and picked up the pouch and opened it. 'Thank you, Chief Protector,' he said mimicking his accent so accurately that Robinson gave a start. He recalled that in Van Diemen's Land the people there too were good mimics and had used the ability to learn English so well that they often spoke it better than some of the convicts. Maree, Crow's wife, came to fling a few sticks onto the fire and he remembered that she had come to his office and left without telling him what she wanted. He asked Crow about it and found out that she had come for tobacco. He nodded, then pulled out his watch to find that it was one o'clock and time to get home.

Robinson got onto Gardiner's Creek road and walked to one side of the lines of deep ruts. It wound for about half a kilometre through almost virgin bush to where the punt-road track joined it. The bush was so hushed that it brought to mind the free days in Van Diemen's Land when he and his trusty little band marched through the wilderness. Those had been the days! Soon they would be his again. Soon he would be marching through the wilderness far away from all white men and feeling that heady sense of freedom again. So he romanticised from the depths of his boredom at having a steady job and a comfortable future. He reached Punt Road and turned off onto the smoother surface. Heavy carts did not use it much. As he ascended the long slope beyond which lay the Yarra Yarra and across it the steadily growing settlement of Melbourne, he looked around with the eyes of a man judging opportunities. If only the government divided this land into building lots, he might pick up a few cheap blocks as an investment. In only a few years the population of Melbourne had grown from less than a hundred to six thousand, and if the trend continued, land prices were bound to rise more quickly than they had in Hobarton. The block on which he had built his house had been purchased from a gentleman suddenly in need of ready money after a loss at the races. That had been an excellent piece of business and now others, at least two of the townsmen, Robinson corrected himself, were thinking of building on Forest Hill.

When he reached his house, he was puffing heavily. Old age was catching up with him, but he still had a few good years of travel and adventure in him. He felt a faint urge to return one day to the old country and then travel over Europe, seeing the marvels he had thought he would never be able to see. Now it was all possible. Just a few more years and a few more opportunities and he would return a gentleman of leisure, able to devote himself to writing his memoirs. His house had only three rooms, including the kitchen. The servants lived in huts that were little more than shelters at the back. The convicts had their hut on one side of the block and the Aborigines on the other. The Chief Protector still believed in the separation of the races. He entered directly into the main room crammed with the furniture they had shipped from Hobarton. The solid furniture (he always kept an eye open for bargains) looked incongruous in the rough room of unplastered walls and no ceiling. They had moved in as soon as the walls were up and the roof on, but he hoped to effect steady improvements. Trugernanna welcomed him as a dusky servant neatly clad in bonnet and long skirt, but her face passed beyond the disguise she had put on for his sake. She had been one of his greatest successes and also one of his greatest failures, for beneath all the trappings of European culture, she remained a black woman with a black woman's beliefs and ways. This he knew and now as she came to greet him, he wondered what she had been up to. His wife was always complaining about her, and some of the complaints were true and not based on the fancies of an ailing woman.

Mrs Robinson lay trying to rest on the sofa. She lay there like a bloated white whale. The months her husband had left her alone on an island filled by death and despair had sickened her. She was dying, but no-one knew it. She was plagued by obscure complaints and a general listlessness. The local doctor, whom she considered a quack (why else would he be practising in such a place?), found nothing wrong with her and classified her condition under 'women's complaints'. He treated it with a mercury compound to cleanse any pollution she might have picked up from her stay among the savages. But the woman continued to pine and fret, and to have vague aches and pains tethered to dull throbbing headaches. Her husband had little sympathy for her and often wondered why he had married such a vulgar worthless woman. He thought this now, as he entered.

'George,' the woman called from the sofa, 'that Lalla Rookh disappeared for a whole two hours this morning. She couldn't be found anywhere, and that convict cook of yours, he was not to be found either. Don't blame me if your lunch isn't ready. You can't expect me to have everything ready, if I have to rely not only on criminals, but also on Aborigines. It's impossible! They don't listen to me, and then I am sick, George, I am not well! If only we could go back home to England. You have enough money now. We can live on that if we take care, and you won't have to work. You can live the life of the gentleman you so ardently desire to be.'

'Yes, dear,' he said as he picked up the latest copy of the *Port Phillip Gazette* and began to read the small print.

No land sales were scheduled.

'It would be easy, and you must show some consideration. Didn't I follow you half way around the world?'

'Not until I had sent you letter after letter of importunity,' Robinson muttered, distracted by the woman's prattling. If he had not been a man of moral sense, he could have put her out of mind and taken a convict lass as had many others, he thought, then hurried away from the thought by concentrating on the *Gazette*.

Trugernanna, still on her best behaviour, entered and began laying the large dining table which occupied the centre of the room. Robinson acquired objects as bargains, but his wife clung to them as possessions. He equated money with security, but she with things, and so the table pushed them to the margins of the room and the little spaces between chairs and sideboards and cupboards and dressers. At night, in the darkness, movement was impossible and he would have sold up the lot if it had not been for his wife who was still babbling on: 'We could sell the furniture. There's a scarcity of good furniture and if you found someone with money—some arrive with so little. We could sell it and why, that would cover our passage home. It would cost us nothing to leave this dreadful place. And then there's the house and the land—Why,' her voice rose in wild hope, 'we could leave tomorrow. We could, we could—'

'Soon, soon, just stay calm, Marie,' her husband counselled, knowing how hysterical she could become. He saw the wild look come into her vacuous eyes and a tic start on her cheek. 'Just a short year, Marie, just a short year and I'll have my pension and we'll be on the ship going home to a comfortable retirement. Just think of how we have advanced and of how we must stabilise our position before I resign my post. Marie, I have my responsibilities. I am a civil servant, The Chief Protector of Aborigines!'

'You may be that,' his wife cut in bitterly, anger quelling her sobs, 'and you may be something more. They call you an interfering nigger-lover in town, and people look down on me for being your wife. Why do you keep them around you? Shouldn't they be down at the camp with the rest of them?' she snarled, turning on Trugernanna who had just finished at the table.

178

'Marie, they have to be trained to take their place in our society. They must be able to earn their living just like anyone else.'

'They'll never make good servants and you know it! That Mrs Free-and-Easy there and that waddling husband of hers are far too lazy. They take what they can get from you and give you nothing in return. They only work when they feel like it.'

'But, Marie, cast your mind back. Just a few short years ago that woman you see before you was a naked savage suffering in the jungles of Van Diemen s Land.'

'And that Mr Free-and-Easy, that one that waddles like a duck, he's still a savage as far as I can see. Look at his hair and that red stuff he smears all over it. Why I caught him using some of my lip rouge, the jar I keep to remind me of home. His hair looks just like a nest of red snakes. Why don't you get him to cut it, and get that other one to do it too! He's even worse a savage,' and she began sobbing again. Her face became all red and twisted, and Robinson looked away in disgust.

'Marie, my work requires me to contact the local Aborigines. I have allowed these two to keep their hair long so that they may contact the local people without arousing fear.' How tired he was of his calmness; how tired he was of this woman. Thank God, he would soon be off.

'Yes, yes,' the woman cried, her face quivering with hysteria. He took refuge in his thoughts and remembered when he had arrived back at Wybalenna to find that his charges had reverted to savagery. He had had to right things quickly before handing them over to his successor—but, on considering his new position, he had thought that some of their customs might prove useful in New Holland. He would soon put this to the test, as he intended to use the methods that had proved so successful in Van Diemen's Land. His natives would first contact the local groups and he would follow behind them. Then after he had conciliated them, they would be concentrated at the stations which were now being established, and the work of civilisation would begin. He would not be doing that. Missionaries would be sent out from England to do the teaching. Thus he thought through his wife's ranting

179

and ramblings. He hurried through the meal, then left to catch the punt . . .

'Weenerop wangan,' a Port Phillip man challenged Ummarrah and Wooreddy resplendent with their locks dripping lip rouge and new blankets stamped all over with the government mark. They held their own heavy spears, different from those of the mainland, and scorned the foreign wooden shields and spear-throwers. Wooreddy began to introduce himself, using the polite introductory sentence of Van Diemen's Land culture. 'Pallawah nirree, pallawah ngune, Wooreddy,' he said, giving his status, clan and name; but Ummarrah replied in a different way. He had risen to the challenge and held his spear pointed at the man who shouted out the question again. The Chief Protector decided that mediation was called for. Crow was the tool for the job. He went to him.

'Tell your people that they are friends from across the sea.'

Waau went to the group of men and began arguing with them, or rather explaining that Ummarrah and Wooreddy and their women were with the Chief Protector and shared his privileges. He would vouch for the strangers and introduce them into the country properly. They too were Aborigines and would accept the proper way of doing things.

He then went to the two from Van Diemen's Land and introduced himself as Tankli, a crowman of the Bunurong people. 'Those men,' he said, indicating the ones that had accosted them, 'are Wurundjeri and rough fellows. You will see this in their dancing. We are the masters of any ceremonies here. But we are doing only rubbish dancing today, just for the white fellows. When we dance in the proper fashion it is a joy to behold.'

Wooreddy and Ummarrah re-introduced themselves, this time using English, the common medium. They explained that any misunderstandings had arisen because of the differences in language. 'We hope that we have caused no ill-feelings,' Wooreddy said. 'It is not our way to act roughly, but since most of our people are no more, we have lost touch with many of our customs. There seemed little use in trying to keep them up. The white man we travel with has told us to follow his ways and this makes us act in the wrong fashion.'

180

Waau accepted their apologies and with a few deft questions worked out how they stood in relation to one another. They were of the same generation level, and there seemed little to stop them from treating each other as equals without restriction. Crow arranged for a formal ceremony in which they would request permission to be on this land. This would be held immediately.

Wooreddy informed the Chief Protector about what was going to happen. A number of people had gathered around him to learn of the day's events and he took the opportunity to enlighten them that they were about to see a real savage ceremony. 'Today is a unique occasion,' he told them. 'You are about to see an authentic ceremony used when strangers seek permission to enter the land of another nation. If they did not do this, they would be speared,' he informed his audience, stretching the facts a little, but he always dramatised those ceremonies he had a hand in organising. 'They were about to be speared, when I intervened,' he whispered to one of the ladies present—a Miss McCrae who gave herself social airs, though she was not English, but Scottish.

Wooreddy and Ummarrah and their wives made a fire and waited until the sticks were well alight. They took a brand in each hand and, leaving their women at the fire, began to walk towards where the local people stood. Waau and the men of his clan came out to meet them. He introduced them to each of the men who presented them with boughs, showing that they could make use of the forests of the country; plants to show that they could eat the vegetables growing thereon, and herbs and grasses favourite to the different food animals— they were allowed to hunt these for meat. After this, the women came up, and Waau took them to a fallen tree where he had left his family.

At ease among friends, they began talking about their home island and how the white people had acted there. Hearing the sad stories, Crow replied: 'If they try to do the same we too shall resist them, but perhaps things will be different here—'

He looked at his numerous clan members painting their bodies for the dance. They were strong and could fight.

They marked their bodies with meaningless circles of red and yellow ochre and striped their faces with white pipeclay. 'We decorate our bodies differently,' Wooreddy observed. 'We emphasise our degrees of initiation more.' He opened his blanket and showed his neat rows of cicatrices. Taking some of the red ochre and white pipeclay he began to circle and connect them in a pattern. Waau indicated his own relatively unscarred chest, and said: 'We do not over-scar the body, but our main mark is the absence of a front tooth.' He opened his mouth and showed the gap. 'That indicates the basic initiation.' The good doctor would have liked to question him further on such matters, but Crow got up and hung around his waist a belt from which fell fringes both front and back. He tied bunches of leaves around his ankles and was ready for the dance.

While this was going on, Trugernanna and Ummarrah's wife, Dray, her girlhood friend who had survived in the South West and then had connected up with Ummarrah, were regaling Maree with tales of horror in a mixture of English and sign language. Dray told her how she had held her dying sons in her arms when they had come to stay at Wybalenna. 'It was really bad there, though we had gone there to get away from bad things. And when we got on the ship to come here many people had been attacked by the coughing demon. I don't know how many are still alive,' she said, and began to sob. The two other women began sobbing in sympathy.

The dancers took up their clapsticks and went to the centre of the paddock. Waau was not taking part and sat with his guest. Maree took the two strangers to sit with the rest of the women who sat in a semi-circle and who had stretched their possum-skin rugs tightly over the cavity between their crossed legs. Wooreddy could not guess the reason until the entertainment began, but he recognised a songman when he saw one come forward.

'I gave him the job,' Waau whispered. 'I am the best artist in these parts, but I refuse to perform in such a rubbish entertainment. I do not waste my talents. How are you with songs? . . .' Then the songman clicked his sticks and the women took up the rhythm, beating the skins with the flat

182

of their hands. The songman took a few steps and sang:

Kooeem tangarboom yerrin oot—

One group of men began imitating a herd of feeding kangaroo while the others put themselves in the position of hunters and began stalking the animals. The songman intoned: *Konga gee darak pardeyang.* The women joined in the singing and repeated the words at a higher pitch: *Konga gee, konga gee pardeyang, pardeyang.* The hunters attacked the kangaroos. Some fell writhing in death, others bounded off in alarm, and one man, a masterly mimer, dragged himself as a wounded kangaroo into the scrub. Then the dancers gave a loud, shrill cry and ran off the ground.

'The next ones will be better. Those were just youngsters,' Waau explained to his guest. Then he began talking to Ummarrah and found that he was homesick and wanted to go home. This horrified Wooreddy and he exclaimed: 'But it is no longer a home for us. We have nothing there. Everything's gone. Those of our people who remain are on Flinders Island and only a fool would go back there!'

'I could live in the islands with the sealers. They always want workers and they hate the government as much as we do. My wife wants to return too—and as for Trugernanna she feels that she wants to go back to see Bruny Island. It is not good to stay away too long from your own soil. We want to leave here!'

Wooreddy could only gape with astonishment. He knew there was no going back, that there was nothing to go back to! They would wander homeless until the end of the world.

But Waau agreed with Ummarrah, and said: 'Yes, it is not good to stay away from home. It makes you sick. And there might be a way for you to go across the sea to your land. Down where the land faces the sea across which you came, often white men put into the bays there. If you go down there, you might be able to get a boat to take you across.'

'I won't go back,' Wooreddy declared. 'I have seen my earth polluted, the last of my people die—I'm sick of death! To stay here or to go there is no choice, but if Trugernanna wants to go back, let her go with Dray. Perhaps one day I will feel like going back,' he finished with all the wistfulness of an exile.

'We all have been in this place for too long,' Waau said. 'It is time we went south. You can travel with us, but we go slowly. Perhaps Wooreddy can travel along with us, and you others can go straight to the southern seashore if you are in such a hurry. If you do find a boat, leave us a sign so that we will know, if you do not meet us down there. You will see our smoke.'

Wooreddy did not have to arrive at a decision. He thought of the kitchen duties at the Robinson house, and how he disliked them! He thought of the convict cook, and how he disliked him! He thought of the place where he slept, and how he disliked it! He thought of the clean smell of the forest and the joy of being on the move. He did not think of the Chief Protector!

II

Long since the four Aborigines had concluded that all that they owed their friend, Conciliator, Commandant and Protector was death and destruction for the calamity he had brought on their people. They had no qualms in leaving his employment as servants for which he paid them in keep. The Chief Protector, from his days in the bush, was an early riser and they saw a light come on in the house as they strode off into the dawn. It did not matter, for by the time he found them gone, it would be too late.

They walked along the ruts of Gardener's Road until they came to the thick girth of an ancient Eucalyptus tree, then turned off along a narrow path which would bring them out at the camp. The prospect of being free of the whites and their ways ended the long depression they had laboured under. They came to a fallen tree beside which a thicket of saplings thrust up. Upright in this they had hidden their spears. They pulled them out and sat down to sharpen the points. After this they took off their white men's clothing and greased their bodies. Their wives dressed their hair and at last they were ready to enter the camp.

184

Waau greeted them. The women had packed their few possessions into baskets and they were ready to leave. Crow too had taken off his clothing and had packed it in his wife's basket. Whites were known to shoot naked blacks, but hesitated if they saw anyone dressed in their clothing. He eyed Ummarrah's and Wooreddy's spears and put out his hand for one. 'Too heavy,' he grunted, as he balanced it. 'Impossible,' he said, as he tried to fit the end into his spear-thrower. 'Our weapons are superior,' he declared fitting spear to woomera and letting fly at a tree. His stone point shattered and it whanged off. Ummarrah smiled and showed his skill. His spear thudded into the tree and stayed in the tree. Waau was impressed enough to try a throw. He failed to reach the tree. Wooreddy lifted his arm and his spear thudded next to Ummarrah's. Then they tried the mainland way of using a spear thrower and with the same disastrous results as Crow had had with their weapon.

The sun was up and it was time to be off. The men left the camping area in a group. The women picked up their baskets, rounded up the children and followed after. Dray and Trugernanna were with Maree.

As they walked along the track which would bring them to the edge of Port Phillip Bay, Ummarrah boasted of the exploits of his little band of guerrillas, before the inevitable sadness of those days overcame him. 'But we were so few, so very few,' he said softly as he looked at the thirty or so men strung out along the track. 'We were so few, and fewer and fewer—' He sank into the sorrow evoked by the memories of those days and Waau felt his pain. He had talked to these two men; heard about their sufferings, and felt the bitterness and bewilderment as they tried to understand what had happened to them, not as individuals, but as an entire people. How he hoped that nothing like that would happen on his own land and to his own community! There had been some sickness and deaths, but since Mr Robinson had arrived to help them, there had not been any. Things had improved and might continue to do so. Wooreddy, too, thought of Robinson and of their travels together. Those had been the good days. Plenty of food and women, of visiting new places and seeing new things. But then they had been taken to the Island of the Dead and the days had turned bad. How many were still alive? When Mrs Robinson had arrived, she had told her husband that the coughing demon had attacked not only the Aborigines, but the whites. She had accused him of leaving her behind in the hope that she would die along with the wretched people exiled there. 'Well, you have succeeded in ruining my health,' the woman had cried, 'and this place will see the end of me!' Wooreddy sighed while he recalled her exact words. Death had been his companion for so long that it was a friend. Then the joy of travelling took away the gloom. This was the life; he smiled and thought of going hunting. He would ask Waau about it. Perhaps they could go together and test their different methods.

They came to the edge of a small swamp and made their first halt. The men gathered wood and carefully positioned their own fires in the ordered pattern which showed the family and clan alignment. Waau's guests continued to share his fire. The women came up, put down their baskets, and went to gather vegetables from the swamp. The men relaxed and smoked as the food was being prepared. An hour or so later, they got up and moved off along the track. The women and children followed. The next stop was at a waterhole just behind the beach sands. They halted only for a drink before moving south along the flat beach.

After seven kilometres, they came to a second waterhole hidden in the screen of ti-trees backing the coast. Waau and the others approached carefully. It was explained to the strangers that not very far away was the hut of a white man and working there was an Aborigine who had killed a woman. They had pursued him to bring him to justice, but after they had speared him in the side, the white man had given him refuge and refused to surrender him. As this was being explained, three men came toward the waterhole. Two were white men and the other an Aborigine dressed in European clothing. The white men carried muskets, but the Aborigine appeared unarmed. He only had a coat draped over his arm and hand, but undaunted he came up to the group of men and shouted: 'You are not to come here. You kill cattle. You will not get me, but I will get that one who wounded me in the side.' There came a sound like that of a stick being

186

broken and a close relative of Waau's fell back. The barrels of the muskets lowered and the muzzles covered the men.

'Well, well, that's the end of that little to do, isn't it, Jacky,' a rough blonde-haired and bearded giant of a man stated. 'Now we'll just get ourselves a gin or two and be on our way.' Just as he realised that the group was all male, they were off and away through the ti-trees. Ummarrah and Wooreddy kept close to Waau because they were uncertain about the country. A short distance from the waterhole, they stopped to regroup. A man was sent to warn the women of the danger and Waau, furious at the death of an uncle, decided to go back to reconnoitre. Raging, he whispered fiercely to Wooreddy: 'That brother of yours has been saying how good you islanders are. Now come with me to the waterhole.' He glided from the spot, and Wooreddy followed, every bit as skilful, though the nature of the country (sand and spaced-out clumps of ti-tree) did not require a great amount of skill in moving silently and unseen.

Except for the badly wounded man lying where he had fallen, the clearing was empty. Leaving the shelter of the trees, Wooreddy knelt at the man's side. He had had experience of gunshot wounds. The bullet had smashed into the chest and lodged beside the spine where it could be felt like a small pebble.

'A doctor can suck that out,' Waau said with hope in his voice.

'He will die from his wound if we don't stop the bleeding,' the good doctor replied. 'There's no clay about, but we can use the ashes of the old fires. We'll pack that into the wound and when we get back to the women, we'll tie it up with rags.'

He did this, and they carried the groaning man to the beach where they found the rest of the community grouped. After fashioning a stretcher out of the European clothing and thin ti-tree trunks, they laid the man on it and continued along the beach away from danger. They came to an outcrop of red sandstone. In it was a circular well. They removed the stone lid, gave the man a drink of water from a shell, then had one themselves. They pushed on to put distance between them and any possible pursuers. The women and children hurried along the beach, while the men moved through the

187

scrub with their spears at the ready to defend them.

Waau had calmed enough to resume his duties as a host. He pointed out the spots where the waterholes and wells were as they went along. Towards nightfall, they left the beach to ascend a steep slope to the top of a cliff. A large spring of water bubbled here and they decided to camp. The rear guard came in to report no sign of pursuit and they settled down. Waau ate damper while planning revenge for the relative who had died just as the first fire was lit. 'Tomorrow morning we will bury him, then I myself will go and put an end to the life of that miserable wretch. I vow that he will be dead before three days are over.'

The good doctor noted that these people had the custom of burying their dead, then volunteered to help him on his mission of revenge. 'I am a stranger and my tracks are unknown to most. After this I will return to the Chief Protector and will wear 'boots' so that my tracks will never become known. We of Van Diemen's Land have fought them and have won against them. And we still want to fight them, as revenge against the slaughter of our people. I am your guest and it will be a way of repaying your kindness to us.'

Waau agreed. If fighting ever broke out between the two races, he would need the knowledge and now was his chance to pick some up in the field. Early next morning they scooped a grave out at the base of the cliff and lined it with paperbark. Then as the women were wailing out their sorrow Waau and Wooreddy began the return journey. The good doctor carried a half dozen heavy spears he had fashioned in the night. They rushed back along the beach and rested at the waterhole. Behind it and some distance inland lay the shepherd's hut.

It stood right in the centre of a large cleared open area and the men could be seen cutting down another tree on the far edge. The Aborigine was chopping wood near the shanty. He had no chance of seeing Waau and Wooreddy creeping toward him sheltered by the bulk of the hut, but he had every chance of feeling the sudden rip of Waau's spear tearing open his side. With a scream he dashed inside and the white men looked across just as the avengers dropped to the ground. They began edging towards the safety of the hut, Wooreddy stood up and hurled his heavy spear. It picked up the foremost man and flung him dead on top of his mate, who gave a shriek and charged for safety. Wooreddy grinned. This is what he had wanted. The man vanished through the door. It slammed shut after him.

The walls of the hut were of the usual wattle and daub. The poles could be easily wrenched out of the ground, but it was too dangerous. Two holes of windows covered the front and the walls were thin enough to be fired through. The chimney was a huge misshapen affair of turf down which anyone who did not value his life could climb. The good doctor looked at the roof and smiled. Dry sheets of bark held down by a framework of poles. The same as in Van Diemen's Land and, in dry weather, the best way to get at the prey within.

They kindled a fire on the blind back of the hut and when it was blazing thrust the ends of rolled up pieces of bark in it. When these took fire, they flung them onto the roof. With an audible 'poof', the entire roof erupted into flame. From the inside came a scream of agony. A shot blasted out from a window. With his clothing on fire, the white man came charging out with a pistol in each hand. But Wooreddy was waiting beside the door and as he raced past felled him with a single blow from the axe he had snatched up from the wood heap.

He picked up the unconscious man and flung him into the flames, then did the same with the other body after taking out the spear. 'That's how we did it in Van Diemen's Land,' he declared in satisfaction. 'They had an accident and burnt themselves to death'—then for some reason tears came to his eyes and he had to look away.

They slowly retraced their steps. Now there was no hurry and sooner or later they would catch up with the rest of the people. Seafood was plentiful and Waau had no qualms about entering the surf to harvest it. This horrified Wooreddy, and he explained to the man about how bad the sea was and how Great Ancestor protected them from its evil. 'That may be possible,' Crow replied, 'Our Father too protects us just like your Grandfather of Grandfathers. See that huge rock standing off the point there. That is him, or a part of him, and he stands there to keep the waters back. He walked all over this land and I will show you some of the places he camped as we go along. But to what clan do you belong? I am, as anyone can see by the name I go under, a crowman, but what are you?'

'My real name is Poimatapunna, phoenix, and thus I am related to both fire and to all birds. We are not only brothers by generation, but are connected also by religion.'

'Yes, but strictly speaking the firebird does not appear in my connections, perhaps owing to an oversight. I am related to the hawk, the rabbit rat, the kangaroo, emu, iguana, and other creatures, but then even our learned men leave out things on occasion. It is true that the crow is connected to fire and is even a fire bird of sorts. So we are both birdmen, just as you say. The crow is a marvellous bird and I will take you to see what he did just an hour's walk from here.'

They walked along the top of a high bank of a creek choked with brush until they entered a flat plain of dark basalt. The stream ran in a gorge through it, clear and sparkling and free of vegetation, but they turned away from it and walked down a slight slope which steepened as they went. The dark rock turned into the paleness of limestone. Wooreddy's feet began to hurt from walking on such a hard surface, but Waau assured him that they were almost at their destination. The slope steepened still more, and the sides closed in until they were clambering down a hole. They reached a wide ledge around the hole which still fell down and down into the darkness. 'Our crow ancestor made that hole,' declared the crowman. 'Once he was angry with us, we had disobeyed his laws, and to bring us to our senses as well as to punish us, he cast down from the sky an egg of stone. Long ago we used to meet here to make our boys into men. We were here at that time and the stone crashed down on us and through into the earth. That egg is still down there, so far down that it is so cold that it cannot hatch. One day it shall!' He picked up a pebble and let it fall into the hole. Wooreddy listened and felt that he could see the pebble falling down and down into the coldness where the egg, slightly glowing, lay. Subdued by the hole, they walked off to the creek and followed it inland. The land began rising

190

steeply. A kookaburra began laughing and Waau explained to the mystified Wooreddy that just as they had phoenixes in Van Diemen's Land so they had laughing birds here. Wooreddy nodded and followed his pointing finger to where a large brown bird sat on the dead branch of a tree. A writhing snake hung from its beak. 'Watch this,' Waau said, fitting his spear into the wommera. He cast it, and the bird dropped the snake and flew off. 'Now we have our supper,' Waau said, killing the serpent with the end of his spear-thrower.

III

'In the very old days, long ago, five women lived at this waterhole,' Crow said, his long beard jutting toward five small boulders edging the rock pool. 'They used to dig up these yams,' he went on, getting up and walking to a patch growing not far from the pool. 'Women's work,' he explained, 'but, if one is not around, we do it.' He carried the pile of yams he had dug back to an old fire site and began making a fire there. 'Those five women used to be the only ones who had fire. They were selfish and kept it to themselves.' He pushed his firestick into the centre of the pile of bark and twigs. It caught instantly in the dry air, and he put some of the yams on the coals, while saying 'To Waau, my crow ancestor, they used to give a root or two, thinking that he would know no better. But crows are clever and curious. One day he hopped to a cooked one and pecked at it. It tasted so much better than those he had been eating, that he decided then and there to eat only cooked ones. Then he had a problem, he needed fire and those selfish women would not give him a single spark, let alone a live coal.' He took up a twig and poked at the roots to see how they were cooking. 'So that was his problem,' he repeated as he began dragging the yams out of the fire. He pushed some in the direction of the good doctor.

Wooreddy gingerly put one to his mouth. They were not

native to his land. He found them to be sweet and soft, a little like possum flesh. 'One day,' Crow said, then stopped as he saw that Wooreddy had finished the roots. 'Let's go on!' They continued climbing up the ridge. Far below they could see the coastal plain and the bay. Clouds began to race across the sky as they came to an ant-hill. 'Here is where my ancestor came,' Waau said, jerking his beard towards the ants' nest. 'He caught some snakes and hid them in the ant-hill. Then he sat on that long stone there. It was a log then, and he called down to the women. I have found an ants' nest, come and dig out the eggs. They are much sweeter than your yams. Those greedy women ran up and knelt down and began digging into the ant nest. You can see the marks of their knees on that slab of rock there. They knelt and began digging at the spot where Crow had hidden the snakes. They reached them and those snakes hissed and lashed out angrily. They slithered out after those women. See, the lines of their tracks there. The women ran off, to that big boulder, then turned and began hitting out at those snakes with their digging sticks at the end of which they kept their fire. They hit out so hard that the burning end of one of the digging sticks broke off and landed where that patch of red clay is. My ancestor pounced on that burning fragment and hid it in his kangaroo skin bag.' While Crow was telling the story, he was cleaning up around the marks of that long-ago encounter. He removed all dead grass, sticks and leaves. 'The women suddenly realised that they had lost the burning end off one of their digging sticks. They began looking for it and could not find it, nor could they find Crow. They knew that he had the fire. The women saw him and chased him to the top of a very high tree. It is that tree right on top of the ridge, just where it begins to dip down to the well of sweet water made by the moon man.'

They made their way past the tree and from the distance Crow pointed out a column of rock like a dead tree stripped of branches. He said that Wooreddy could not go close because nearby was a keeping-place of the Crow Clan. Then they went down a track leading to the waterhole. A rustle in the undergrowth made them hesitate. They stopped and waited. Thud, thud, thud, a kangaroo? — no, a wallaby from the lightness of the feet striking the earth. Crow gestured to Wooreddy to move away a few metres. The good doctor side-stepped, then began to creep towards where the sound had stopped. Crow did the same. They inched forward to the edge of a glade. A wallaby bent over munching the clumps of grass. Wooreddy lifted a foot and put it down. The animal's head rose and its ears twitched. He could even see its nose quivering in his direction. He pretended to be a rock, but it continued to look at him. A swish came from nearby. Something streaked through the air to lift the wallaby and throw it down. Wooreddy ran in and brained the animal. He picked up the carcass and they walked on to the waterhole.

'All this area is the place of the Crow and belongs to our clan,' Waau said. 'After Crow got the fire he came here to stay. His brother, Eaglehawk came to him to demand his share. 'Give me some fire, I want to cook this kangaroo,' he shouted. He had a kangaroo just as we have a wallaby. But Waau and Bunjil had been quarrelling and Waau refused to share his fire. Two of their uncles saw this and they came down from their home in the sky to put things to rights. They took the fire from Crow to divide it, but accidentally dropped it. It burnt Crow and all this country and that is why both are black to this day. Here we are at the waterhole. Once moon man flung his spear at Emu here. He missed and caused this hole in the earth. The spear was tipped with poison, fatal to Emu, but nectar to men. That is why the water is so sweet.'

Waau cooked the kangaroo in an earth oven. They feasted on the meat, then lay back content as the evening fell and stars began flickering in the purple sky. The far distant campfires shone out to them, and Waaau pointed out where his ancestor's fire glowed, then those of the sisters who had retreated into the sky with the others of that period. They were all up there in the skyland, and, what was more, they waited for the present day people to come to them. Wooreddy listened to Crow, and then began to tell him about Great Ancestor. They held similar beliefs and there was little conflict between the two men. Wooreddy relaxed and somehow felt that Great Ancestor was very close to him. It was as if he were looking down directly at him.

Around the hollow holding the spring flowed the coolness of the dark forest. The day birds had ceased their calling and settled for the night, but rustles in the undergrowth showed that life was on the prowl. With a great flapping of ungainly wings an owl flew over them and through the dartings of a bat. The weather was warm and no shelter was necessary. The men lay on beds of fern fronds on opposite sides of the dull glow of the fire. For once the night held no fear for Wooreddy, and he did not feel the need to keep the fire blazing. He relaxed, letting the darkness sweep over him. His eyes looked up at the sky, identifying the familiar star patterns. At ease, but with a certain feeling to which he could not put a name. It was as if certain forces were operating, as they always had, but now consciously. A sickle moon floated up. On either side were his two children. He stared at two stars which Waau had said were his Crow ancestor and his brother, Eaglehawk. They were the campfires of the two ancestors flickering. One even briefly spurted up as more wood was added. All around were the fires of their relatives, their children, their children's children and so on down to the present. He saw the black streak along which the dead walked to the Islands of the Dead, and then the bright return road leading up from the sea. He stared at a dark spot, which resolved itself into the top of a tall tree. Up this tree men climbed one after the other. Strange men, clever men, with the power to ascend while living into the heaven world. He watched men chasing game, and saw a streak of light where a community was on the move, burning the country before them as they travelled.

He floated up through the darkness surrounded on all sides by the sparkling of countless campfires. A steady hum vibrated all around. Strange, indistinct beings travelled with him. They stretched hands towards him, tried to grab, but could not. He moved on, they dropped behind as he passed over a place beneath which all the land was ablaze in a great circle of fire. From the fire projected lines of light like ropes leading further up. He caught hold of one of these and felt himself pulled higher. All around were the campfires of his ancestors, but beyond was another land. The streaming rays of light stretched up. He clung on and was pulled higher

194

and higher until he was lost in a nothingness. He clung on to the light ray, clung on in solitude in a nothingness pierced by other rays but without clinging figures. All was light and he awoke to the morning. He told Crow of his dream and of the journey. The man looked at him with respect and said: 'Let's go to the ocean. I want to show you a cave.'

They moved off in silence. Not having the need to talk, they did not speak. The land sparkled under the morning sun. It was summer but the earth was still damp from the winter. As they progressed tendrils of steam began rising, and they moved through a strange misty landscape of which Crow knew not only every landmark, but how they had been formed. Sometimes he detailed a mark with a terse sentence, but more often he did not break the peace. The trees stretched high into the sky—and here and there Wooreddy noticed that the land was falling into disrepair. 'The white men have taken part of the land near the coast, and they will not allow us to burn any of it now,' Waau explained—and the magic and peace of the day disappeared into the harsh reality which the strangers had given them. Wooreddy sought his dream. Could all of them ascend into the sky, beyond the harshness?

And they came out onto the sea and Wooreddy recoiled from it, but Crow took him along through sand dunes and right to the edge of a cliff at the foot of which the ocean boiled in fury. Wooreddy looked down at the sea lashing away at the land, lashing away as it always had done. At one part it had bashed its way right through a stone wall to create an arch. The spray came up to wet his face as they made their way along the cliff. They edged between the ocean and the matted vegetation massed to protect the land. Then Waau led him down a path which was but a crack in the cliff face. The ocean battered at Wooreddy hurling wind and spray in an attempt to dislodge him and sweep him into its domain. But as they descended the tide fell and by the time they reached the base of the cliff, they could walk on land reclaimed from the sea. Somehow it seemed sacred.

'*Puliliyan* is our *Ria Warrawah*, but unlike you and your people we face him and gain powers,' Waau said matter-of-factly.

195

'And some of us too have faced *Ria Warrawah* and gained powers, 'Wooreddy asserted. '*Puliliyan* and Our Father are close relatives,' Waau stated. 'Everything comes in twos, but behind them stands only one.'

Wooreddy felt himself recoiling from what the man was saying. The sea boomed not far away, though close at hand it appeared calm—too calm, and he wanted to run and hide. Suddenly, his boyhood experience lived again in his mind. It had ruled his life and thus *Ria Warrawah* had ruled his life. This he suddenly realised with a shock that threatened his sanity. To steady himself, his mind clutched at what Waau was saying: '*Puliliyan* controls all these waters, and he is neither evil nor good. He only is, and is even kin to my Crow ancestor. He controls all the ocean, and loves the waters and in his way loves the land too. He likes sporting in the sea, paddling in the warm shallow waters and diving deep into the cool green depths. He thumps and threshes the waters just as the women thump the rolled up possum skin rugs in our ceremonies—'

Wooreddy began to feel a terrible dread rising in him. It seemed that all that he had believed, the scheme that had supported his life, had been but part of the truth. Things were not the simple black and white he had imagined them to be.

Waau guided him along the sand. The very water retreated at their feet. 'Once *Puliliyan* thumped the water until it became very thick, as thick as mud and he could no longer see far down into the depths. Something appeared to move in the murk and he took a branch and divided the waters to see what it was. He saw a pair of hands, but not as big and strong as his own. He broke a twig off the branch and fashioned a hook which he let down into the water, and he drew up those creatures. They were similar to the ones Our Father had created on land. So he took these two strange creatures to him. Our Father took them and gave one each to the men he had created. They were women and were to be their wives. He gave each man a spear and each woman a digging stick, then told them to live together and divide the work between them. That is a story about our *Ria Warrawah*...'

'And here is where it all happened!' He pushed Wooreddy

196

toward a cave and he slipped on the slimy rock floor and skidded inside. His head filled with a strong sea-smell which reminded him of women. He saw fish swimming in clear rock pools and his mind opened. The women had guarded their underwater world and denied it to the men. He trembled all over and kept in the light falling through the cave mouth. Great spears fell from the roof. Great Ancestor casting down his spears to keep *Ria Warrawah* at bay—but other spears rose from the floor to join them in a oneness. They met and there was no conflict as he had always thought that there should be—that there had to be! And his skin did not itch at the proximity of *Ria Warrawah*, and he did not feel threatened by the new truth, though he felt beyond his old life. *Ria Warrawah* and Great Ancestor came from a single source and somewhere was that source which he had been seeking in his dream. He moved further into the dripping darkness of the cave and it did not panic him. It was the origin of all things. Suddenly rays of light pierced through to him from the entrance. His second great flash of enlightenment came. The first ships had brought him the news of the ending of the world, now the light told him that that end was near and with it his life. His mind flashed and a pattern came which he could not explain. Only a few more steps existed to the end. Both his life and the collective life of his people were at an end. His mood and thoughts evened out. He found himself outside the cave and without a word let Crow lead him up the cliff path.

IV

They climbed up off the beach and began to cross the base of a point jutting out into Bass Strait. Waau led the way. He was passing a thicket when a slight rustling made him hesitate. Wooreddy calmly waited to see what had caused him to stop. He was not disturbed when Ummarrah, Trugernanna and Dray left the thicket and walked to them. Each one carried a musket and had a bag for ammunition slung over a shoulder.

They exchanged greetings and walked with the men. Waau said that they were making their way towards where his people were camped. Wooreddy only smiled. They continued on and Trugernanna fell back to walk beside her husband. She began to speak in the old Bruny language which they had not used for years.

'You saw that Paddy, that *num* a long time ago when we still lived at home. He was raping me and you did not try to stop him. I don't blame you for that. You could do nothing. None of us could. Well, we were going along the coast looking for a boat to take us across the sea, when we saw these ghosts. They had landed in a bay close by here. One of them was that Paddy. He treated me worse that day than he had the need to. It was inhuman! Well, I have paid him back. I shot him and Ummarrah shot one of the others. But the rest escaped in their boat before we could grab it. Now Ummarrah feels that it's just like the old days and wants to stay in the bush and fight them. I don't know what to do! I suppose we'll have to keep to the coast and try and find a boat. But those ones that got away, they'll be able to identify us as Van Diemen's Land Aborigines, and they'll track us down in this strange land. I don't know what to do! I don't want to go back to that island, to that place Robinson calls *Wybalenna* (Black-fellow's place).'

Ummarrah broke in also, using his own dialect. 'The ghosts are dead and nothing can bring them back to life—but we are not going to surrender. We are staying here, away from the white people. Later on we will find a boat and sail to Wybalenna and save the people that remain alive. We will take them back to Van Diemen's Land, back home, and take to the mountains. I left only because everyone else had. This time we will all be together.'

Wooreddy nodded his head. Nothing concerned him. He too had killed a ghost with a casualness that had frightened him, but now all that killing was at an end. Soon all problems would be abruptly solved with the end of the world, and so he said: 'Come along to the camp with us. Tomorrow we can discuss what to do.'

'We'll do that. There are few ghosts around here and they won't be after us yet.'

Waau knew nothing of what had happened: If he had he might have taken precautions and moved the camp away from the cattle ranch which had been established a few kilometres away. When they approached the camp, the women saw them and called out. The men shouted in return. Waau related how the outlaw had been executed and a feeling of well-being settled over the camp. Things had been put to rights. The site was an excellent one which had not been visited for some time and bags of seafood were collected from the rocks.

That evening the people feasted and the visitors from Van Diemen's Land were prevailed upon to dance. At first they refused, saying that there were too few of them and that it would be a mockery. But Waau, who was a great songman, knew that Wooreddy also was a songman and finally got him to agree to teach the basic movements of a dance to a group of young men. He was overjoyed when Ummarrah volunteered to lead the group while Wooreddy and the two women sang. Ummarrah did not decorate himself for the ceremony. He only dressed his hair, removing the lip rouge and replacing it with red ochre. He put a little on his face. The Port Phillip dancers were more extravagant. After they had rehearsed the steps and motions, they began painting themselves with red and yellow ochre and pipe clay. They put on a feathered head band, a bone through their noses, a long fringe hanging from their waists in front of their bodies and bunches of leaves around their ankles. They held two clap sticks to mark the rhythm. The austere Ummarrah waited for the equally austere Wooreddy to set the rhythm and begin the song.

In a clear ringing voice, Wooreddy sang:

Nica plokarna puneneme memmalee

And Trugernanna and Dray repeated the words while the rest of the women began to pound their rolled up rugs, giving a distinct Port Phillip sound to the song.

Nica plokarna puneneme memmalee

At the end of the refrain, Ummarrah led his bedecked dancers into the area illuminated by the fires. It was a modern dance. Half of the men stooped down and put their hands on the backs of their companions. Imitating horses they galloped around the ring while Wooreddy and the women sang:

> *Larekoyer koey henna warame*
> *Larekoyer koey henna warame*
> *Kolelebe bekonena tarlarne may*
> *Mar mar porrenne toomatta*
> *Tar payar marawoe*
> *Tar payar marawoe.*

Ummarrah pretended to have a long whip. He flicked at the horses to make them go faster. A dancer mimed a dog and ran about the horses. Wooreddy and the women increased the tempo of the song.

> *Mar ya margana narename parewurhe*
> *Mar ya margana narename parewurhe*

One of the riders dropped his musket and began to run. He whipped up his horse. Faster and faster went the rhythm. The ghosts went running to the east and to the west as they came under attack.

> *Plarelape peengemma ill la name*
> *Paymarpar maymarpay may marpar.*

The dancers began to shake their heads and bodies and to stamp their feet. The horses were in a panic and the dog raced around in circles snapping at their heels. The final chorus began. One man left the circle and raced out. With a whoop the rest followed and Wooreddy's words rang out over the empty arena.

> *Naymarkar parname larera namemenna*
> *Naymarkar parname larera namemenna.*

Waau came over and thanked them for the gift of the dance and said that it would live on as it had a distinctive style. In return, he said, his people would put on a composition with similar subject matter from the Murray River area north of Port Phillip.

Giving a series of sharp taps with his sticks, he began to recite in a slow chant:

> *Enagurea nung ngalourma barein gurukba murhein*
> *Burunbai nganungba lilira muringa.*
> (They come across our tracks,
> Like stone chips the bullets will fly.)

The women began a slow boom-boom rhythm over which the now keening voice of the songman soared. A group of dancers entered the area. They mimed a herd of cattle. Some lay down and chewed the cud, others stood scratching themselves with hind feet or horns. A second party of dancers entered to stalk them. They speared two head and went through the motions of cutting them up. Waau sang:

> *Perr toneebit tangeit; perr toneebit tangeit.*
> (Let us roast and eat them.)

He changed the rhythm just as there came the sound of horses galloping towards them. Real horses!—for before they realised it what seemed to be a whole army of white men swept in from all directions, yelling and shooting their muskets over their heads. They ran this way and that way, but there was no escape. 'Don't shoot any of them, not a one, or we'll have that Protector down on our heads,' the leader of the party shouted. Quickly they separated the Aborigines of Van Diemen's Land from the locals and tied them on the spare horses. It was over, and Captain Powell, the leader of the party, had Waau brought before him. He said: 'These fellows plenty no good. They kill, one, two maybe three men. We take and give to governor. You no go with such bad fellows. Or we take you too and hang from tree like these fellows. You come town and see.'

Waau nodded his head numbly. The captain wheeled his

201

horse and the whole party dashed off. It had been a successful night's hunting. They had their quarry and would see them hang!

V

Robinson marched along the muddy street towards the gaol which held the Aborigines he had brought with him from Flinders Island. They had repaid him for all the attention he had bestowed on them by going on the rampage. He had not expected such ingratitude, and it gave his enemies the opportunity to point the finger of scorn at him and his endeavours. God knows he had done all that was in his power, but that had not been enough. Underneath the thin veneer of civilisation had lurked their savage natures waiting to emerge, and they had! Now he had the nasty job of explaining to them that they had stood trial that morning and that after due deliberation Ummarrah had been condemned to death. It had been obvious that Alpha suffered from senile dementia and could not follow the proceedings. The women had been treated as accessories and given the benefit of the doubt, thus leaving Ummarrah to feel the full weight of the law.

He was allowed into the cell which held the four Aborigines. Wooreddy sat with a vacant smile on his face. A broken clay pipe lay beside him. For one moment, the Chief Protector wished that he could have put all the guilt on this madman, but the man looked so feeble-minded that no court would have believed him capable of a crime. The two women sat together smoking. Lalla Rookh looked up at him and got to her feet. 'Fader, what will they do to us? We did nothing wrong; we were only trying to get back home! That man that was killed. Long ago he raped me. Black women can be raped too! We can feel pain and we do not kill without reason. We are not savages. That is only your excuse for not listening to us.'

'Lalla Rookh,' Robinson scolded: 'A man has been killed,

or rather, two men have been foully murdered in cold blood. Ummarrah has acknowledged his guilt and he will pay the supreme penalty. Both of you women are to be returned to Wybalenna on the first available ship. And I declare that it is your own fault. What you have done is beyond my comprehension and understanding. It is also beyond my forgiveness and I wash my hands of you. You Lalla Rookh, you Dray and you poor Alpha will return from whence you came and that will be the end of it. May you see the errors of your ways! I have come to spend a little time with Ummarrah. Tomorrow he is to die.'

Ummarrah looked at Robinson and laughed. He filled his pipe with tobacco and began smoking.

'We shall pray together,' said the Chief Protector. 'This day will be your last. You will not be pardoned. Make your peace with the Lord.'

'I am at peace because I will never return to Wybalenna,' Ummarrah replied.

Just then a warder brought in the prisoners' rations of a half loaf of bread and a mug of tea. Ummarrah began eating his half loaf with gusto, washing it down with great gulps of hot tea. The others had no appetite. The women were crying. One was losing a husband, the other a lover, and both a friend. Wooreddy alone remained unmoved by the drama. The ending of the world was occurring in his mind. Ummarrah stopped his eating and said: 'I am like Wooreddy, I don't care a fig for anything. This world is yours and you can have the ruins. I will walk with Wooreddy and forget all this. I have three heads and only one of them belongs to you—that one I lose on the gallows. The second one will go to my homeland and the third I take to the grave.'

Robinson looked at the condemned man with concern. 'That may well be so, Ummarrah, but tomorrow you are to die. I have come to tell you this. I have been able to let your three companions stay here with you. Tomorrow I will come to take them away.'

Ummarrah looked at the two women. They were still crying, just like women! For some reason he thought of the guerrilla leader, Walyer, and of how she had given up so easily and died so easily. He had not given up until there

203

was little left to give up. He was leaving behind only this woman, Dray, who had been his wife and borne him two strong sons, only to see them die in exile. He shrugged and grinned his old grin and said: 'Cheer up. It's no fun living in a white man's world. I leave it without regret.' This only caused the women to wail hysterically. Wooreddy sat on. Perhaps watching the land beginning to fragment. Suddenly he left his trance to look at Ummarrah. 'You know,' he said, 'they don't even believe that we can speak like this or choose our own destiny. We have chosen to go away and we are going. Soon everything will end and they will have only ashes.' He saw the tea and reached for a mug. He gulped it down and lapsed back into vacuity. Robinson left and Ummarrah smoked his pipe. All at once it hit him that he would die and at the hands of the ghosts. He shuddered and felt a numbness creeping through his bones. His zest for life strove to reassert itself and failed. He sat staring at the wall until morning. A lost black man in grey clothing and with closely cut hair.

Robinson came early next morning to collect his three charges and take them to the ship. He would put them aboard, and they would sail out of his life for ever. He felt bad about the whole thing. This ending had no feeling of triumph about it. Had he failed? How difficult it was to eradicate their savage natures! He waited in the gaol yard as Ummarrah was led out for a short religious service before being taken to his death. He looked sullen and angry. The Chief Protector walked to him for a last farewell. The condemned man looked him in the eyes and said: 'Just about all my people have been killed or murdered. We only killed in self-defence or for injuries inflicted on us. Lalla Rookh killed that man for raping her when she was a young girl. He was an ugly brute. The other was killed when he came to his assistance. This is all that I have to say.'

Trugernanna, Dray and Wooreddy respectable in European clothing, and with the man's head closely cropped, were handed over to him. Wooreddy was still in his trance and the women seemed to have joined him. All three shuffled along listlessly. A crowd waited outside the walls to see the murderer, and they hooted and jeered the three black people. Robinson had great difficulty in escorting his charges through the mob and was still trying to get them away when the crowd gave a great collective sigh. A body of mounted troopers cantered through the gate. Between their columns rolled the death cart. The mob began to laugh and shout remarks at Ummarrah. 'That crow ain't so chirpy now, is he!' Someone called out next to Robinson, who immediately bristled and declaimed to those around him: 'That person is a human being, sir, and perhaps a better man that some of you.'

'Shutup, you're the one that brought those murdering savages here, and it's your fault. We won't rest 'till they're all hanging from the trees,' a voice mocked.

Surrounded by the crowd and the troopers, the cart wheeled out of town and to a low rise where once the local people had camped. The area was like a park, studded with tall trees and cropped grass. On the rise a rickety wooden stage had been erected. Two stout posts had been sunk into the ground and on top of them, a distance of three metres from the ground, a beam had been nailed from which a rope dangled with the noose just above the platform which had been set on top of piles of bricks a metre high.

Ummarrah rode slowly along in the cart and perhaps some feelings of humanity had overcome the crowd, for it had parted to allow his three companions to walk beside him. They alone kept the condemned man from panic. He had never imagined that the execution would be such a circus with hundreds of people watching him die. He felt sick and giddy and was thankful to hear Robinson's voice say: 'Steady, Ummarrah, you are still among friends.'

Trugernanna and Dray let the tears flow down their cheeks. They muffled a shriek when they saw the construction on which their friend would die. As they approached, a strange humming began underlining the noise of the crowd. The trees were filled with Aborigines. Waau and his people had come to farewell the stranger they had lately welcomed. The men were wiping their eyes and the women were openly crying. Ummarrah looked up and saw them. He felt ashamed to seen without the glory of his long locks. He looked down and saw his fellow islanders. The sight of Wooreddy moved him the most. He looked old and bald and shabby.

The cart stopped at the scaffold. He was pulled down. He waited while the chaplain read an offering of prayers which ended with: 'O Lord, we beseech thee, mercifully hear our prayers, and spare this sinner who confesses his sins unto thee; that he, whose conscience by sin is blackened, by thy merciful pardon may be absolved; through Christ our Lord. Amen.'

The prayers served to numb him and he ascended the scaffold without help, though the loose planks making up the platform swayed alarmingly on their stacks of bricks. Then the hangman had to balance there while he put the noose around the neck of the condemned man. The chaplain began to read the burial service and Ummarrah, in spite of himself, began violently to shiver. 'In the midst of life we are in death' was intoned, and the hangman kicked away at the central plank. He felt his body falling, then he began choking for breath. His legs began kicking and his body writhing convulsively. Robinson gave a cry of horror and vomited as Ummarrah gave a last vigorous kick and went limp.

The Chief Protector hurried his charges away from the dreadful sight. He took them through the bush to Hobson's Bay where a small boat carried them out to the ship which would deposit them back on Flinders Island. One of the officers settled them down amidships where they would be out of the way and told them not to move. 'I'll send you some grub every now and again,' he said. Robinson left the ship and the disagreeable episode came to an end for him.

The ship passed through the heads without mishap and entered Bass Strait. The captain expected a quick run to Hobarton with only a short stop at Flinders to let off the three crows. But the vessel was no sooner in sight of the island than a fierce storm blew up. The ship had to take shelter in the lee of a small island. It anchored there. The three Aborigines sat on the deck and tried to remain unseen. The two women were sunk in apathy. They hated the very thought of the future and were thankful when one of the sailors exchanged a bottle of rum for one of the shillings Robinson had given them as parting gifts. They swigged on the liquor and felt warm and uncaring. They had nothing to care about! Wooreddy refused to drink. He just sat there with his eyes on the side of the ship. He sat there until one of the sailors who carried food to them nudged him. The old Aborigine fell over on his side. The sailor saw that he was dead and brought an officer. The captain was informed, and he decided to bury the old crow ashore. It would give him a chance to stretch his legs. They rowed to the island and dug a shallow grave in the sand. They rolled the body in and shovelled sand over it. No prayers were wasted on the old heathen, and the captain, after strolling over the barren island, went back to the ship.

Trugernanna stared towards the shore. The last male of Bruny Island was dead. There was a great hole in her which could never be filled. She tried to think of the people that might be alive at Wybalenna, but all she could see were the faces of the dead passing before her eyes. Each face passed, sunk in death and each face bore a name and once had been a living person. What was life? It seemed that all that she had ever known was death. Now her husband was dead and lying in a shallow grave on that beach. She wished that she could have taken his corpse and burnt it in the proper way. Then she saw him with his *num* clothing covering his shrunken old man's body and his shaven head. No, the real Doctor Wooreddy had disappeared before they could get to him and inflict further humiliation upon him. She found herself sobbing and sought the arm of the tearful Dray. They clung to each other and let the tears roll down their cheeks as they watched the shore and the storm clouds clearing away. The yellow setting sun broke through the black clouds to streak rays of light upon the beach. It coloured the sea red. Then *Laway Larna*, the evening star, appeared in the sky as the sun sank below the horizon. Suddenly a spark of light shot up from the beach and flashed through the dark sky towards the evening star. As it did so, the clouds closed again and the world vanished.